THE PETTY QUEEN

THE PETTY QUEEN

Hell Hath No Fury

QUEEN

B. E. SCOTT

ISBN paperback: 978-1-0880-5403-1
ISBN hardcover: 978-1-0880-5416-1

Contact the author at BEScott@writeme.com
Follow the author at www.goodreads.com/BEScott
Cover design by Alice Briggs of Kingdom Covers.
Map created by Thomas Rey.
Edited by Stan Timmons
First Edition

PROLOGUE

NORR, A KING of the gods, came from the Boreal ice and created all the lands that made Amor. He had six sons that made up the kings of the six provinces. They sat together as the Pantheon of the Gods. This is the legend, but it is a complete work of fiction.

Norr was a king, but not a god, and his wife was Anora, a woman from beyond the desert in the east. Norr came from beyond the desert, but little is written about his origins. Anora had incredible powers to move the continents by raising soil from the ocean. Using this power, she created all of Amor. The world before existed only to the east of the Mirror Mountains, and Amor was nothing but ocean.

Amor was not created in a single motion and Anora's husband Norr played an important role. The name Amor came from a composite bastardization of their names. Together, they created great harmony in the world they made.

Norr had four brothers and two sisters. They made up the rulers of the provinces and as soon as one died, the others would push to absorb their lands. It was slow at first, and then the wars became longer. The cousins and children of the original kings would become more bloodthirsty and even more desperate.

The wars claimed all the harmony that Anora created. When Norr died, she fled to an island to the south. There she had her only child, Elnora. The gift of her mother had survived through her. The children of the elementals would continue through the centuries as the continent was in a never-ending war. The power of the Queens and Kings of Elnora kept their secrets and protected them.

The conflict on the continent led the provincial historians to craft godhood for Norr's siblings, ignoring him completely. It was not until years later that Norr was added to the Pantheon of The Seven Saints. Beyond the Kingdom of Elnora, Anora was largely forgotten.

This story is best told from oral legend. Two thousand years of truth lies beyond the endless desert and the mirror mountains.

From the writings of Lord Edwin Ulrich – The Legend of Amor

THE PETTY QUEEN

CHAPTER 1

THE SUN HAD never been so bright in the sky. It had been two days since the gala and Lucien had left shortly after. Kate missed Lucien more than anything, and thinking of him made her feel love all around her.

The sky was light blue and autumn was upon the province. The Free Marshes was a desolate place in winter, so they had already spent the last month storing extra wood. A cold dry wind blew to the east and the leaves had changed to a speckled orange and red.

Kate was hunting alone for the first time, east of the city. Lucien had shown her there were good spots for game, but today the boar rooting location was empty. It was fine, because being out alone somewhere she had never been was exhilarating. There was so much she could do now that the king had given her the rights to hunt in Dulimore and Westfall.

Kate had never been to Westfall but she looked forward to visiting. It would have to wait since Lucien would not be back for a week. There were some issues with the army- rumors of forces east of Dulimore, and of course his father, King Delvin.

King Delvin by now had heard about the two of them, and Lucien would have to receive his approval if they were to be matched. It made her nervous thinking about being a queen. There had not been one in Elnora for several decades, and there would be no queen mother to train her. That was a relief, but at the same time she never felt pretty enough to be a princess, let alone a queen.

The responsibility made Kate anxious and queasy. The people always looked to their leaders, and the prosperity of Elnora was definitely going to make it hard for her to fit in. They had luxuries while she was used to only the most basic things in life. She could imagine wearing hunting gear and the local nobility turning their noses at her. She would be on the outside looking in for the rest of her life. Her head spun just thinking of how it would affect Lucien.

Kate was finally on the east road. It was mid-day, and she felt she had better go back to the city. Viola had talked about spending some time together. Edwin being gone had made her bored. It could be fun for them.

Kate knew how it felt to be bored and lonely. Lucien had kept her so occupied for the last few weeks that she hardly knew what to do with herself. The company would be good for her. Hopefully Viola wouldn't talk of just Edwin, though. That would not be pleasant and the two of them gushing on each other was stomach-churning enough.

The walls of Dawnbridge rose into view now as Kate approached. The guards at the east gate had gotten used to seeing her the last couple of days and they passed her through with just a wave. The news of her being the hero left people with mixed feelings.

Some of the province thought it was good news that finally women were recognized, and the rest could only gossip about her attire. Kate figured at least none of them wanted her to be kicked out of the court. This was a positive outcome, considering there were no women of prominence in the king's court, not that he had much of one. Kate grimaced at the thought of their poverty; it was a wonder Lucien was oblivious to it. She was grateful that the castle guard seemed to give her more respect, and some referred to her as the huntsman or hunter.

The best part of it was that people did not notice her much anymore, now that all the information was out. They knew she was at least very good friends with Crown Prince Lucien, even if that wasn't formal, and they knew her father worked as chancellor for the king, in an official capacity.

Kate had now made it to her home near the gate, the adviser's house. She would drop off her cloak, bow, quiver, and spear to be a little lighter, then see what Viola was doing. She could imagine her sitting and staring at the crumbling mortar in the castle walls as she waited for the visit.

Kate hoped Viola would be in a mood to maybe walk around the city. There had to be some spots that were interesting.

The stairwell north of the adviser's house took her up to the main manor. Kate felt warm all over as she passed the room where Lucien stayed. The last time she was there, she spent the night in an embrace with him. It made her arms break out in gooseflesh at just the thought of their bodies entwined.

The corridor in the manor was a long walk to the hallway by the throne room. Once there, she just needed to take the adjacent hallway and up a spiral staircase to the royal quarters. The guard there could barely look her in the eye after the fiasco with her threatening to kill Viola, not to mention Edwin's naked bottom. It was best to make a quick move to avoid any questions. Kate lowered her head and the guard pretended not to see her.

Viola's door was open, so Kate just knocked on the frame.

"Hello, your highness." Kate said, and bowed slightly to be proper.

"Kate, thank the gods you are here. I am bored out of my mind." Viola stood up abruptly from her desk.

"Well, I just came from a hunt east, so I wanted to check and see if you were planning anything interesting."

Viola giggled with excitement. "Gods, what I wouldn't give for a hunt! If I leave this room I have Arnold following me like a shadow. I am going mad in this castle. You have to help me escape."

Kate rolled her eyes and sighed. "Well, we could go hunting, but I am sure that Arnold would make it difficult for us to have much fun. He is rather imposing."

"Yes, that, I agree. I will have to sneak out." Viola tapped her finger to her pursed lips and narrowed her eyes in thought.

Kate was already getting anxious thinking of the two of them deliberately trying to avoid Arnold, and not telling anyone what they are doing.

"Tonight, I will sneak out my window. I will use the sill on the outside to steal around to the garden on the north side of the manor. There is a tree, I think I can climb down into the courtyard. You can meet me there," Viola said, her voice quick and decisive.

"No. No, absolutely not," Kate said, underscoring her refusal by holding her hands up and shaking her head.

Viola held her hands together as if in prayer. "Please, Kate. I would do anything for you. I will owe you something special if you agree. How am I supposed to survive in this room while Edwin is gone? I cannot bear the monotony."

Kate crossed her arms in mock-haughtiness. "Well, you knew that your escapades with Edwin would get you into trouble," she lectured.

4

Viola turned her head to the side and raised her chin. "Humph! Edwin and I were together just a few times in my bed, and I am still as pure as the day he met me."

Kate struggled to keep from laughing. "You can't possibly think I would believe that. I saw him completely naked in your bed."

Viola waved her hand with a huff. "Kate, there are more ways to pleasure a man than with just your body. You should learn that soon. You have to know a ruffian like Lucien will need encouragement not to stray."

Kate covered her ears. "Gods, no, I do not want to think about how you are keeping Edwin from wandering, or what you do in your bed."

Viola grabbed Kate's arms and pulled her hands away from her ears. "You have to help me. If you don't, I will go alone. How could you live with yourself if I were to be hurt?"

Kate sighed and grumbled, "What would we do, even if you could get out? They would find us in a day or less. There is no point in trying to get free only to be locked down even tighter after they capture you." Kate could not hide her excitement about the trip, no matter how hard she pretended to not want to go.

Viola turned away from Kate. "I don't care. A day free of this place is worth a month of imprisonment."

"You might be imprisoned in the dungeon if the king even thinks you are doing impure things. Anyway, where would we go?"

"Well, there is an estate just near the mountain. We could hike there, and maybe even go to South Pier. We could even smuggle aboard a ship to Elnora, like bandits."

"Gods, you are mad. The Elnorans are hyper-reclusive. I have never even heard of anyone going to the island. If we were found out they might just throw us off the boat mid-trip."

Viola turned back to face Kate, her arms folded over her chest. "Where is your sense of adventure?"

Kate motioned to her stomach and grimaced. "I have three nice wounds on my stomach that account for all the adventure I can handle. If we go west, we can hike to the estate. It's a long trip, though. Can you stand camping through the night?"

"We can stay at your old home in Galebridge. Do you still have anything there? Did you have boys there, Kate, who could give me juicy Kate stories?"

"That is an incredibly bad idea. I have my camp there, but I am not sure about the two of us staying in any camp, let alone near the village. The people there are awful."

The boys from the village attacking her entered Kate's mind, in addition to the bandit attack at Tallin. It was pretty scary after those incidents to stay there. Maybe she was just becoming more cautious, but she could tell Viola was desperate. Still, it could be fun. "Well, we could make my camp, but the estate is a long walk. It might take us all day to reach it. You are sure we can stay there?"

Viola nodded. "Sure, it is abandoned."

Kate could only rub her head in worry. *This is a very bad idea.* "Viola, are you sure about this? I can travel and hunt, but you could get into trouble, and I am not sure it's safe."

"I will meet you in the courtyard after sundown," Viola screeched.

"All right. I need to rest up, then, and tell my father I am going hunting west for a day or so. I will be careful to omit that you're coming."

As Kate was leaving she looked back at Viola. "Don't be late, I won't wait forever. I don't want someone to see me there any more than you do."

Kate walked past the guard and down the spiral staircase. It was a foolish thing they were doing. It was a thrill, and the idea of it was something Lucien might come up with. As she thought that, she wondered what he was doing right now. *I hope he thinks about me when we're apart. I think about him all the time.*

Kate made the journey back to the adviser's house, although she thought of it as the chancellor's home. The quill and book on the shingle hanging by the door identified it as a scribe's shop also.

Kate went inside, where her father sat at the counter in the shop area, working on some papers.

"Hello, Kate. How was the hunt?" Brian asked, barely looking up from his papers.

"It was nice to get out in the open air. It is autumn and the trees are almost completely changed, but I didn't have much luck."

"Humph, I'll bet. Your head was in the clouds, thinking of that scoundrel Lucien," Brian chided.

"You mean his highness, Crown Prince Lucien. Don't forget, you are chancellor now. It would be a diplomatic slight to insult him," Kate lectured, trying – and failing – to sound serious.

"May they lock me in the stock, but I breathe easier now that the scoundrel is far to the south. The trouble in Dulimore will no doubt bring him back, I am certain of it," Brian said with a smile.

Kate looked at him, curious. "Lucien, when…what have you heard?"

"Kate, you sound too eager. You won't catch a man by being desperate," her father said glibly.

Kate crossed her arms and cocked her head to the side. "You were just teasing me?"

"No, he will return. The Elnoran army is in Porin now. The port is teeming with Elnoran knights. They plan to hold the fort and send a message to Elgin if he makes a move into Dulimore."

"That must mean Alaric is there. Do you know of Edwin? Did he join the army?"

Brian tapped his quill into some ink, continuing to write as they talked. "No, he is with Lucien in the south. They will be there soon enough. It is a day from Elnora to Porin, so if they want, they can get there anytime. I suspect the king is giving them a scolding for their recent behavior."

"I hope it isn't too bad," Kate said, and frowned. Lucien and Edwin had made some trouble, and it was worrying what punishment the king might have for them.

CHAPTER 2

THE RED RING of Lucien's eye expanded as he focused on a bead of sweat making its way slowly down Edwin's forehead.

"I...I...I...I assure you, my lord, my...your majesty, that these, or these...the rumors, or rather...Brian simply misinterpreted what he saw in the bedroom. You see, my, I had a flower. I happened to drop it on the floor, and in bending down to pick it up, my trousers fell as I was...I was adjusting them...beforehand," Edwin stammered, shifting his weight from foot to foot, glancing from Edwin to King Delvin.

"Are you an idiot?" King Delvin asked, as he stood in front of Edwin.

"No, no, your majesty...I simply...rather pointing out...some factual...or possibly factual inconsistencies that might exist in Brian's version of events."

"Edwin, you were caught with your pants down in Viola's bedroom. There is no factual inconsistency other than your intelligence. What is inconsistent is that you can speak, but are so stupid."

9

"I..."

"You know, Edwin, King Elias and I had a nice conversation on capital punishment. He is of the mind we should return to more firm punishments. I don't know, let us say...castration."

Edwin looked to Lucien, his face covered in diamonds of perspiration as he mouthed, *help me*.

"I agree, castration it should be, my lord. It's just...if she were to be with child...It might be a bigger mess if you were to castrate him now, you see. Perhaps give it a few months to see if her belly grows. We can certainly castrate him anytime, really," Lucien said, waving his hand demonstrably about.

"Don't help me anymore," Edwin whispered to Lucien.

"Lucien, I will get to you soon enough. Edwin, your father wishes to have you stripped of your status, your army commission, and sequester you to the vineyard. He happened to mention this at the same time he said it might be a good idea to send a diplomat to negotiate with King Elias. He is known to be a reasonable man, and that you are not the worst match for Princess Viola. You and your father are very similar: you both talk out both sides of your mouth."

Edwin nodded quickly. "Very prudent, my father."

"Lucien," the king said, and struggled for composure as his jaw tightened.

"My lord," Lucien replied, a devious grin on his face.

King Delvin paced around the two of them with his hands behind his back. He seemed to be searching for something on the floor as he went around and around many times.

"I cannot fathom what I could possibly say to you. You vanish before my eyes, and then wind up nearly dead in Dulimore, yet rescued again by one of your rogues gallery. If that was not enough, I hear of you taking a woman three years your senior into your bed, after." The king stopped pacing in front of Lucien, holding his finger up to him. "This, after her father, in no uncertain terms, warned you off. The father who is now Lord Chancellor of the Free Marshes!!! Do you honestly have nothing to say to all this?"

"I believe things worked out rather well, and Brian is aware that his daughter is still pure. I would not sully her, or her reputation."

"So are you telling me this girl is to be your wife then?"

"Well, we are very good friends. I am certain my father would have to approve, and there may be nothing to it in the end."

The king studied Lucien carefully, and then looked to Josephine who was taking minutes of the audience. Josephine did not show any emotion, but Lucien could pick a few things up.

Lucien could never feel his father's temperament, but he felt distrust from Josephine, as well as something unsettling in whatever his father was planning.

"Very well, then, if there is nothing to it, then there is nothing to it. I am sure you will no doubt have other ladies of interest, such as the Princess Zara, whom you told you were already smitten with someone. Princess Zara of Westfall. Gods, Lucien, we are trying to hold the continent together and you cannot even entertain the poor girl. Her father's letter was soaked in disappointment with us."

"Ah. Well, if there is a silver lining it might be that she was quite grateful that I was with someone, as she would rather have preferred suicide to me."

The king shook his head. He raised his hands and turned away from them. Climbing the two steps to his throne, he stopped before it. "You both are to report to Porin, where Alaric will be expecting you. I pray you do not make a mess of things there, and by the gods, if you do, perhaps Elgin can rid me of your problems."

Edwin and Lucien quickly left the throne room.

"You ass, when the king suggests castration, the first thing you are to say is no, no to castration." Edwin shook his fist as they hastily moved down the corridor.

"Well, he wasn't going to castrate you, at least not right away," Lucien said without even a sideways glance to Edwin.

Edwin gingerly rubbed his groin area. "How very comforting. What is with you and lying about Kate?"

"Edwin, leave my love life to me, and I shall leave yours to you. Stop rubbing yourself or they will start spreading rumors that you are some kind of pervert, even more than you already are."

"Bastard, don't change the subject. No, you are no longer wearing the blindfold, and you are known on the continent as crown prince. That means I am a concerned citizen. Perhaps I should ask Josephine to bring it up to the council."

"I don't want Josephine and that evil council of busybodies kidnapping her in some scheme to force me to breed with her. It's kind of gross to think about, but I got a distinct vibe from her that she is happily considering it."

"She is nineteen, nearly twenty. In this era when thirty-five is an old man, you should probably approach it with an open mind."

"Edwin, she is not some broodmare, she is the future queen. Don't you think there might be some decency to our love? I will get to that point someday, but she is a woman of the woods and likes her independence. I like her as she is. She may not even want children, and what then? You will be happy with Anne being used for breeding, even though she would only be doing it out of obligation?"

Edwin and Lucien had finally made it to the castle courtyard. There were two ships at the port.

"Lucien, you aren't going to make me sail all the way to Porin? There is no way to just, you know, get us there?" Edwin exaggerated a wink at Lucien, but received only a blank stare in return.

"I am afraid not. I have never been to Porin before. I think this time we will have to take the old fashioned way."

Lucien boarded the boat, and Edwin was just behind. Edwin noticed a soldier heaving his lunch over the side. He could only think it would soon be him.

"I would pray to Sossius, but I am certain he would curse me for wasting his time with such a short voyage." Edwin slowly boarded the galley, crab-walking his way up the gangplank. "Gods, I hate the sea."

CHAPTER 3

KATE ARRIVED AT the courtyard early. She had struggled to sleep during the night and her father did not say much about her going hunting early in the morning. She did not mention Viola, and when she said early in the morning, she meant just after midnight.

It had been on her mind since she lay down to rest that Viola might be her first friend, and that it may also be the reason she would do such a foolish thing as going out to the mountain with her.

Kate stood alone in the moonlight, thinking. She knew it was safer than it had been in the past since Elias had control of the mine gallery at the base of the mountain. There were guards, but no miners that she knew of. Elias had searched the province and even attempted agreements with Dulimore and Westfall to get miners, but so far there was no progress.

Kate had sympathy for Viola, as Kate knew that being royalty in these times just meant you spent most of your time hiding. Their lives in the castle never looked glamorous, and it was something she never wanted.

Kate was unsure what life on the island would be like with Lucien as crown prince. It couldn't be more dangerous than the continent, and she was sure that it would be hard for bandits to hide from him, even with his powers suppressed while she was around him. Her effect on him would make the island less safe from outside invasion. If he could not sense ships approaching, it would mean less time for him to act. King Delvin was a superior king in this regard. *Maybe someday Lucien will get used to my powers. I can only hope.*

The thought that the two of them may not be a good match caused a sinking feeling in her stomach, but that was instantly replaced by fear as she heard someone behind her.

A dark figure covered in a cloak approached.

"It is me," Viola whispered.

Kate was surprised how small she looked all wrapped up in the cloak. Almost like a child.

"I am surprised you made it. Did you have trouble with the ledge and tree?"

"No, the guards fell asleep, I just walked out the front," Viola said, and giggled.

"Gods, what is coming to this world? Let us go out the east gate. The guards should be easy to pass. They never question anyone leaving."

Viola nodded to Kate and followed behind her.

They made their way south through the courtyard, past the adviser's house, to the east gate. They were careful to stay in the shadow of the castle walls as they went, just in case anyone looked down from a window above.

Once they reached the gate, they were able to walk through unchallenged. The guard there was too busy relighting sconces along the gatehouse to notice them. They were able to sneak behind him just as he turned in the direction opposite to their path.

The east gate was a long walk to the west around the walls. It wasn't dangerous, but unsettling and eerie in the dark.

It took some time to travel all the way south then west into the swamps once they saw the torches at the gate.

"That was easy enough," Viola said as they made it to the road.

"We just need to go a good way to the west and then there is a path south to my camp."

They walked quietly for a long while. The moons were bright tonight, making it easy to see. Autumn air was a lot cooler at night, so they both had their cloaks wrapped tightly around them, and their hoods down.

The path south was so familiar to Kate she could do it with her eyes closed. It would have been a lot easier if Viola hadn't stopped every now and then to pick up things on the ground. She was picking herbs, weeds, and even some bushes that had berries or some kind of seed on them. Kate was not sure what that was about, but Viola had a satchel filled with bottles and small bags that she added the items to as they went.

Kate's camp looked cold and damp, and there were still patches of hoarfrost on the ground.

"Shall we make a fire?" Viola knelt down next to the scorched pit at the camp.

"I don't know. The villagers might get suspicious if they see a fire here. The guards can see light from the palisade too."

"Well, I don't think we should worry about guards. I would like to cook some things. Do you mind? I am capable of lighting it myself."

Kate thought about it as she looked at Viola's hopeful expression. It was cold and the shelter was damp. The fire would dry out the ground, and make it easier to rest.

"All right, but just a small fire; don't get carried away."

16

Viola gathered up some dry brush and sticks. She had a very nice flint and chisel set that she used to start the fire. It took just a couple of strikes to make the sparks that grew into a fire.

Kate couldn't help but wonder what it would be like to have pyrokinetic abilities like Lucien and just light a fire without any effort. She smiled when she thought how amazing he was, but that turned to sadness when she worried that his father was almost certainly giving him trouble about her. It was the last thing she said to him before he left. *You don't have to tell your father if you don't want to, I will understand.* She knew all too well the pressure he would be under to acquire something in return for his marriage.

Viola moved logs around into a nice overlapping pyre and the fire was very nice and warm, but small enough it hopefully wouldn't draw attention. *Viola is a natural at fire crafting*, Kate thought.

Viola sat some small ceramic bottles around the fire.

"What are those?" Kate gestured down at the row of bottles.

Viola pointed to the individual bottles as she answered. "These two are soup, the other is water I want to boil." She pulled a small wooden bowl and stone pestle from her satchel. Viola put some ingredients in the bowl and ground them with the pestle.

"What are you doing?"

"Making some potions for our trip, just in case we get into trouble."

Viola removed a wood block with many holes in it from her satchel, and in the holes were small wooden vials. The vials were sealed, and she struggled to remove each plug as she opened them. She put some water in each of the vials, and a pinch of whatever she was grinding.

"These poplar plugs are horrendous. If we ever get access to cork again, I will buy ten stone of the stuff."

Kate's eyes widened watching Viola carry on. She was clearly making alchemicals. She would be turned away from the castle if they knew of this.

"You're an alchemist," Kate gasped.

"What of it? Who do you think gave you and Lucien all those potions? There is no decent alchemist in the province."

"It was you? It is forbidden though. What if someone finds out?"

"Don't be silly, almost everyone knows I dabble in some ointment or other. Maybe they don't know I make potions, but the old superstitious nonsense of witches no longer matters. People just want to settle their upset stomachs. People continue to eat so much fish that they would rather keep from emptying their bowels, too."

Kate's mouth made an *o*. "Does Elias know?"

"Of course. He gets potions from me all the time. How else would he in such good health on a poor diet? Martin knows too, and he is well aware I make potions before I travel. It's why I hoped to make some here."

Kate knelt down next to Viola, surveying what she was doing. She couldn't help but touch the vials and look at them.

"Be careful," Viola warned, and grabbed the vials from her hand. She returned them to the wood block, meticulous in putting them back in their proper order. "If you're not mindful, you will put them back in the wrong order. I don't have anything to mark them with, so I just have to remember which hole I put them in."

Kate could see numbers carved in the block for each of the vial locations.

"I have to say, it is rather surprising how good you are at this."

"Well, I go mad in that castle. I started reading about alchemy when I was younger. The books were always interesting in their talk of ailments and items you can treat them with. Also, there is a lot of culinary use as well. The soup is dewberry, cattail tuber, and some venison I was able to get in the market."

"Venison? Was it dried?" Kate asked.

"Oh yes, you rarely get fresh meat anywhere these days. I bought it from a back street scoundrel. If Arnold wasn't there, I don't think he would have sold it to me. Blame the small minds of men, unwilling to trust a woman with a little coin."

"I think I might have sold that to him. Before the gala I had turned in some dry venison for sale. It was a stone's worth."

Viola smiled. "I know it was you. Elias cursed your name for the past few years that you never brought game to the market. He knew you couldn't sell it, as you were a woman. When he found out about the venison, he paid double, and put in an advance in case any more meat came in. That is how we got the boar for the gala. There was a time when Elias was going to have you arrested. It isn't legal to hunt without a permit in the forests. You're lucky your father paid a tax to Elias for your hunts."

"A tax? He never told me that."

"He didn't want to get you upset. You seemed happy in the woods. It wasn't much, but it came out of his wages."

Kate felt bad. She had given her father such a hard time about everything, and all this time he was looking out for her and she did not even know it.

"I have everything done," Viola said, putting the block of vials back in her satchel. "I will leave the soup near the fire so it's warm. The water I will just use later if we need some that is sterile. I think I will rest, I am exhausted from all the excitement."

"All right, I will try to rest. You can lie in the shelter next to me."

Kate pulled her knees up to her chest as she lay next to Viola. The fire had dried the ground nicely, and the shelter blocked any wind.

Kate felt it was a fun trip so far, and already she was learning new things about Viola. Maybe they were going to be good friends after all.

CHAPTER 4

THE BOATS MADE good time to Port Porin. The port city was like no place Lucien had been. It was as large, if not larger, than King's Port in Elnora. There were not many boats docked, but there were many slips for them.

The port was well defended. It had high walls with steps up to a rampart above the docks. If anyone attacked through the port it would take many casualties trying to move men under fire. The land here was very level, with open fields to the east and a small forest to the west. The castle was connected to the docks, but set up high on a hill west, overlooking the entire area. The town was partially inside the walls, and some of the houses and shops were spread north of the docks.

Lucien could not help but notice how well everyone dressed, and the upkeep on the castle and port was done well. *It looks like a proper lord must keep things in order,* he thought. He did sense unease among the population. It was hard to read them as they were all new to him, but the overriding emotion he could sense was one of concern.

Lucien pulled his hood down low, stepping onto the docks.

Alaric was there to greet them. "Well, if it isn't the lord-lings, come to join in the festivities. I heard the king gave you both a proper ribbing. He assured me that there would be no more Karl, and no more Viola for either of you."

"It is Kate," Lucien growled.

"Kate, Karl, it makes no difference to me. You are both to be on good behavior, and completely celibate for your internment at Porin."

Alaric looked past Lucien.

"Did Edwin survive the trip?"

"He is a bit under the weather. Sailing east into the wind made for a choppy ride."

"I know how he is feeling. I will give him a proper greeting when he is able to remove himself from the boat." Alaric had a devious smile.

"What can you tell me, if anything, about the plans of the king or Elgin?"

"You don't waste time. It is as bad as you expect. There are several hundred, possibly a thousand knights east of Omskov. They made camp in the grassland across the border near a stream. The official word is that they are doing some training for winter."

"The unofficial word is?"

"Invasion. King Richter sent a letter requesting the release of his daughter. He claims she acted without his knowledge and she will be confined to her quarters until she is properly wed. This was all said in a threatening manner in which he would take her by force if she was not released."

"I suppose the lords didn't like the sound of that. King Elias has probably already given in," Lucien said, rubbing his forehead.

"Surprisingly, no. King Delvin wants her imprisoned to force Elgin's hand. King Icel of Dulimore is furious at the refusal to give her up."

"That isn't surprising. Elias's kingdom is not about to be invaded, but Icel has cause to worry."

"Icel is very weak. I would almost say weaker than Elias. He has no true allies, and his army might be five hundred knights, at best. The rumor is he will accept vassalage from Elgin in exchange for him to keep Drommer."

Lucien let out a laugh. "Drommer and Porin are the only cities in Dulimore. What would Elgin get in that deal?"

"Elgin wants you dead, and that is all that truly matters to them," Alaric said, fixing Lucien with a stare.

Lucien's hood hung low over his face. He stroked his chin, deep in thought.

"I am to kill him first, I suppose."

"That didn't sound like a question." Alaric glanced at him before noticing Edwin on the ground.

"By the gods," Edwin said, crawling on his hands and knees from the boat. His face was sheened with sweat, and his flesh had a greenish tint about it.

"Edwin, I was wondering if you survived the trip!" Alaric clapped his hands, rubbing them together with a giddy laugh.

"I would give anything to never get on a boat again," he croaked.

"Well, lad, get your legs about you. Lord Jan is putting us up in the castle manor. The rooms are small, but the beds are big. I have enjoyed his company. He has made a dinner in our honor."

"A feast. I don't think I could eat for a year. I have no appetite at all. Just show me to my bed."

"Why not let me tell you what we are having?" Alaric put his hands on his knees, bending at the waist to look down at Edwin. "Raw oysters, you know, the very gooey and slimy kind."

"Gods." Edwin tried to hold a hand over his mouth while crawling to the edge of the pier. "I am going to be sick."

"Oh yes, and some runny eggs." Alaric and Lucien shared a laugh.

Edwin dry-heaved over the side of the pier. He seemed to feel better after, even though nothing came out.

"Let us go, Edwin. We have to play our part. I hope you can pretend to be decent for the evening," Lucien said, and reached out his hand to help.

Lucien and Alaric hauled Edwin to his feet. There were several stairs leading up to the castle, and they had to carry-drag-walk him most of the way.

The castle wasn't huge, so it wasn't as far of a walk as King's Port, but it was a nice-sized city. Lucien was still amazed at how well maintained it was. People took care of their homes rather well, and to the north he could see farms with freshly harvested fields. It was unsettling to think that Elgin would get all of this land without even so much as a fight.

By the time they reached the manor, Edwin had regained his composure. Alaric and Lucien looked over their rooms. They were on the north side of the manor and each had windows overlooking the battlements. Just beyond their rooms was a chemin de ronde, a raised walkway behind the castle battlements that guards patrolled with clockwork frequency. From this distance, the approach to the castle looked treacherous. The road wound east around the castle, and to the north there was a cliff that collapsed west down into the forest. It would be almost impossible to attack from the west or the north. Lucien wondered if this town was worth the trouble to take. It looked heavily defended by fortifications, and in excellent shape. The guards wore well cared for armor, and seemed to take their duty seriously as well.

Lucien wondered if there was more to this place. It seemed to be extremely well taken care of for a backwoods port area. His sense told him there was something under the surface in people's minds. The worry of something was with them, but he could not tell what it was. Worry, yes, but not fear of the war.

The thought of this city being traitorous was a distinct possibility. If it was, the army of Elnoran knights here made it a dangerous position for Alaric and his men.

Lucien heard Alaric in the corridor asking Edwin to come to the dining room. Lucien joined them as they walked down to a large entryway foyer at the end of the hallway. To the left was an open dining hall with a vaulted ceiling, almost as big as a cathedral. There was a large table extending from one end of the room to the other, and smaller tables set further back on either side of the main table.

A big man in heavy armor stood next to a young man, perhaps not quite twenty, sitting at the head of the table. He wore a dark orange tunic with a red belt around his waist that held an incredibly long sword. It nearly touched the ground, and had an extremely narrow blade. His hair was auburn, but cut very short on the sides, with some length on top. His hair was similar to Lucien's, save for its coloration.

He rose to greet them.

"Greetings, I am Lord Jan. This is my master of the guard, Petric. It is an honor to finally..."

He paused as Lucien removed the hood from his head, and stared at him.

Lucien's eyes were solid black, blacker than anything Jan had ever seen, almost like a void, with a solid thin red ring around the center. Jan's face involuntarily showed his shock, but he was quick to recover.

"I am very sorry your highness, I was told to prepare myself for your arrival, but seeing is believing in this case. I ask your forgiveness; it is quite unsettling at first glance, but I will get used to it."

"It is just Lucien, and there is no offense taken. I am used to it by now, and just glad no one in the village took off running and screaming," Lucien said, trying to lighten the unease he felt from Jan and Petric.

"I am grateful, Lord Lucien. It is a pleasure to meet you and Lord Edwin. Your reputation precedes you with the glorious support that your father offers, and Alaric has been a distinguished guest already."

Alaric guffawed. "Ease up, Jan, we are friends. None of these lord-lings will make trouble for you. I will put them in their places if they do."

"Very well, Alaric. It is always good to be formal at first, to let them know you can be. I am sure they are famished from their boat trip, and are looking forward to a decent meal. We have breads, cheeses, and some chicken to eat. Eat all that you wish, I will fetch more if need be. I don't suppose you boys are permitted to drink wine, but there is some excellent cider that they make in the village you should try."

Edwin and Lucien looked at each other. They seemed taken aback by the hospitality.

"Thanking you, your lordship. We are grateful for your hospitality. There are dark times approaching, I feel." Lucien gave a strong push of his powers to see what he could feel from Jan. There was very little hidden, but there was definitely the same feeling he had when he arrived. The entire city was on edge about something, but it wasn't as simple as just the war.

"This city is unique to others on the continent. It is a manor city. The castle, city, and surrounding lands are part of my private estate. They have made up an Arch-duchy for several centuries, even during the imperial times. I have been titled Archduke, similar to Archduke Franz before he was killed at Chaplain Hill."

"The city is well taken care of. It is not normal on the continent to see such prosperity," Lucien said, allowing his gaze to wander the room.

"We have access to fresh water, hunting in the forest, crops, animals, and some trade, but it's rare for trade lately."

"I have heard my father used to ship wine here, but that over time it was stolen by Elgin," Edwin said.

"Yes, well, at first, trade with Elgin was fruitful. They exchanged many goods for some of ours. The wine they had a particular interest in, and over time they decided to just steal it and anything else as a result."

"You don't sound too pleased," Lucien observed.

"There is little we can do. King Icel has given us strict orders to pacify Elgin, and we must obey. They are cruel to the workers in the port when they come, but they rarely come for more than one day a month."

A young girl entered the room as he finished. She seemed quite thin and petite. Her face was neither pretty nor ugly, and she had long, light brown hair.

"Ah, please meet my darling sister, Celia. She is not yet of age for the gala, but for two more seasons," Jan said with a watchful eye toward Edwin.

Lucien and Edwin rose as she sat down.

"When are the next Elgin boats supposed to arrive for their extortion?" Lucien asked, scowling distastefully.

"Two days ago the boats approached the port. When they saw the knights, they turned away. I suspect word by now has reached King Richter of our refusal, or news of the knights in the port here," Jan said, unable to hide the quiver in his voice.

Lucien could sense now more closely that Elgin was the issue with Jan. And not just Elgin, because when he mentioned Icel, he seemed rather uneasy as well.

"Are you married, Lord Jan?" Lucien asked.

"No," Jan answered simply, and took a bite of food, feigning disinterest.

"It is interesting that a man of your years has not found a wife. You seem quite eligible with this estate."

Lucien could feel it now. These questions were raising Jan's temperature. He was angry about something, and Lucien demanded to know what.

Alaric gave Lucien a reproachful look.

"I do not see any heirs other than your sister, and whoever would marry her would gain all this estate. It almost would stand to reason you would have married much more quickly than you have."

"If only it were so simple, your lordship. You, of all people, know the power of the crown and their wishes are above all else. King Icel has denied me access to the gala, and also I am not allowed to marry until Prince Oswald has. That is not to say he has not threatened to take my sister as a bride for the prince."

Edwin and Alaric looked sharply at Lucien. The idea that Oswald would marry a girl so young clearly meant they planned to kill Jan if any marriage took place.

"I see, so your future is not your own." Lucien finally understood the issue that was on everyone's mind. Jan was going to lose his estate to Oswald through marriage and possibly assassination.

"My father refused the king when he wished to have my sister when she was only ten years old. Soon thereafter, he was found dead in the woods from a hunting accident. I have not ventured far from these castle walls since."

"Does King Delvin know?" Lucien wondered if his father knew exactly what he was doing by sending him here.

"Yes, I asked him for help. I am not sure I could trust Elias. He is too close to Icel for me to risk it. Oswald has been hiding in Dawnbridge for nearly a year now. I could not risk him finding out, either. To ask for a foreign king to send soldiers is an act of treason."

"A king trying to steal land from a patron is also treason. Icel should not get away with it. Have you conspired with Elgin, hoping they might aid you?"

"Yes. At first, Richter liked the idea of my lands staying in my possession. It didn't last long, however. As soon as his daughter was of age, he pushed for a marriage between us. She is not wholly terrible. I would have seriously considered it had she been a member of a family with any decency. I needn't tell you of her or her father's behavior. She, after all, tortured Lady Aela mercilessly. I am not certain on whose orders: hers or her father's."

A wave of heat flushed through Lucien's body, his face. He didn't like to think about Elena and certainly didn't like some foreign lord talking about Aela. He tried to look away from Jan, tried to regain his composure, but rage was building. What did he know of Aela? The two of them were almost of the same age. He must have been a suitor.

Edwin noticed immediately how uncomfortable Lucien had become, and so did Alaric. Edwin looked to him to try to calm him down. Lucien had to know what he knew of her.

"Most people know her as Kate. Have you two met before?" Lucien tried not to grit his teeth or grimace as he spoke, but his tone was curt.

"I hope she has not spoken of me negatively. I was not kind to her when she came out at the first gala. The rumors about her were tawdry, and her father seemed very desperate for a match.

29

I did not care for her appearance either. I hope it hasn't soured your opinion of me, I know you two are friends.

"It is a sad thing. She did not get any interest, and no one would speak to her. I tried to keep my distance. Today, I am ashamed of myself." Jan was genuine in his reply.

Jan took a bite of food and was relieved after the air was cleared.

He had a large smile on his face. "You know, I am still quite taken with Lady Anne. I have heard you were cousins?"

Edwin spit the piece of chicken he was chewing halfway across the table with a violent cough.

Alaric looked to Lucien and Edwin in total shock.

"Edwin, I hope you are all right." Jan looked on, concerned.

Lucien tried to find some way to respond to this. The idea of Archduke Jan with Lady Anne would be an incredible match for Elnora. It was the first time in his life he felt like selling out a close family member for political power.

Lucien caught the look in Alaric's eyes that warned him not to say anything foolish.

"You know she is only interested in girls, I am afraid," Lucien said casually, taking a bite of cheese.

"Gods," Alaric said as he spit up his cider. He coughed, trying to catch his breath. Edwin rested his hands on the table, afraid to take another bite that Lucien might say something else shocking.

Jan had a very hearty laugh after hearing Lucien speak of Anne. "I have to admit, I had my suspicions. There were many suitors and she did not seem keen on any of them, although most were dreadful bores. I was much too shy in those days to approach her. She is quite the beauty. You will have to give her my regards."

"The meal is quite good, your lordship," Alaric said in a feeble attempt to change the subject.

Jan's mood had changed from being one of concern to being quite jovial. Lucien could feel he was getting more comfortable with them.

"You know, I have heard Princess Viola is quite fetching. I know you both have met her. Is she truly the beauty they say she is? I think a match between us would be quite good," Jan said with a wry smile.

Edwin's heart pounded like an angry fist at a closed door, making the vein in his neck pulse in time with it. He was going to say something, but Lucien spoke before he could.

"You know she is quite fetching. I think that might be a way out of your predicament. If you were to marry her, you could get Elias to push back against King Icel." Lucien smirked, turning to Edwin.

"How dare you?" Edwin slammed his fist on the table, standing to face Lucien.

The entire room exploded in laughter. Even Celia was laughing at the spectacle. Edwin felt like a complete ass when he finally came to his senses. He tried to put a smile back on his face, but it did not feel right or genuine.

"Gods, Edwin, Alaric said you had a temper but I didn't believe it. How you could not know that the entire continent is aware you are randy as a jackrabbit for Princess Viola is beyond me," Jan scoffed, and laughed. "Surely, boy, you must know that being princess to a king like Elias is not exactly drawing suitors. The marshes are horribly poor and most are starving. They have little to offer, and the rumors of you would easily turn away any serious suitors. You should rest easy."

"I have tried to tell him that myself but he is farcically jealous," Lucien said, smiling.

"I am sorry for my outburst, your lordship. I am quite keen on Viola, and perhaps a little sensitive to comments about her."

"Do not worry yourself. I have seen much worse," Jan said with an airy wave of his hand.

"Your lordship, perhaps we should go over what we discussed yesterday...the preparations?" Alaric leaned forward on his elbows, turning to Jan.

"By all means, I think sending the boys up to the Elgin camp is a solid plan. I just don't think King Delvin would agree."

"Lucien, this may come as a surprise, but I want you and Edwin to go north and scout the Elgin forces. They have made camp just inside the Elgin border near a stream. So far we do not know if they are still gathering, or if they are truly just training. I think, from experience, they were waiting for the bulk of the army to arrive before marching north to Omskov, then west toward Drommer."

"I see. It is no wonder you don't think King Delvin would approve. Last we spoke, he was telling me that Edwin and I would be marooned here under your guidance. Now, first chance you get, you send us out to scout. I think it is a good idea, but don't think I won't make a move if I get there and think they are preparing to invade. You need to explain to me what the real plan is for when they do." Lucien sat back in his chair, his fingers steepled together before him.

"The plan is to defend, much as King Icel has proclaimed, as well as King Delvin. The problem with that plan is we can hold cities, but the towns will be gutted or destroyed. If we let that happen it won't matter if we win, there won't be any people who would dare trust us to rule again," Jan said, shifting uneasily in his chair.

"That is my fear as well. I think we have to make some sort of effort to slow them down, so we can defeat them before they lay waste to the countryside. It is no secret that Richter wants you dead, either. If you go and people see you, he will definitely come looking for you," Alaric cautioned.

"That doesn't sound like a good idea. He may invade just to get to me. That would be a mistake on our part, they clearly outnumber us."

"It is a calculated risk. We know he will invade anyway, and getting him to come after you is a good plan."

"I suppose it is worth a try. If they come for me, I will find a way to slow them down. Edwin, if you want out, now is your chance." Lucien looked to Edwin with a smirk. Edwin only nodded. "It is a good plan, and sitting here doing nothing is going to only help Elgin. I think we should be cautious though," Lucien added.

Edwin smiled. "I am always cautious, at first."

Alaric looked around the table and then back to Lucien. "Good. It is settled. You both can leave in the morning. I want you there and back before midnight."

CHAPTER 5

KATE WOKE UP still tired from the night before. She looked to her left and Viola was already awake.

"Morning," Viola said as she sipped her soup. She was more chipper than she had a right to be.

Kate's eyes felt grainy from too little sleep. "Ugh, I forgot how rough it was to sleep on the ground."

"You sound like an old maid," Viola laughed. "It is amazing to be outside so early in the morning. It is so amazing to be free. We could do anything, you know. We could head north to Westfall, even."

Kate shifted herself gingerly with a sigh. "Gods, Viola, we are just doing a bit of hiking, is all. Maybe hunting if there is some very obvious game in our path. Otherwise, we need to be careful. I can think of a dozen shifty nobles who would love to get their hands on you."

"Well, you will have to be my bodyguard then. I just have a dagger, and I really use it mostly for picking herbs and berries." Viola sighed, waving the dagger about.

"You will know what to use it for when the time comes, I promise. When in danger, you learn quickly."

Kate stood next to Viola and brushed the leaves off her clothes and checked herself once over. Viola looked like she'd been up for hours.

"Where do you get all this energy?" Kate asked as she yawned groggily.

"Try the soup," Viola said, and winked at her.

Kate looked at her suspiciously. She picked up the flask of soup and removed the cap. She sniffed the steam rising from it and thought it smelled rather good. Carefully, Kate took a small sip.

"Wow, it is pretty good." Kate's eyes widened and she smiled.

"Sure, it has herbs that restore your energy and help you start the day."

Kate did feel better as she took a few more drinks.

"Let's head out, then." Kate put the cap back on the flask, and placed it in her satchel.

Viola jumped to her feet. "Let's."

Kate led Viola west along the paths toward the south road.

"You know it's not too late to head to South Pier and sneak aboard a boat to Elnora. I think it would be a thrill of a lifetime to go there." Viola grinned impishly.

Kate rolled her eyes at Viola. "I am sure you would, but I would rather not be killed as a spy."

"Kate, you need more of a sense of adventure. I know you are becoming an old lady now, but you have to live. We need excitement in our lives or we get old and stale, like bread."

"I am not an old lady. I am just much wiser than you are. I was, after all, beaten and tortured not too long ago."

"Well, you made it out alive, and that should embolden you. What are the chances of you getting beaten and tortured again in such a short time?"

"Higher than I want to admit," Kate said sarcastically.

Viola giggled and hopped as they went. "Just remember, the offer stands."

It took several hours to reach the south road, long enough that Kate thought they could take a break at the halfway point. She stopped, found her flask of soup, and took a few sips. Viola must have had some left as well, as she did the same.

"Why did they abandon the estate?" Kate asked.

"It's far from the city, and there was no one left to man it. The servants were almost all killed along with the family when the plague hit. It is very sad because Elias spent some of his childhood there."

"That's too bad. I know my father told me about some scheme Elias and he had made to marry me to the blacksmith. If I agreed to raise his children, they would let me have Elias's sister's estate by the mountain. Do you think it's the same?"

"It could be. It is of little use to him, and you might actually like it there. It's far enough from the mountain to be safe, and far enough south to make trips to South Pier if you wanted."

"It doesn't sound too bad. I guess I will see for myself."

Kate and Viola walked south awhile and then continued west along the paths toward the mountain. The western path was not familiar but Kate remembered some of how it went after her boar hunting. They were a little farther north of where Lucien and she had traveled to the mine gallery. She would have to take a southwestern direction to get to the location that Viola mentioned.

"How much farther, do you think?" Kate asked.

"It should be coming into view soon. I think if not we are starting to get an incline up the base of the mountain. The estate is not that close. We may need to head south a little more."

They turned south and it wasn't long until they could see a wood palisade in the distance. It looked in disrepair. It was getting colder, but just seeing how inhospitable the buildings seemed made Kate shiver even more than the cold did.

"It is amazing, isn't it?" Viola held out her arms as she ran inside to what would have been the courtyard area.

Kate followed cautiously. The palisade gate was open. Inside, most of the buildings showed the effects of their age. There were four buildings. A large stable just to the right of the entrance, and across from that was a workshop with a forge. The main manor was at the back, and there was a bunkhouse that probably once housed soldiers or servants adjacent to that. The area in front was open between all the buildings; it was in the shape of a horseshoe.

"It doesn't look like anyone has been here in ages." Kate looked at the collapsed roof of the stables.

"No, it doesn't. Let's find a way inside the manor. We can stay the night there," Viola said as she went to the door.

Viola tried the door, and then noticed an open window. She began to climb through.

"Be careful, I don't want you getting hurt inside there." Viola did not hear her. She tumbled through the open window with a laugh, followed by a muffled thump as she hit the floor.

It was no more than a moment before Viola opened the front door. Kate entered carefully, checking each way as she crossed the threshold.

The main room of the manor was completely open from front to back. There was a great hall in the center and two wings of rooms on each side. The large fire pit in the dining area had a high ceiling with an open floor, and there was a fireplace on each wall beside it. It was clear that someone of wealth must have built the place. The size was the most shocking part as you could easily seat over twenty people at the tables.

There was a lot of furniture strewn carelessly about, and there was wood stacked by the walls. *It would make sense they left everything. The plague killed thousands and thousands*, Kate thought.

"I am going to get a fire going in one of the fireplaces," Viola announced.

Kate wandered around the manor as Viola knelt down by the fireplace. She could never admit it, but she felt uneasy in this place. It was so big and so empty, it would be hard to feel at home here. The space and its emptiness made it feel like someone was watching, and it made her feel trapped inside.

Lucien was on her mind. No matter where they were together, she always felt safe with him. Even in the end, when she thought she would die, he was there to make her feel safe. She felt very sad that he was gone, and even more anxious about when she would see him again. *I miss you, Lucien.*

"I don't feel comfortable here, Viola. The place is so wide open, there isn't really any place to hide or defend," Kate said, looking around uneasily.

"Don't worry, I think we are safe. There is nothing out of place here, and not really anything of value. What would people want in this tattered old estate anyway?"

Us! They would want us, she thought. Kate paced around, rubbing her shoulders. If she was getting older like Viola said, it may very well be true. The fear of loneliness was strong before, and now she felt especially alone in this place. The last thing she wanted to do was scare Viola with stories of the mountain people.

Kate sat down with her back to the wall next to the fireplace and watched Viola. She had her blanket unrolled and was laying out all kinds of herbs on it. It was a mess of dust-like substances and other odd-shaped weeds. There was a small pile of what looked like dried skin. Kate recoiled, grimacing. It almost looked like human flesh.

"Gods, Viola, what is that?" Kate asked, pointing.

"This?" Viola took a bite, smiling.

Kate's mouth dropped open.

"You really are jumpy. It's just dried venison. It will be our dinner. I was going to make us some more soup. We can have half now, and half in the morning when we head for South Pier." Viola chewed as she moved the flasks and added the ingredients she had laid out.

Kate let out a sigh of relief and rubbed the nape of her neck. Viola was a new element in her life and it was taking some getting used to. Kate's imagination was running wild, and she had an idea why.

"That soup you gave me before doesn't make you anxious, does it?" Kate tried to take a deep breath to calm herself down, but the more she tried to calm herself, the more anxious and agitated she became.

"It might; perhaps I will lower the dose some in yours. Your eyes seem more dilated than usual. Here, drink this." Viola handed her a small vial.

Kate opened it and took a sniff. It didn't smell bad, and she took a drink. *Gods, that is powerful stuff,* she thought. Her heart began to slow, and her breathing was steady almost instantly. Her arms dropped to her side and she tilted her head back against the wall and she let out a huge sigh and smiled.

"Do you ever, you know, medicate Edwin?" Kate laughed, looking up at the ceiling.

"No, he is pretty unbalanced on his own," Viola said, fidgeting on with her herbs.

"He is so smitten with you. I don't know what you could be thinking of him. You seem to enjoy it."

Viola smiled at Kate. "I do, but it isn't all easy. Being a princess is stressful. I can feel how much pressure Elias applies to Martin, and I am no different."

"What kind of pressure?"

"Look right, talk right, and soften myself."

Kate couldn't help but laugh at the comment about softening yourself.

"Elias must be spending too much time with my father. I can tell you he has said 'soften yourself' to me over a dozen times. I get furious with him."

"You have to see his point. You aren't exactly soft. You're tougher than Edwin," Viola said.

"I take that as a compliment. Edwin is a bit of a dandy for my tastes," Kate said.

"He is plenty manly for me. That ruffian Lucien, gods, what you see in that man-boy. He will never grow up."

"He has a lot on his mind. If you knew him like I do..."

Kate trailed off, thinking about Lucien's secrets. It made her very uneasy talking about them with Viola. They were rival kingdoms and she swore never to talk about them.

"What is it?" Viola asked, furrowing her brow.

"It is just...Lucien has a lot of secrets. I don't want to betray his confidence."

"Have you seen him without the blindfold?"

"I have, and it is frightening at first, but he is still the same, even though he looks that way."

"Edwin says people just overreact because he is different. I do see his charm, though. Lucien might be the only decent prince I have ever known. I could even imagine being with him, you know."

What! Kate shook her head without even noticing and became very warm, and her face got red imagining Viola smiling at

Lucien. She was a princess after all, and Kate had no way to compete with a busty and dainty little blond girl like her.

Viola rocked back on her haunches, looking at the fire. "Kate, you should calm down. I meant nothing by it. You have to realize how it is for me. Elias would give anything for me to marry Lucien. It would unite the kingdoms in a way nothing else could."

Kate was not only angry, but horribly sad. Viola was right. They would never be safe, and Lucien was very decent compared to the likes of Oswald and Elena. She did not even like Henry of Westfall. He smelled of arrogance and condescension, a terribly rancid perfume of entitlement.

"You may not know this, but King Delvin offered a full alliance if I agreed to marry Lucien."

"I am not surprised," Kate answered, and was surprised to hear how raspy her voice was. She looked away and closed her eyes.

"I even agreed. When Lucien first met me, Edwin asked him point blank if he would be with me. He said no, he didn't like me. I was very hurt because I felt he could easily come to like me, seeing as not many did."

Kate looked back to her seeing now how hard it must have been. "Gods, Viola, I am sorry. I was so jealous I just... never thought you might feel that way. I can be so sensitive about Lucien. I never realized what you might feel."

"It doesn't matter. Edwin went on and on about how he loved blonde girls, and how I was so perfect. He was rabid." Kate noticed when Viola laughed, her nose wiggled. "He told me his mother was a curly blonde beauty when she was younger, and I was twice as pretty. It was nice to have his affection. He liked me for me, and really he has little to gain from a marriage with me other than my affection. You should already know his father may be the wealthiest in all of Amor, but he loves his freedom just like you do."

"Wow, there is a lot I didn't know about Edwin. He seems to be a lot sweeter than I give him credit for. I guess I always felt his jealousy of me and Lucien. The loving stuff between you was also pretty sickening." Kate put her hand over her mouth to stifle a laugh.

"Well, get used to it, because I plan to marry him. Just as soon as Lucien is married," Viola said, her voice trailing off.

"What do you mean?"

"Kate, you have to clearly understand that no woman in all of Amor can marry until Lucien is. They all have to wait until he is off the market. If there is even a chance, our keepers will make us hold out, hoping to land a marriage. I assure you it's the same in Westfall, The Vale, and especially in Elgin. Elena might hate you, but she hates her father more. I can't help but feel like she has been hurt the most by her wicked father."

Kate pulled her legs up to her chest, wrapped her arms around them, and rested her chin on her knees. *What a sickening thought.* She wasn't even able to marry Lucien until his father gave his approval. This would be possible only if both their families worked together and right now, she wasn't sure King Delvin even knew. Her own father may not make it easy.

"That is horrible. I feel very guilty just thinking about being with Lucien now. It is difficult to accept that people are that desperate, but if they are desperate enough to starve the marshes with trade, they would certainly deny marriage for their children until a key alliance is beyond their reach. It is hard not to see this world as a horror."

Viola smirked and said, "I am just glad that Edwin is with me. He doesn't care if we marry right away, and being friends with Lucien gives him inside information as well. Maybe we can have our weddings together."

"I was comfortable thinking no one wanted to marry Lucien. It might still be the case, but the politics are far worse. The kings and lords of the continent are far more interested in him than any woman."

"Maybe we can get them together, and they can marry him," Viola struggled to finish her sentence as she burst out laughing.

Kate was laughing at her comment before they both stopped to quietly smile. The fire was going very strong now, and the house was cozy as the warmth spread throughout. Kate leaned against the wall and once again let her mind turn to what Lucien might be doing.

"You know, Lucien isn't much different from Edwin," Viola said.

"You mean they are both little boys pretending to be men?" Kate asked, and raised an eyebrow. "I know. Believe me, I know."

"No, I mean the stuff about Edwin's mother. He has a particular taste in women, and I just so happen to fit that. Lucien is the same. Edwin told me about the soldier girl who rejected him."

"Yes, I have heard something about it as well. She rejected him when he got too close."

"Is it surprising? Lucien had no mother. He spent his entire time at the fortress and never had any female companions, other than wicked maids. Then he spent the last five years or more with the army. Maybe he sees girl soldiers and that is what he knows. It is also what he likes, someone who fits into his life with minimal change."

Kate smiled, thinking Lucien liked her because she was different. It would be hard to find a girl who lived as she did. The thought had occurred to her before, that maybe Lucien likes someone who can take care of herself, but also might be a companion to take care of him.

"I think he just likes to have someone around to get him out of trouble," Kate said, and giggled. "Once Edwin is married, the two of them won't be spending as much time together. That probably worries Lucien. He is the youngest, and being alone can be miserable."

"Well, I plan to stick with him. We are good together, and I could not imagine being with anyone else. It won't be easy having to be queen and accepting that I won't be able to travel as much as I would like, but being around him is all I really want."

"Certainly, it is a perfect match. I think so, anyway. Once you two are married, it doesn't have to be boring. You can still travel. Lucien's father will be around at least a few more years."

Kate straightened her legs and clasped her hands in her lap. "I hope so. Lucien and I need to run off together and just spend time getting bored with each other."

"That might be a wish that remains unfulfilled. I thought after a couple weeks of Edwin I would get tired of him, but I just want to be around him even more. The more I'm with him, the more I want to be with him. Does that make any sense?"

"I could spend every day with Lucien and never get bored. He has his schemes working, always. The war and politics are on his mind, not to mention making trouble for his minders. When I say this right now, it cannot be far from your mind that the two of those scoundrels must be up to something that would make both of us blush."

Kate lay down on her side with her cloak balled up as a pillow, and her blanket pulled over the top of her. Viola did the same.

"I can only imagine. I would probably be more worried than embarrassed." Viola yawned. "We will have to go to South Pier in the morning. Maybe play some dice."

"Gods, the thought of you playing dice sounds like one of the most dangerous things you have said yet. You better have some crowns because I am skint for sure. That reminds me: Lucien hasn't paid me back for the horse wagon we took to Omskov. Maybe he is a scoundrel."

"I hope he does not get himself killed with one of his mad schemes in the meantime. Edwin is no help in that department. When the two of them are together, they are nothing but trouble. " Viola closed her eyes and drifted off to sleep, but the smile did not leave her face for quite a long, long while.

CHAPTER 6

"GODS, IT IS tough getting used to porting," Edwin said, brushing off his clothes. "Where exactly are we?"

"We are standing in the exact spot where I fell unconscious and Elena took Kate off to be tortured to death," Lucien said, spreading his arms to take in their surroundings as he turned in a slow circle.

"That is comforting," Edwin responded wryly. "So, which direction do we go?"

Lucien put his finger in his mouth and held it up to the slight breeze, as if that could tell him anything. "Hmmm, east?"

"I guess this is why you keep me around."

Edwin removed a map from his cloak pocket and opened it over his knee.

"We should probably head south to avoid Omskov, and then head east until the hills level out some."

Lucien slapped Edwin's back and said, sarcastically, "Good plan, I'm glad you came along!" Lucien surveyed the area, shading his eyes with his hand.

Lucien couldn't help but paw at his blindfold. *I thought I was done with this thing.* He did not want to wear it anymore, but Jan's reaction left him concerned about anyone who might see his eyes. When he finally confessed to Kate who and what he was, he thought it would not matter anymore what anyone else thought. When he felt the unease of the people in Porin, he changed his mind. *Just when I am out and about meeting new people, I hope.*

His sense picked up a lot more around Omskov now that Kate was gone; her power over him was incredible. Lucien could feel the Elgin forces nearby. They were an hour or more away. Their discomfort was obvious to him and easy to pick up. It might even be dread.

Lucien and Edwin walked south to the east road. The road was rubble and the terrain was rocky hills with some mountain grasses among the flat areas.

"Kind of desolate," Edwin said, looking down the road. "It makes Porin look like paradise."

"Precisely why Icel wants it- the lands of Dulimore are a wasteland. If there is one thing they have on the marshes though, it's that there is at least some grazing land and plenty of minerals. They could use timber. It is amazing they are so petty as to not trade since the marsh is full of the stuff. Stone for timber seems to be the easiest trade in the world."

Lucien and Edwin continued walking down the road for more than an hour and the land began to level. The rocky hills gradually became more smooth and rolling, and the elevation sloped down. It was just a moment after they met a steep hill that they could see a drop down into a river valley.

From their elevation they could see the river basin below and grasslands stretching out far off in the distance.

"This must be the stream that Alaric mentioned. It's really not much of a border between the provinces," Edwin commented, looking at the map. He rolled it back up. "It looks like we need to climb the hill here north. We should see the camp once we are up there."

Lucien and Edwin climbed north up the hill. Once they reached the peak, they could still not see. There was a dip and then another hill further north. They continued down into the gap between the hills and made their way to the top. Just as they reached the peak of the hill, the sound of voices drifted toward them.

"Wait," Lucien said. "Do you hear voices?"

Edwin paused for a moment. "No, must be you picking them up on your senses."

Lucien listened again and didn't hear anything, but he felt overwhelmed with dread. The soldiers took no pleasure in their position and the impending war. They had no interest in fighting, and most were considering desertion.

Lucien and Edwin stood up to see another hill. There was another hill just beyond it.

"Gods, these hills seem to go on forever." Edwin climbed up behind Lucien on the next hill.

Just as Lucien stood to go over the top of the hill, an arrow whizzed past his right leg, close enough that the breath of its passing made his cloak flutter.

"Get down!" Edwin grabbed Lucien and they both dropped behind the rise.

Lucien removed his bow and nocked an arrow. Edwin pulled his sword.

"Watch this," Lucien said with a cocky wink.

Lucien stood, drew his bow, and released the arrow. Edwin had his head above the crest of the hill just in time to see the arrow miss high.

"That's not as impressive as you seemed to think it would be," Edwin snorted.

The soldier below was wearing black armor and a black metal helm. He had his bow drawn just as the arrow whizzed by over his head. He released his arrow, and it fell short of its mark, spraying rocks and dirt in Edwin's face.

The soldier then began to charge up the hill.

"Lucien, any time now," Edwin yelled, watching the man drawing ever closer.

Lucien aimed his bow again and let the arrow loose. It missed the soldier by an even wider margin than the first one. The soldier continued up the hill, making Lucien think absurdly of a metal stove suddenly given the gift of mobility. Lucien would have laughed if the soldier wasn't so quickly closing the distance between them.

"Lucien, we have to run," Edwin said. When Lucien didn't move, Edwin drew his sword and stood ready to meet the attack.

"I have him." Lucien calmly drew his bow, and steadied his aim. The soldier was closing, and was within a few yards, then a few feet. Lucien released the arrow and it struck the soldier square in the head.

The arrow ricocheted off his helm, striking sparks where it hit, and flew back towards Lucien, nicking Edwin on his right cheek. The soldier stumbled, dropped his bow and swung his arms like windmill blades, trying to regain his balance. With a curse muffled by his helm, he fell backward, and tumbled down the hill with a crash and clatter. He was nearly in control of the fall when his head smashed on a jagged rock. The helmet made a bell-like sound and crumpled where it struck the rock. The soldier lay motionless as blood dripped from his visor, torn loose by the impact.

Lucien quickly turned to Edwin with his finger in his face. "Not one word," he said to him tersely.

"I..."

"Not. One. Word," Lucien repeated as they moved down toward the dead soldier.

"I feel safer with Kate," Edwin blurted out as he wiped at the wound on his face.

Lucien stared down at the dead soldier, wondering how he could miss him three times. He did not want to use his power because he was getting too dependent on it. If the final arrow had not hit him, Lucien probably would have burned him alive. That would not have been a good way to go.

"I definitely need to practice more with the bow." Lucien rubbed his chin, unable to look away from the lifeless soldier.

"What now?"

"We technically didn't kill him. He fell to his death, so it's not as if we broke the peace. It was self-defense anyway. He fired first without even a warning."

"Right," Edwin said with a nod.

Lucien seemed to notice the blood on Edwin's cheek for the first time.

"The wound doesn't look too bad," he said after a moment's consideration. "It probably won't even scar."

This only made Edwin even more aware of it. He rubbed at it, checking his hand for blood.

"Well, let us- carefully- climb to the top of the hill east. We should probably see someone now." Lucien calmly began to climb.

The two of them stayed low to the ground as they climbed to the top of the hill. Peering out across the peak, they could see hundreds of tents in the purple shadows of the valley below. The majority of them were far off in the distance on a small stream that came off of the river. The river was not that wide- more of a creek with several fingers reaching in several different directions. The basin was a floodplain and a grassy marsh. It was dry this time of year. Lucien could hear Edwin counting the tents under his breath.

"How many do you count?"

"It is at least a thousand," Edwin sighed with resignation.

Lucien winced. "So, not a training group then?"

"No. What do you pick up from them?"

"What I've felt all along. Dread. They are not looking forward to the invasion, or the war."

"What do we do?"

"I don't know. We can go back and tell Alaric, although I suspect there is little he can do. This army will pillage the countryside with ease. I doubt they will lose a single soldier from the looks of them." Lucien absently drummed his fingers on his chin.

Edwin shifted his eyes back and forth over the army trying to come up with ideas. "Well, I think we have to slow them down, at least. Maybe burn a few tents?"

"Maybe, or I could port south, get my armor, and try and scare them into running." Lucien said, only half-serious.

Edwin could hardly imagine how horrifying it would be to see Lucien in that armor. It was made of obsidian and was designed to look like skin stretched over bones, with inlays of scales like an alligator. The pauldrons were shaped as claws down to the gauntlets. From the cuisses to the greaves, the design was animal legs with three-toed hooves for feet. If all that wasn't terrifying enough, the helm resembled a demon skull with two sets of horns on top and a small vertical opening at the mouth that linked with two small openings for his eyes. *Peering out from behind that demon skull was the stuff of nightmares*, he thought.

Edwin rested his chin on the back of his hand. "Well, maybe in the daylight they won't be so afraid. Just give it a try."

Lucien shrugged and disappeared. Edwin slid down the hill, away from the top to make sure no one would see him. It was possible the soldier they encountered was part of a patrol and his fellows might be looking for him. Just as he thought that, Lucien appeared in the black demon armor.

"Gods!" Edwin said, his throat suddenly dry, his voice little more than a whisper.

Lucien's red eyes peering from the demon helm were terrifying, perhaps even more terrifying than the demon armor.

"All right, well, in the daylight it's far more frightening than I thought. I swear you look a lot taller." Edwin struggled to regain his composure.

"The boots are thick and the helm is tall as well. I will just pop in and see if they will try to fight. If I can burn some of the tents, they might break and run. I will push some of the ground and add to the fire. If I get in trouble, I will warp back and switch out of this ridiculous thing." Lucien waved his arms with limited mobility, mostly shifting at his hips.

Lucien pulled his scimitar. "Well, here we go."

Edwin crawled to the top of the hill to peer out over the camps. Lucien reappeared in an open area between the middle rows of tents. The men looked and immediately screamed. There was pandemonium as soldiers scattered in all directions.

Edwin couldn't help but laugh at the spectacle. Lucien shot fire into the sky and ignited several of the tents with flames from his hands. Anyone who had not run initially did now. The fleeing soldiers scattered in all directions, but the majority went toward the border north with the Vale.

In the distance a man wearing a red cape and riding a horse came into view. He shouted and waved, trying to rally the men around him. Lucien disappeared and reappeared at the camps further in the distance where some of the men had tried to hide. He ignited several tents and the men dropped their weapons and fled.

The caped man must have been the general or commander. He yelled to the men, "Stop running! He is just a man, and like any man, can die!"

Lucien appeared behind his horse and slapped it with his hand. The horse reared, whinnied, and threw its rider. The man landed on the ground with a grunt next to Lucien.

"Just a man." Lucien's red eyes peered from the darkness of the demon helm. "Could just a man do this?" He spread his fingers, palms down, summoning flames that burned a circle around them. Lucien grabbed the general and ported, reappearing at the river.

"If hell's flames aren't to your liking, perhaps this will be!" Lucien growled, and threw his screaming captive into the shallow river.

Edwin laughed wildly and covered his mouth as the men fled from the field. The general had struggled out of the water and was running for his life now, heading east to the Elgin capital, City of Saints.

Lucien reappeared behind Edwin. He looked and felt terrible. There was blood leaking from his mouth, nose, and eyes, and his breathing was as ragged as a dog's on the hottest day of summer.

"Gods, it took a lot out of me, going back and forth," Lucien gasped, sitting on the hill next to Edwin. He had returned to his normal clothes and blindfold.

Edwin could only smile. He put his hand on Lucien's shoulder.

"What do you think? Did it work?" Lucien panted.

Edwin slapped Lucien's back. "I don't think you will see some of those soldiers in Elgin for a decade. They dropped their swords and ran for their lives."

"Let's hope so. I can imagine it will embolden King Richter. He will see through the tricks."

"Maybe, but it definitely will live long in their memories. I would imagine in a few days all of Amor will hear of the attack from the demon prince."

"I can barely stand. We should head back to Porin. I need to rest." Lucien struggled to catch his breath, and tears of blood ran down his cheeks from beneath the blindfold.

Lucien grabbed Edwin's arm, and they vanished.

CHAPTER 7

KATE SLEPT SOUNDLY in the night. She enjoyed Viola's company and felt they were fast becoming good friends.

As Kate turned over in her bedroll, a hand clamped over her mouth. She was fully awake now. She struggled in the darkness as someone wrapped their arms around her legs. She reached for her sword but it was gone.

"She is strong, grab her and tie her hands," a man's voice growled.

Kate kicked and struggled but the pressure of a large man on top of her made it difficult to breathe and left her weak. They had a gag wrapped around her head by now, and her legs were tied. Her hands were bound in front of her and a hood was pulled over her head. A moment later, she was picked up and thrown over someone's shoulder.

Panic was setting in. Her heart pounded and fear spiraled through her body. Kate heard only two men, but did not hear Viola as they carried her away. Maybe they grabbed her before.

They walked for what seemed like forever with her over her captor's shoulder. Her hips and stomach ached in pain. The weather was getting colder, and she sensed snow in the air. They must have been going up a path to the mountain.

Slavers! Kate tried desperately to get her hands free, but they were bound so tightly she could no longer feel them. She shook with fear, and fought back tears. She knew there was nothing they would do until she was sold or gifted to whoever wanted her. So she tried to comfort herself. *Stay calm, you will get your chance to escape. Be brave. They will underestimate your strength and ability.* Tears swelled in her eyes as she tried to focus. If only Lucien were around, at least she could hope for a rescue. Viola could be dead or captured, and even still she was no fighter.

Kate had lost track of time and was convinced the trek would never end. She was surprised when she was suddenly and roughly thrown to the ground. She grunted in pain, landing on her left side.

"Well, what do you think?" a man's voice asked.

"These marsh women are so small, I am not sure if they would parlay for something so little," a different voice said.

Someone removed her hood. She blinked in the dim light. She looked at the men before her. They had shaded skin, and the one kneeling beside her had long black hair and paintings on his face. He was very large, and had two swords on his back, and was covered in animal skins. The man to his left was lighter in complexion. He had a large scar on his face and a bow on his back, with two daggers at his belt.

"Maybe the Taiga will give us something for her," the man kneeling beside her said.

"We just took three of theirs, they will not trade. We are best to take the three and this one to barter. If we can give four for two, they might agree," the man with the scar said.

The kneeling man removed the binding from Kate's mouth.

"Who are you, girl? You dress as a boy, but are far too small and frail to be one."

Kate didn't answer. She knew talking would get her into more trouble. It was best to stay quiet. It had worked in the past. The man looked unhappy and frustrated.

"Girl, you will talk or I will leave you to my men, and who knows what they would do to you?"

Kate's hands trembled and her heart was racing. There was no escape and she didn't want them to abuse her. She had to buy time.

"Kate."

"Where are you from? There are no settlements in the marshes near the mountain."

"I am from Dawnbridge."

"The city? You are far from home, girl. Why did you come so far to the mountain?"

"I am a hunter. I was tracking animals." Kate's voice was broken and meek. She prayed he did not sense her lie.

"We will not harm you if you cooperate. We have no use for such slender things on the mountain. You are for trade only. Do you understand?"

"Yes," Kate said, nodding.

"I am Tel-son, and this is my tribe," he said as he stood and waved toward the huts around them.

Kate sat up and looked around. They were so high in the mountain that the sea was hidden just beyond the horizon. The camp sat in a large cave in the side of the cliff, and she could see a small path down the side of the mountain. *That must have been where we came from.*

"If you want money, I know someone who would pay to get me back," Kate bargained, hoping beyond hope he would be interested in the offer.

"Well, girl, I am afraid we are not interested in money," he said as the two of them laughed. "Someone took something from me, and I want it back. You are to be traded in order to get what I want."

Kate nodded hastily, biting her lip. There was a small fire nearby where she was thrown. She could smell meat cooking. They had a drying rack for animal skins near the huts. *The camp is well isolated and defended*, she thought. Kate's stomach was in knots. *How long will it take for them to trade me, to whom, and what happened to Viola?* she wondered.

CHAPTER 8

VIOLA WOKE BEFORE dawn just so she could see the sun through the trees. The freedom of being able to move without restrictions and do things alone was such a thrill. She wanted to pick some rare flowers that bloomed only at dawn-time.

She quietly left the estate and picked thistle near the stables. It was going to be a beautiful sunrise and she looked off in the distance where the sun smudged the horizon as it climbed higher. She walked and picked flowers and herbs as she went north of the estate. She was about to head back to start the morning meal when she heard struggling from the palisade and the sound of two men talking. They were just far enough away she couldn't make out what they were saying, but the tone of their words told her it wasn't good.

Viola crouched down close to the stake wall and overgrown shrubbery to conceal herself. The men left the yard and exited by the gate. One went south. Viola did not see Kate with him. She let him get ahead of her, then followed from a safe distance. As she followed she looked back at the other man and noticed he was carrying something over his shoulder. It must have been Kate. Something that looked like Kate's satchel was slung over his other shoulder. A surge of adrenaline slammed through her system, and she started to worry what they might do to her.

Viola had tears in her eyes, imagining them brutalizing her on the mountain. She had to do something. *What would Edwin do?* she asked herself. It was clear: she had to kill the bandit and circle back for the other.

Viola followed close behind the bandit. She took out her dagger and dipped the tip of it in a potion from her satchel. The man slowed and began to relieve himself on a tree. Viola nearly gagged in disgust. *The savage*, she thought as she came up behind him.

Just as she was going to stick the dagger into his back, he finished and turned. He was startled, but regained his composure quickly. He backhanded her, knocking her to the ground. His blow split her lip, and she thought he might have loosened a tooth.

"Well, well, what have we here?" he asked with a hideous, toothless grin.

Viola swiped at his leg with the dagger and nicked his thigh. He cursed and knocked the dagger from her hand, then grabbed her around the throat.

"Look at you! What runty girls they have in the marshes." He lifted her by her neck into the air with ease.

Viola could not breathe. Black speckles exploded in the periphery of her vision, their sparks spreading across all of her sight. She was losing consciousness, and if she did, that would be the end of it.

"Normally I'd throw something as small as you back, but I think I can find...can find..."

He spoke thickly, confusedly. He dropped Viola and clawed at his throat. He gasped for air. Foam poured from his mouth as he struggled. He flailed as he collapsed to the ground.

She lay on her back, eyes closed, gasping for breath, trying to calm her pounding heart but managing only to make it race harder and faster, like a horse that has kicked down its fence and is galloping over all the hills in all the world.

She heard a sharp, rattling wheeze. The man she thought was dead sat up, his eyes wide. The froth around his mouth was flecked with blood, but he wasn't dead yet. The poison was killing him, but it might not do its deadly job before he could kill her.

Her fingers scrabbled in the dirt for her fallen dagger. She touched the hilt with her fingertip and tried to inch it closer to her hand. The man bellowed in agony. Black and purple splotches appeared on his face and neck, and now the bloody foam was leaking from his nose.

He did not lunge for her so much as he fell toward her, but Viola had the dagger now and the tip of the blade entered his chest with a wet punching sound.

He breathed his last into her face and the smell was horrible.

She struggled out from beneath his pinning weight, afraid to look away from the man in case he decided death was not for him.

Freed, Viola covered her mouth in horror, trying not to vomit. Tears streaked down her cheeks. She retrieved the dagger from his chest with shaking hands. It came out even easier than it went in. Bloody knife in hand, she took off running in the other direction. *I killed that man*, she thought, *but the man would have killed me in a few seconds had the poison not made it to his blood first and weakened him enough for me to escape. But I killed him.*

Viola wiped at the tears on her cheeks. In the distance she saw the man with Kate. They were far ahead, at the base of the mountain, and the man was taking a path that led upward.

Viola did not know what to do. They were too far for her to catch them, and if he dropped Kate she could fall off the side of the cliff. She pressed her back against a shallow declivity in the rocks, willing the man not to turn and look toward her.

Viola palmed her tears away. When she was sure she'd given them enough time, she slipped out of hiding. All she could do was follow them. She realized it didn't matter how far ahead they might be as long as there was only the one path they all followed. The only other way off the mountain was over the side, and she didn't think that was the man's intention.

She hoped it wasn't, at least.

The path became narrower but the man followed it with the surefootedness of a mountain goat.

Around the final curve, the path widened into a clearing and Viola managed to step back into hiding before anyone could see her. She held her breath, afraid someone would hear her, and peeked around the rocky wall.

Viola could see smoke from a campfire. She almost gasped as the man tossed Kate roughly to the ground. A large man approached Kate and spoke to her. Other men came out of a cave entrance and gathered around their captive. They did not behave violently toward Kate. *Yet!*

There was little else she could do here, so she made her way back down the path and squirmed her way into the narrow fissure she'd hidden in earlier. She needed time to think, and a place in which to do it safely.

A few light flakes of snow began to fall, then more.

Just as Viola settled, she heard the shouting of men down below. They had come up the path a little ways to yell up at them.

As near as Viola could make out, the argument was something about children and a goat.

There was no way to tell how many men were in the caves above, or on the path below. It wasn't even clear to Viola if the men below would welcome and aid her, even though they seemed to be at odds with the cliff dwellers. She just didn't know what to do.

Viola wrapped herself in her cloak and decided to rest while she waited to see if Kate would get free.

CHAPTER 9

THE TEMPERATURE HAD been dropping steadily since mid-day, and now fat clots of snow were falling. The wind was howling like a drunk in a tavern and it was as cold and sharp as a knife's edge. Kate tried to stay close to the fire.

The wind seemed to hold its breath for a moment, allowing the yelling of the men on the paths below to reach the cliff's top.

"Tel-son, we know you took our children. We won't leave until you give them back," a man's voice drifted up on the wind to them.

Tel-son and several of the members of the tribe pulled their weapons and strode to the cliff's edge.

"Ulfr, you killed my brother. He was worth more than those three runts we took. Consider us even and be done with it," Tel-son warned.

"Your brother stole our goats. He died a thief. You now steal our children. You will meet the same fate if you do not return them."

"Are you calling me a thief? I will kill you where you stand!" Tel-son cried as he raised his weapon in warning.

Tel-son grunted and dropped his sword.

"Balls," he muttered.

He swayed unsteadily, as if uncertain whether to fall or continue standing. A powerful gust of wind decided the matter for him and he toppled slowly to the snow-covered path. The shaft of an arrow jutted from his chest.

There was a shout from below followed by a fusillade of arrows. Many whacked against the rocky outcropping; a few arced high over the cliff's edge and rained down on the camp. Most were blown off course by the powerful winds, the archers' aim spoiled by the sheets of snow.

But the men below were getting their range and the next volley of arrows would not be so ineffectual.

"Hurry, get him inside!" the man with the scar ordered, dragging Tel-son across the snowy ground.

Kate slid herself as far away from the fighting as she could. Her back was against the cave wall, but still close enough to the fire she did not freeze to death.

Several people tended to Tel-son as the arrow-fire into the camp stopped. For now. The men took defensive positions, and had nets full of rocks brought up to the path.

They laid Tel-son next to the fire. His breath was thready, and blood came from his mouth. Kate couldn't help but think that he was dying, and wondered why he wasn't already dead. These people dressed in fur, and seemed to have less than nothing. *Why did they stay on the mountain?* she thought.

There were several very large women who came out and dressed Tel-son's wound, but his breathing was still labored. Blood soaked through the bandages almost as soon as they were applied, and the women who tended Tel-son dressed the wound once more with clean cloths.

Kate could tell they had little knowledge of medicine, and that she could help him. It frightened her to think what might happen if she tried to help and he died. They might blame her.

He became frustrated with their doting over him and told them to leave. Tel-son noticed Kate had been watching him.

"What, enjoying my suffering, marsh runt?" he gasped, and there was only disdain in his voice.

"No, I might be able to help if you untie my hands." Kate lifted her hands up to him.

"I am dying. The arrow struck me true. Those Taiga scum kill another of my people."

"They said you provoked them. Is it true that your brother stole from them?"

"They killed him for a goat. We are starving, and they live in peace and harmony north beyond the mountain. Could they not spare a goat for my brother's life?"

Kate felt only sadness for him. These people lived in a dire situation. She knew they were savages, but they killed each other and stole children. The barbarism was hard for her to understand and harder still for her to accept why they did not leave.

Kate grimaced at the sound of his pained breathing. "Would you not have done the same?"

"Yes, I would," Tel-son responded with a strained laugh.

"Let me help you. I know something about medicine, and you will pay me back with my freedom." Kate hoped he would agree.

"I would rather die than free you. The Westfall monsters took my daughters. I do not wish to live so long as they are made whores of that petty king."

Kate could not believe what he said. Why would Westfall take his children?

"Are you certain Westfall took them? I know men of Westfall and they are decent people, incapable of doing something as unconscionable as you claim."

"You know nothing, swamp runt. They treat us like we are cattle to them. They steal from us, lie to us, and kill us for their entertainment."

Kate's heart sank at the thought. People saw them as savages, not even human. *Less than human.* Maybe what he said was true. She only knew them as decent people, but even in the marshes there were criminals. If she could help him, she would. He deserved that much.

"Tel-son, I will help you. I don't want to be a slave either. You have to let me treat your wound and promise not to let me be given as a slave. I will get your daughters back, if you trust me," Kate begged, and tears pricked the corners of her eyes.

"Why do you think that you can get my daughters back?" he asked, and coughed violently. She waited while he forced himself up on one shoulder and spat out a wad of bloody phlegm.

"I know people who are powerful. They are more powerful than the king of Westfall. I can get them to return your daughters, I swear. Just believe what I am telling you, and it will work."

Tel-son paused to give it thought. He took more strained breaths as he clutched at his chest. His brow furrowed and he blinked pain-sweat out of his eyes. He was dying, but his eyes were still full of fire.

"If you lie, I swear on my ancestors, I will see you and everyone you love dead. I will burn your home and I will kill everyone who flees, and then I will salt the ground where your home stood."

Kate crawled to Tel-son, and held out her hands for him to free her. Just as he reached up with his knife, the scarred man jumped to his feet, exclaiming, "What are you doing, brother? Are you mad from fever? What about your daughters?"

"Hear me, Earie, I am dying. This girl thinks she can help heal me, and more importantly, she thinks he might be able to get my daughters back."

"She lies! She would say anything to save herself. She is Taiga, just look at her skin."

"If she is, I ask you to seek vengeance in my name. I cannot live without my daughters, and this wound will take me before I can save them. You have to trust her, if she can help. It is my last hope." Tel-son wheezed a mist of blood and took Earie's hand.

Tel-son cut Kate's bindings. Her hands and feet were numb. She struggled to move them and the numbness quickly passed. She opened her satchel and reached in. Earie grabbed her arm. "Careful, runt. If I see a dagger in your hand, I won't hesitate to slit your throat, no matter what my brother says."

"No dagger," Kate said, and rummaged through her satchel. There was lichen and a small marigold potion. She held them up for Earie to inspect.

"Please drink this. It will help heal you." Kate gave Tel-son the marigold potion. Earie grabbed the vial, removed the stopper, and sniffed it.

"It isn't poison," he said, and held it to Tel-son's lips so he could drink. Half of the potion spilled out of his mouth as he coughed.

"Gods! Are you certain?"

Men are all babies when they are sick, she thought, and the thought made her want to laugh, but she knew this would not be a good place or time to do so.

Kate carefully opened his jerkin. It was stuck to the wound and she teased it free as gently as she could. The wound still bled. She looked for the arrow they had pulled from Tel-son, but they hadn't. They had only broken off the shaft. The arrowhead was still buried in his chest. The entry wound looked like a jagged set of lips. Kate spread the lips with the thumb and pointer finger of her left hand and slipped the same digits of her right hand into the wound. She could feel the arrowhead. It was lodged tightly, possibly in bone.

"Brace yourself, but I must remove the arrow." Kate struggled to remove it, digging into his chest.

It wouldn't pull straight out so she had to gently jiggle it from side to side. Each movement brought a new freshet of blood and a stifled grunt from Tel-son.

"Gods! Either pull it out or drive it into my heart, but end this!" Tel-son snarled.

The arrow broke free after Kate shifted it side to side and gave it one last mighty tug. Tel-son was falling unconscious as she began to work with the lichen and bandages. The bleeding had slowed with the removal of the arrowhead and the lichen she packed into the wound. She wrapped the strips of bandage around his chest as hard and tight as she could to keep pressure on the wound.

Earie watched closely as she worked, wary of any signs of deceit or treachery. "He better live, girl, or you won't."

He stared at her and then walked out of the cave. She laid Tel-son flat on his back near the campfire. It was beginning to die down, and she threw a few more branches onto it, kindling it back to life. Kate only hoped she'd done as much for Tel-son. She covered him with a blanket of furs that they had laid on his legs. He seemed to breathe steadily and easily.

She had done as she had promised. The next few hours would tell the story. But right now, Kate needed to find out if they knew anything of what happened to Viola.

She approached Earie standing at the cave entrance.

"Earie, do you have my weapons from the estate? I need to look for my friend." Kate swallowed hard before asking, "You didn't kill her, did you?"

"What, another runt like you? You were all we saw, but another of the tribe is missing. Here are your weapons. You run from this camp and do not return, we will hunt you. All of us."

Kate's stomach lurched at the idea of them chasing after her. She knew the violence and cruelty they were capable of. She hoped Viola had not abandoned her, or worse. If she was going to get those girls free in Westfall, Viola would have to help.

CHAPTER 10

LUCIEN LAY EXHAUSTED on the bed. He used a rag to wipe at the blood from his mouth, nose, and eyes. Porting to the island and back was too far. He was lucky he didn't lose consciousness or have a brain-bleed. He had felt lightheaded as soon as he arrived in the obsidian armor. It was very dangerous to push too hard and he very well could have collapsed on the battlefield. It had happened before, in Omskov, and it was an experience he was not keen to repeat. The only thing that mattered now was whether it worked or not.

He had heard Edwin in the hallway. Edwin had spoken to Jan and Alaric by now and would have information from the spies about the Elgin army. The news would get across the continent with or without the spies as the army scattered, and the Vale would be the first to know since most of the soldiers fled north.

It was difficult to shake the feeling Lucien had picked up from the Elgin soldiers. There were almost none who wanted to be in that army and even the general who had tried to rally them seemed to have little interest in staying to fight. It was possible that Richter Elgin was just as bad as everyone said, and those men were conscripted. They looked well armored, and had good weapons, but by no means did they look like seasoned knights. It was more likely they were men-at-arms, or common guards from the castle.

Lucien was relieved it was over now. The room in Jan's castle manor was small, perhaps half the size of the ones in Dawnbridge and King's port, but still afforded the same luxuries. There was a huge bed with excellent bedding and at least one large window in the outer wall. There was a desk, wardrobe as well, and a nice animal skin rug on the floor. These were luxuries intended for a lord. It stood to reason that the king of Dulimore was uneasy with the prestige and power of having the manor city.

The sense of unease and distrust Lucien first felt when he arrived in the city seemed to have lessened considerably since their talk at dinner. Lucien continued to wear the blindfold in hopes of keeping his identity suppressed and put those around him at ease. There was no reason to push their good-will further.

If Lucien could help Jan, he might be a good ally to have, even if Icel was upset with the relationship. *Jan has to get married or he is going to be assassinated,* he thought. King Delvin had to be informed of the situation first thing upon their return. *If they returned.*

The door creaked as Edwin peered into the room.

"I'm awake," Lucien said.

Edwin approached Lucien where he lay in bed, still fully clothed. It was just afternoon now, and it would be better to try to stay awake until the evening.

"How is it?" Edwin sat on the side of the bed.

"It took a lot out of me. I feel my strength coming back."

"That's good. Alaric and Jan have sent out spies to get a survey of the positions. They even sent someone into Elgin near The

Saints. If they get a look at the capital there is a good chance to find out if they will raise another army."

"Did they say what they were thinking?"

"They both seemed to want to get more information. So far, they see this as a positive outcome. It should make Richter think again before invading, and the morale of his forces has to have taken a hit. Jan seemed unhappy you didn't spill some blood though. He was pretty frustrated you didn't kill at least half the forces. If they go north they could just join up with Vale forces, and make them stronger."

"Why would he care? They have Westfall to deal with, not to mention the Boreal raiders in the north. They should be happy with the lands they have now. It is a blessing to have Elgin brought to heel. That would give them the opportunity to seek trade without fear of Elgin attacking to blackmail them."

"I doubt it." Edwin shrugged. "You underestimate the hatred all these kingdoms have toward each other. They all seem to think they should be ruling the entire continent. Well, everyone except Delvin and Elias, at any rate. It could be why they get along and the others don't. I suspect that might be why we are in Porin. Jan doesn't seem to want to rule or get involved in any fighting. He wants to be left alone and perhaps get some trade."

Lucien thought about it a bit. There were a lot of problems all coming together at once. It was nice to have Jan as an ally. He sensed he was very grateful for the help, and when he mentioned King Delvin, Lucien felt Jan's hopes rise.

Edwin looked as if there was something he wanted to say, but couldn't quite find the words.

"What is it? You look like you have something heavy on your mind," Lucien observed, struggling to sit up in bed.

"I told Alaric we would be going to Dawnbridge to report to the king." Edwin frowned and turned away.

"That isn't a bad idea. It will keep us off the island for another day or so. We need to head back to report to our own king too."

"I don't really care about reporting. I just want to see Viola. It has been several days since we last saw each other, and I don't need your powers to know you want to see Kate. Don't deny it. I can see it on your face."

It was true. Lucien did want to see Kate again, but he did not have the heart to confess how bad Kate was for his powers. He suspected Edwin would find a way to stop their union if he knew. The energy he used to frighten off the army had left him very weak, but if he waited until dark, his strength should return enough to port them to Dawnbridge. Unfortunately, he would become weaker still, once there. Kate's very presence would make it hard for him to get back to full strength.

The mention of her name led to thoughts of her soft lips, her woodsy smell and warm eyes. Lucien knew then just how desperate he was to see her again, and the longer he was away the more doubts he had that they could be together. He needed to see her and make sure she was all right and that they were still strongly in love. *I am so in love with her.*

"Let me rest. We can port in a few hours."

"You are sure?" Edwin stood quickly, trying to stifle his smile and show concern at the same time.

"Yes, as you said, I want to see Kate just as much as you want to see Viola. It will be nice to finally meet up with them after a few days."

"Good. You rest and I will come back in a few hours."

CHAPTER 11

KATE WAS SHAKING from the cold as she made her way down the mountain path. She wrapped her cloak tightly about her body and pulled her hands inside the sleeves to keep warm. Dark was still a few hours away, and she wanted to try to find Viola, if possible.

The path was narrow and steep in places. It wound down and around in a series of switchbacks to the base below. She kept low to the ground, looking out frequently over the edge. The Boreal tribesman must have moved farther into the woods because she did not see them below. She knew they were down there, somewhere, but did not think they would bother with her.

Her caution over being spotted made the walk longer, but she eventually reached the bottom of the path. Even at the base, the elevation was enough to see out over the copse of trees. There was no sign of Viola or the Boreal, and to explore further would only expose her to a greater possibility of being spotted. It might be best to head north to the estate. Judging by what she remembered of the distance, they were farther south than the mine gallery. It made her wonder if the Boreal came from the north or the south.

She moved southward and downward, mindful of her footing. The steep incline would be punishing if she made a misstep here.

Kate heard a soft rustle from the cliff above and to her right. A moment later, someone landed on the slope and slid down into her.

Kate struggled to keep her balance as the man tackled her, but the incline was too much and they slid down the mountain face to the woods. Somewhere in their wild, unchecked tumble, she lost her bow.

Her attacker was tall, but not bigger than Lucien, and he slid just behind her, pushing her to the ground the moment they reached the trees.

Kate pulled her sword even as she leapt to her feet. She was ready for whatever her attacker had to offer.

In the moment they stood facing each other, she noticed he had light skin and was covered in animal furs. His head was shaved except for a red mane of hair over the top of his skull, and his eyes had blue paint like a smear across them. He drew two small bone or rock daggers, holding one inverted to slash, the other upright to parry.

"Lay down your weapons, Tel-son criminal," the man commanded with a growl.

Kate positioned herself to fight standing with both hands on her sword. She wasn't the best with a sword, and this new sword was completely different from her old knife.

The man swiped at her, but she stood back and did not parry. The effort from the swipe was weak and much too far to reach her.

"I am no criminal," she said, and held her sword to the side to strike.

"I saw you come from that Tel-son camp. I know you are one of them. If you were able to walk free, you are one of his scouts, which means you can either surrender as a slave or die where you stand."

He lunged at her with the dagger, but she sidestepped and struck his shoulder with her sword. It was a weak blow, and drew just a small cut through the heavy fur he wore.

"I don't want to fight. I am looking for my friend. They took me in the night. If you stop and talk I can help you get your children back."

"What do you know of my children?" the man roared, his face convulsed with rage.

He swiped closer this time, and the stone blade skipped across her leather armor. Kate stumbled, reaching for her side, instinctively checking to see if she'd been cut. The distraction allowed him to move closer, and Kate swung wildly. She missed him, but it made him step back. He was already in position to strike again.

"Tel-son wants his own daughters back. He took yours out of desperation. I promised to help him get them back, and if you let me, he will free your children as well. You need to listen to me," Kate yelled breathlessly. Swinging a heavy sword wasn't as easy as Lucien made it seem.

"Sorry, marsh runt, your luck has run out."

Just as he said that someone behind Kate kicked the backs of her knees. She hit the ground hard. As she fell, her sword slipped out of her hand. The man quickly kicked it aside, and the two men jumped on her to bind her hands and legs.

Kate was in a stew of emotions as they dragged her into the woods. It was twice now in one day she had been tied up and taken against her will. The fear was nothing compared to the disgust she felt for herself that she didn't try to run or wasn't able to defeat the man.

The two men approached their camp, dragging Kate along the ground behind them. They sat her with her back to a tree and tied her hands behind her, just beyond the warmth of their campfire.

"Ulfr, what is this? We do not take from the marshes. This is not one of Tel-son's soldiers," a man with a large gray beard and bushy gray hair said. *He looks as old as Roger*, Kate thought.

"Stigr, I saw him come down from the camp. He is one of his thieves or murderers," Ulfr said.

"You're wrong; he stole me and let me go so I could help him." Kate gritted her teeth, struggling. "I can help you too."

"Is this true, Boden? Did he come from the mountain?" Stigr asked.

The large man with a wooden helm sat down by their fire. "He came from the mountain, but he looks nothing like Tel-son's soldiers," he said with a nod at Kate. "I know the tribes and if he took a boy so weak, I don't think he would keep the respect of the others."

"What, you are challenging me that I am a liar? That scum took my children! I will have all of them killed," Ulfr raged at the other two.

"Calm yourself, Ulfr. We will get the girls back, but sometimes it is better to think than to act. What if this boy tells the truth? Tel-son might have taken him, thinking he was a girl. He is as frail as an old woman," Stigr said.

A light snow had begun, and the air was freezing. Kate shivered from the cold and the thought of them leaving her like this overnight. She could not even cover herself with the cloak.

"Please listen to me, I am not an enemy. Tel-son took me in the night for trade. He needed to collect four girls to take to Westfall in hopes of swapping them for his daughters."

"So he steals my children to save his. He is a savage! He blames me for his brother's death. He came into our camp at night and took our goat. I did not know who it was, and a single arrow pierced his chest and he died. He should not have stolen from us. We are not any better off than they are, but they have stolen our chickens, and animals' skins we set to dry. They are thieves. Worse than thieves, to steal scraps from starving men!" Ulfr crossed his arms as he stood and paced around the fire.

"Ulfr, listen to the words of this boy. He speaks true. Tel-son's men probably mistook him for a girl. No one would trade for a boy, and not for one who's such a runt," Stigr said. He picked his teeth and gestured at Kate.

"I am a girl. His men knew that when they took me. Your arrows wounded Tel-son and I saved his life. As a reward, he released me and said I could look for my friend. There are people who can free his daughters without trade. I just need you to believe me."

The three men looked at her. Ulfr got close to her face and took off her helm and coif. Kate's hair was tied tight to her head, but the men could tell by her face she was a girl.

"I do not understand why Tel-son would free you. He had what he wanted then, to trade for his daughters," Ulfr said, puzzled.

"I told you. He didn't want to take your children. He did it because he had no choice. The people to blame are in Westfall, and those are people I know. I can get them to release his children."

"Enough, I will take you to their camp and barter you for at least one of my children. They must be willing to do that."

"I don't think he will. Tel-son might be dead by morning if you don't let me find my friend. She can heal him."

"We will do this my way."

Boden and Stigr shook their heads as Ulfr sat down next to the fire.

"Can you please cover me with a blanket? I am freezing," Kate yelled, unable to keep her teeth from chattering.

Stigr put an animal skin over her and went back to the fire. Kate could tell he was not happy with Ulfr's decision. Viola couldn't possibly survive the bitter night unless she stayed at the estate or found warm shelter. Kate could only wonder if she had abandoned her to get help, or something else had happened.

Something worse.

CHAPTER 12

VIOLA WAS STARTLED awake by the sounds of people yelling. For a confused moment, she thought it was a dream, but then she heard a woman's voice. She quickly came out from her hiding spot to see what was going on. The yelling was nearby and to the north, and she was careful to stay low to the ground as she moved along the cliff face.

She realized it wasn't a dream, but it became a nightmare when she saw Kate pounced upon by two men down by the tree line of the woods. Stealth, not brawn, would win the situation, so Viola circled south in a wide arc, following from a safe interval.

She spotted the glow from a campfire in the distance ahead, presumably where the two men were taking Kate. She watched until they arrived at their camp and tied Kate to a tree. She feared the worst, thinking they would set upon her, but then they started talking.

She crept on her stomach as close as she could to hear their conversation.

Kate was trying to convince them to let her find Viola. She said the man on the mountain was dying as well. There was something about children and goats and the man became angry.

Viola had no idea what to do. *Maybe I can get Kate's hands free during the night when the others go to sleep*, she thought. It seemed sensible, and the risk was slight. She could wait until the men slept and use the cover of the trees and overgrowth to creep up to free Kate.

As Viola lay on the ground considering her best course of action, she became aware of a warm wetness on her feet. She looked up to see the shadow of a man relieving himself on her cloak.

"By the gods, you animals!" Viola screamed as she jumped to her feet. "The world is not your latrine."

"What are you?" Ulfr asked as he pulled up his trousers. "You are the tiniest runt of a woman I have ever seen in my life."

"I wouldn't speak of tiny runts if I were in your boots," Viola said, surreptitiously reaching into her pouch. She found the block of wood containing the flasks and counted by feel from the end of the block to the vial she needed. "Yours is too small to keep. You should consider throwing it back."

Stigr and Boden drew their weapons and spread out around her.

Viola held the potion flask in her left hand and thumbed the cap off. She clutched her dagger and pointed it at the men as they came close to her.

"**Stay back. One drop of this potion will kill you. It will be a slow, agonizing death,**" she said, and splashed some of the flask's contents onto the blade. "Even a scratch is all it takes."

The men stopped, looking at each other, trying to decide if what the runt said was true.

Kate shifted herself around the tree to face toward Viola. "Viola, thank the gods! I was worried something had happened to you."

"You know this...forest gnome?" Stigr asked, his eyes darting from Viola to Kate and back to Viola again.

"Yes, she is Viola. I told you I needed to find her to free the children."

"She was telling the truth," Ulfr said, looking to Boden and Stigr.

"She is a gnome," Boden insisted.

"I am not a gnome. I am Princess Viola of the Free Marshes. You just urinated on me as well," Viola yelled, waving her dagger about.

"Even though you are so small, I was not trying to. If your friend had not said there was someone in the woods, I would not believe you could be a woman. You are even smaller than her." Ulfr absently scratched his beard stubble with the edge of his sword.

"Princess Viola, the Free Marshes," Stigr repeated and looked to Ulfr. "Who is your father?"

"My father was Elijah, now deceased. The king is my grandfather Elias." Viola lowered her potion and dagger. The men lowered their blades. A kind of détente had been reached. It wasn't peace, but it would do.

"King Elias," Stigr said as he looked to Ulfr. "I can hardly believe he still lives. I knew him over forty years ago. He was a good soldier in the imperial army. Ulfr, it looks like this runt girl was telling us the truth after all."

"I did not believe it. Why would a Marshlander care about helping us?" Ulfr grumbled as he cut Kate free. She rubbed some circulation back into her wrists. Awareness returned with pins and needles.

"It was in our interest. We don't want our people taken and sold. If Westfall is doing that, we want to help you stop it," Kate said.

Viola embraced Kate, holding her close long enough for the three men to become uncomfortable.

"Viola, not in front of the men," Kate whispered, and Viola nodded, fighting back tears.

"So, what now?" Ulfr asked.

"Now, I keep my promise. I will go to Tel-son and heal him. Then we will make sure your children are free."

"It is dark now. Do you think they will let you come so late?"

"I don't know, but we have to treat him before morning or he will die, that is a certainty. I can't wait but I will return. You have my solemn word," Kate said. The men stepped aside and let them pass, but they watched to make sure they were heading toward the mountain base.

"Gods, Kate, I am so happy to see you," Viola said, linking arms as they walked.

"I am grateful you didn't abandon me. It was pretty frightening to be kidnapped in the night like that."

"I went to watch the sunrise and when I returned, I saw the man carrying you away. The other man..."

Kate stopped to look at Viola. "What happened? Did the other man...?"

Viola trembled at the memory, which was never far away. "It was awful. He caught me and I had to kill him." she said, and tears bloomed in her eyes and streamed down her cheeks.

"Gods, I am sorry, Viola. I thought you would just run."

"I was too afraid he would come back. I didn't want to live afraid and I didn't really mean to kill him. I cut him with my dagger and he died of poisoning. He had my neck in his hands as he died. He was going to kill me. I had no choice."

"It is all right, don't dwell on it. He wouldn't have given you a second thought if the outcome had been reversed. These are desperate men on the mountain. They do not know kindness and simply do whatever it takes to survive, just as you did." Kate took Viola's face between her hands and used her thumbs to wipe away her tears. "Better?"

Viola nodded and composed herself. She felt relief after having talked to Kate. She still had trouble believing she could kill anyone, but when you are desperate you will do almost anything.

"Viola, let me do all the talking at the camp. Do you have a Lazarus potion we can give him?"

"Yes, it is powerful, though. He may not wake for a day or two after you give it to him."

"Then our first priority is to free the children before you heal him," Kate said.

They made it back up the path to the camp where Earie was waiting by the fire with Tel-son wrapped in blankets nearby.

"I did not believe you would return. This is the healer you spoke of?" Earie asked, nodding at Viola. He was unable to keep the skepticism out of his expression.

"Yes, but she won't heal him unless you free the girls you took from Ulfr," Kate said sternly, hands on her hips. Viola was glad Kate was doing the talking. She doubted if she'd have the nerve to speak so boldly.

"Fine, but if Tel-son dies, you die, too." Earie lifted his chin and fixed them with his cold eyes.

Kate knelt next to Tel-son. "Viola, give him the potion."

Viola opened the small vial and lifted Tel-son's head. Tel-son was asleep and as Viola lifted his head he came slowly awake, recognizing Kate even through the haze of his fever.

His eyes strained to see her. "You have returned."

"I kept my promise. Now, please, drink this. It will heal you," Kate said.

Viola poured the vial's contents into his mouth. He coughed but managed to swallow most of it. She gently laid his head back down to rest and, gods willing, heal.

Earie brought out three small girls, the oldest not more than four summers old, if that. They were wrapped in animal skins, very light skinned, and had blonde hair. Viola watched as Kate clenched her fists hard, her nails digging crescent grooves into her palms, and pushed her anger deep down inside herself to hold back the tears. Viola had difficulty believing the men were going to trade these young lives as if they were no more than livestock.

"Viola, we will take them back to the camp," Kate said, helping move the girls to Viola.

"We will return within a week with Tel-son's daughters. If something happens to them, we will return, no matter what."

Kate and Viola took the children down the path, Kate leading the way, Viola walking behind the children, talking to them, singing nonsensical songs to keep them from being afraid. A guard at the base of the mountain spotted them and ran to tell Ulfr. Ulfr pushed past the guard before he could deliver the news and ran out to greet the strange caravan. He wrapped his arms around all three children, lifting them high in a great hug, kissing each dear face he secretly feared he would never see again.

"We are so grateful! How can we repay you?"

"Perhaps someday we will visit your camp. Can you even tell us where you come from?" Kate asked.

"We come from far in the north along the western side of the mountain beside the sea. Our village is called Einloch. You may never venture so far north, I imagine. Our king is Zell. We will tell him what you have done for us."

"How did your children get down here so far?"

"We come in the summer to hunt in the mountains south of the road of kings. It is tradition, and we have never had any trouble until this summer. I hope that Tel-son will respect us, and we will respect him."

"It was desperation. He meant you no harm, I promise. When we return his daughters, we hope to give him your good will. Please take care," Kate said as they began to leave.

"You won't stay the night in our camp? We have little to offer, but what little we have, we offer freely."

Viola could tell Kate really wanted to go somewhere far away. It was late, but Viola thought they could make it to the estate for the night.

Before Kate could make their excuses, Viola said, "My family has an old estate south of here where we are staying. I hope that you have a safe journey and good hunting."

Viola shook her head to the side for Kate to get moving. Viola didn't have to tell her again.

"Farewell, and safe travels," Ulfr called after them.

Boden and Stigr raised their hands in farewell.

"I still think she's a gnome," Boden said.

CHAPTER 13

"GODS BE, KATE, I don't know how I am going to survive all of this. Today was the most frightening day of my entire life!" Viola bundled herself in her cloak as they walked south. The snow had stopped falling and the twin moons peered between the shredded clouds.

"Try not to think about it. I fear we are just starting. I swore in a week I would have those girls. We have to do everything we can. Tel-son seemed serious with his threats." Kate shivered and rubbed her shoulders; the promise weighed heavily on her mind.

The two of them walked through the swamp toward the estate. The two moons were bright overhead, making the snow-covered path shine like a silver vein through the surrounding darkness.

The trees seemed to part and the path widened as the estate came into view. "Thank the gods," Viola's teeth chattered as she spoke. "We need to barricade the doors and windows. Then we can make a fire."

"Fire first, *then* barricade," Kate corrected, shaking all over, her teeth clicking as bad as Viola's.

The two of them knelt by the fireplace as Viola struck steel to flint, creating sparks. It took her just a few strikes before sparks scattered, igniting the dry tinder stacked loosely in the fireplace. They held their hands over the small fire, trying to warm up.

The main hall was untouched, as if they never were taken. Their bedrolls even lay next to the fireplace where they had left them. The large room had three main entrances, each set into a different wall. They each took a side of the hall and barricaded the doorways using the furniture, stacking and overlapping it in odd ways so that it would offer enough resistance and noise if intruders tried to force their way in that Kate and Viola would surely be alerted in time to arm themselves. They moved the great tables and side tables to make a fort around the area where they were resting, forming a maze that would also slow any potential attacker. If necessary, they could flip the tables onto their sides to shield them against arrows.

Kate rubbed her hands as she stood admiring the great room again. A manor like this could house twenty or thirty guests as well as a full complement of servants and guards. There was a storeroom in the cellar that could keep enough fresh food to feed all those guests, servants, and guards for several weeks. In its day this place must have been majestic.

"What?" Viola asked. "What are you thinking?"

"It is just this house. It must have been a wonder when it was fully staffed. This hall alone would be quite something to see with a fire in the pit across the center."

"It was meant to be yours. I suppose it still could be if you married the blacksmith." Viola laughed until she snorted. "You could hold your wedding here. There's room for friends, family, even Tel-son and his tribe."

Kate laughed with her. It felt good to release the tension of a bad day. Viola's laughter turned to tears as she struggled with her emotions. Kate moved to embrace her and they held each other close near the warmth of the fire.

"I miss Edwin. What a horrible experience. I can't get the look of that man's face as he died from my mind."

"It was you or him. He made that choice for you."

"All right, yes, it was me or him. The look he had when he was choking me, like he enjoyed it. I shall never forget that look."

"It will fade. The men I killed faded, and I accept that it was the only choice I had. You will feel the same, in time. You just have to push it from your thoughts and think of the positive. Three small girls get to see their families again. That man's death allowed their lives to be returned to them."

"All right, I will try to think positive thoughts." Viola sat by the fire, wrapping her cloak around herself like armor against the cruelty of the world out there.

Kate leaned her back to the wall, pulled her knees up to her chest, and stared off into the dark corners of the great hall. *If Lucien was here, how would it have gone?* she thought. Her heart longed to see him and couldn't help but wonder if his heart missed her. She told herself she was being foolish, behaving like a love-struck damsel. She missed him, yes, but boys don't think about girls all the time the same way.

"How will we do it?" Viola asked.

"What do you mean?"

"How will we save Tel-sons daughters?"

"We have to go to Westfall and speak to the king. It is a two day journey if not longer. It won't be pleasant, and by the time we get to the north road I am sure a search party will be out for us."

"Not likely. They won't check my room for days," Viola said with a laugh, rocking back and forth.

"Why do you say that?"

"They just ignore me. Perhaps if a prince wrote a letter or something they might summon me, but so close after the gala, and with rumors of Edwin, I think I could be gone a week."

Kate smiled at the thought. "My father will have them looking for me tomorrow. I think two days is the limit. If I don't check in, he will get worried and send Roger from the village out after me."

"What do you want to do? If it is two days north and then two days back, that leaves us only three days to get back in time to Tel-son."

"Well, if a wealthy patron purchased some horses in South Pier we could save a couple days." Viola raised an eyebrow in response to Kate's devious smile.

"Ah, well, I hate to be the broken wheel that overturns your cart, but I didn't bring much money with me. I have around fifty crowns. I doubt we can get two horses for that price."

"I have twenty crowns, give or take, left from the gala. I can put that in."

"It's settled, then. We head to South Pier in the morning," Viola declared.

"You were so desperate to go there. It will be the opposite of what you wanted. We will go, and then head due north."

"I have never been to Westfall either. If the boys were with us it would be such amazing fun. Can you even imagine what they might think of what we are doing? When we get to Westfall, though, how do you plan to free those girls? We don't even know why they were taken. We could get there and have nowhere to start."

"Admittedly, it is a risk, but what choice do I have? The only hope is that we can get some information from a local tavern or similar avenues. I did meet Prince Henry once. If we can get an audience, it might be possible to get help from him, although I am not sure of his character."

"Prince Henry? You can't be serious."

"What?"

"He is so stiff and arrogant. I wouldn't be surprised if he pretended not to know us. We aren't exactly high society for him."

"Then I will tell him the Dark Lord of Elnora sent me to petition for his help," Kate said with a booming laugh.

"He might have to change his trousers if you say that. You need to be more discrete. Say that his gracious Lord Lucien understood that he would cooperate."

"Gods, that is pretentious. I won't be involved in anything like that. I will be direct, and if I have to be Karl again, I will do it. All that matters is getting those girls free."

Viola yawned and lay back. The events of the day and the warmth of the fire were conspiring to make her drowsy.

Kate yawned, stretched, and curled up next to Viola beside the fire. "What do you think Lucien would do?"

"I have no idea. You know him better than I do."

"Well, he would get wounded somehow, and then more than likely set something on fire." Kate waved her hand dismissively.

"That is horrible," Viola cackled. "When I see him, I will tell him that you were having fun at his expense."

"Just don't tell him that I said anything about his archery."

"His archery isn't good," Viola admitted. "What do you think they are doing right this very minute?"

"I couldn't fathom what goes through their immature minds. I imagine, whatever it is, Edwin is behind all of it."

"I take offense to that. Edwin is always dragged somewhere by that scoundrel, Lucien. He is a gentleman...most of the time."

"I doubt he is that gentlemanly. He has a jealous streak in him and a temper to match. If I were to hazard a guess, I would bet he is hatching some scheme to see the good lady Viola. Why, he may even b--" Kate stopped when she saw the worry in Viola's face. "What is it?"

"What if they go to the castle looking for us?"

It was Kate's turn to be worried.

"That would be bad," she said.

CHAPTER 14

"**W**HERE ARE WE?" Edwin felt around in the darkness. He felt raw wood posts and what might have been a crop, and hanging next to that, a pitchfork. There were a few pieces of hay clinging to the tines.

Lucien's breathing was labored as he answered: "In the stables."

"Yes, I can smell that, but where? Which stables? One stable smells pretty much like another."

"Outside the adviser's house. I thought we should start here, someplace simple to meet up with Kate."

"Not a surprise we would see her first," Edwin groused.

"Well, I didn't really want to pop in on her highness unannounced. If Kate is with us, it looks a lot less like we are going to her room to do untoward things."

"All right, fine, let's go," Edwin quickly changed the subject. They walked out into the moonlight in front of the stables. The cool, clean night air seemed to revive Lucien, if only a little, but it was more likely the thought of seeing Kate once more.

It took Lucien three hours to gather enough strength to port again, but it was still too soon after his earlier exertions and he was laboring under the strain. The two of them had rested and eaten as they listened to Lord Jan and Alaric plot what action to take after they scattered the Elgin army. The two of them were lucky that Alaric was wise to their plans, because they didn't want to get in trouble with the king again. Edwin was already in trouble with his father and the king seemed annoyed with both of them.

The adviser's house was dark. Lucien did not see any light through the windows on either floor. They tried the door but it was locked. Lucien searched his emotions and knew right away she was not there, because he felt normal.

"How late is it?" Lucien asked.

"It is not yet midnight," Edwin said, forming a set of blinders with his hands, trying to peer into the darkened house for any sign of movement. There was none.

Lucien rapped on the door a few times to see if anyone would answer but the silence was still and deep as quarry water.

"Where would she be? Her father should be here at least, shouldn't he?" Lucien had no idea how Kate and her father's relationship actually was.

"Let's head to the castle. Maybe we can see Viola," Edwin paused. "Er…we should see the king and Brian, just to be proper. I would hate to appear in the city and then get caught unannounced with Viola after what happened with the king."

They made their way to the stairwell north along the wall. It took them up to the castle manor and the rooms where they stayed before. The corridor was unguarded, but there were seldom any guests in Dawnbridge so there was no need.

They followed the corridor to the throne room door. The door was open and they heard soft voices from inside as they approached.

Candlelight waved on the walls. The plain room had a few wall tapestries and a hearth. Elias sat upon his throne; Brian stood on the short set of risers leading to the dais on which the throne sat. Standing on the other side of the throne was Arnold.

As soon as the two men saw him, they quickly turned to leave.

"Where are you going?" Arnold yelled across the room.

The king looked past Brian, noticing Lucien and Edwin for the first time, and Brian followed his gaze. His face twisted into something like a feral snarl when he saw the pair.

"You bastards! This is your doing! What have you done with my daughter?"

Lucien and Edwin looked at each other.

Lucien grimaced. "This doesn't sound good."

"No, it is worse." Edwin kept his head down, fearing what was coming.

Arnold crossed the room in a few quick strides and grabbed them by their cloaks.

"This was your idea, Edwin," Lucien reminded him as they were taken to stand at the foot of the throne.

"Well, boys, what have you to say for yourselves?" King Elias calmly clasped his hands together on his lap. "I'm waiting."

"We are innocent. I do not know what you heard in Dulimore, but that wasn't us," Edwin blurted, holding his hands up.

"I haven't accused you of anything. Especially not anything in Dulimore." Elias studied them, his eyes narrowed slits.

"Where is my daughter, you scoundrel?" Brian yelled, his face inches from Lucien's.

"I came here, with Edwin, only to see Viola. I have not seen Kate since the gala," Lucien said.

"Lies, all lies. You had something to do with it, I know it!" Brian gestured wildly with his arms as if he were about to attempt to fly. He rubbed his chin stubble and then his bald head, muttering terrible curses under his breath. He turned to Edwin. "Well?"

"Brian, you're not helping. Boys, what do you know of the missing girls? Aela and Viola have not been seen in two days." The King's voice sounded worried, but he looked hopefully at them.

Lucien had been filled with a low-level worry since his arrival and his inability to sense Kate, but that worry was quickly becoming full-blown alarm. *Now they say Kate is missing and has not been seen in days?* He rubbed his sweaty hands on his cloak, trying to read Elias and Brian. *What happened to them? If someone hurt her, I will destroy them*, he thought.

Lucien cast his net wide, picking up Edwin's confused emotions: he was not sure what to make of it. Surely Kate would keep track of Viola. It wasn't that big a deal, Kate was experienced in every corner of the province. It wasn't that big a deal, and yet...

"We have not seen either of them." Edwin said.

"Tell me what you know." Lucien's voice was flat and direct. His gaze settled on Elias and Brian for their reactions.

"Very little. Kate said she was going hunting. Viola just... vanished. No one has seen either of them for two days, and we did not even know they were missing until Brian brought up Aela's disappearance." Elias shifted on his throne, holding his hand to the side of his face.

"Kate knows it is dangerous. She has not spent a single night in the woods since the attack at Tallin. Since we moved to the city, all but one night has she stayed in the adviser's house." Lucien knew Brian was hinting about her night with him, or rather in the adjacent room.

"How is Viola's disappearance related?" Edwin asked.

"We don't know. When we went to see if she knew where Kate had gone, we couldn't find her, either. It is possible they went off together." Brian paced between Edwin and Lucien.

"Has anyone seen anything or heard of where Kate went hunting?" Lucien's voice warbled, close to breaking.

"I don't know. She said hunting. It would be unusual for her to hunt at night in the east. She isn't that familiar with it. It is possible she went west to her camp."

"What about Viola? Why would she go out?" Edwin looked to Arnold.

"It is difficult to say. She seemed rather uneasy lately about being in the castle. I think she wanted her freedom. It was not a surprise after hearing about Aela's exploits throughout the realm. She may have traveled to get away."

Arnold looked down at his feet. Lucien didn't need his abilities to know Arnold felt ashamed that Viola had escaped the palace guard. "I offer my life in her place."

"Nonsense, she has just run off on some foolishness." Elias waved his hand airily, trying to calm the giant of a man.

Lucien began to probe the area for Viola. Kate could escape his sense, but Viola could not. The thought had occurred to him that Kate could shield others around her from his power, but he did not know for sure if that was possible. He reached down deep into himself and expanded his senses far beyond the city, spreading out like ripples in a pond. He reached past the guards east at the border with Dulimore, and probed all the way to Drommer.

He tried to push farther, wider, and a great clot of blood burst from his nose in a spray.

"Gods, Lucien," Edwin cried, catching Lucien as he crumpled to the floor.

"What is wrong with him?" Brian approached, looking down at them.

Blood came from Lucien's nose and mouth. He coughed blood as he tried to catch his breath.

"It was a long journey. May we rest in the manor?" Edwin asked the king.

"Of course. If you find out anything, let us know immediately. I want this business taken care of, and my niece is the utmost priority. For your sake, Edwin." Elias said meaningfully.

"Yes, my Lord...yes, of course, immediately." Edwin slung Lucien's arm around his shoulders, walking him from the throne room and to the bedroom as quickly as he could.

Edwin helped Lucien lay on the bed and removed his boots. He paced about helplessly, not sure what else to do.

"I assume you searched for them and found nothing?" Edwin asked as he paced. "That's what caused...?" He motioned with a nod of his head back in the direction of the throne room and Lucien's collapse.

"Yes. I did not sense either of them, and I searched far. *So* far."

Lucien was feeling terribly weak and his heart ached for Kate because he knew his adventures likely had pushed her to do risky things. He blamed himself for that, and he blamed himself that he could not tell Edwin the truth: Kate was invisible to him, as were those around her. If he knew that, Edwin would just become more anxious by the moment.

Lucien tried to comfort Edwin, "Kate is tough. She will keep Viola safe if they are together."

"They are together, I can feel it. Viola heard all that stuff about Kate and just wanted to taste a little of the fun. She constantly wanted to hear stories of us. All of the stupid things I have done, it just was too...romantic for her. Now my foolishness has pushed her to her death."

Lucien's face twisted. "You don't know that. Keep heart that she is well."

Edwin paced to the window and looked out, his face pulled down in a sharp frown. "If you cannot feel her, what hope is there?"

"I could only reach to the border with Dulimore," Lucien lied. He couldn't tell him he reached further and still didn't find them. He would assume they were dead without explaining he might not sense them.

"You love her more than anything. How could you not see her immediately? You spent a lot of time with Kate. She would be like a shining beacon in this world." Edwin pushed away from the window and began his aimless pacing once more.

"It just doesn't work that way. The continent has a lot of people, animals, buildings, and terrain. It isn't like the island. I can't just see one person out of all the other distracting things."

"We have to do something! I can't sleep here knowing they are in danger," Edwin said as he stopped pacing in front of Lucien. "Do you know if she could have gone to her camp? Do you know how far it is?"

"Yes, we can go there," Lucien groaned in pain as he sat up in bed. "I just don't know what we will find, if anything."

"I don't care, take us there." Edwin was quick in grabbing Lucien's shoulder and hauling him from the bed to his unsteady feet.

Lucien grasped Edwin's arm, and even in his anxious state, Edwin couldn't help noticing how weak Lucien's grip was.

CHAPTER 15

LUCIEN COLLAPSED TO his knees. The dirt in front of him turned to red mud as he spat a gobbet of fresh blood from his mouth. The pain had brought tears of blood to his eyes. It felt as if his insides were burning and freezing at the same time. His face convulsed in agony as he slumped forward, folding his arms tightly across his chest.

"Will you be all right?" Edwin asked, wanting to comfort him and not sure how to. "Yes...just search for anything." Lucien's eyes were closed as he struggled with the pain.

They had ported in just north of Kate's camp on a path that Lucien had remembered walking with her. Edwin searched for clues in the darkness, walking the path that he could see. He searched the shelter and around the tanning equipment hoping to find some sign of Viola or Kate. There was nothing. He knelt down by the extinguished fire pit, and the ashes seemed fresh. They were bright black and did not show any weathering. It was not much to go on.

Edwin looked through the woods at the torches flickering in the distance. "Do you know anyone in the village?"

Lucien stumbled as he got to his feet. "Maybe Roger. I think he is the captain of the guard. He knows Kate."

"All right, lean on me and we will walk to the village. I can see the fires from here." Edwin put Lucien's arm over his shoulder.

They could see the fires from the village, but could not find the path in the darkness. Both of them ended up getting their boots soaked and muddy in the swamps as they strayed from the winding path. The torches by the gate were the first that came into view as they approached. The gate was closed and a man stood up on the rampart above.

"Who goes there?" a young boy, possibly no more than eighteen, challenged them.

"Lord Edwin Ulrich. I wish to speak to Roger of the guard," he called up to the youth.

"Do I know you?" A man climbed the ladder to the upper palisade.

"No, but we were wondering if you have seen Kate O'Neill?"

"I have not." Roger narrowed his eyes, looking down at them with growing suspicion. "Why do you ask?"

"She has gone missing and has not been seen in two days. The castle sent us to search for her."

"Is that man with you all right? Does he need treatment?"

"No, he is fine, just a long journey for us. Did you see any nightfires in the woods over the last two days? Her camp is there," Edwin said, pointing back in the direction of the abandoned camp.

"Actually yes, two nights ago there was a fire, but it was after midnight when we saw it. It was unusual, but we did not investigate. It could have been her."

Lucien and Edwin looked at each other and nodded. It was the clue they had been searching for. It was possible she had been there and sneaked away with Viola under the mantle of darkness.

"Thank you. I think that was her. Do you know where they went?"

Roger shook his head. "I am afraid not. I would look for tracks. The paths are damp, seeing as it is autumn. We have not had any rain either, so they should still be there, if there are any."

"Our thanks again," Edwin said, and started to help Lucien back down the deceitful path they had just followed.

"You can stay in Brian's old cottage for the night if you'd like. It is rather late to go bandying about in the woods."

"We do not have the luxury of time, but thank you, good sir," Edwin waved as they moved off in the distance.

Edwin carried Lucien out of view of the village, struggling to keep his footing. "What do you think, Lucien?"

"I don't know. It is possible she was there. I am still not sure what is going on. Why would she leave and not tell anyone?"

"Who knows? They are women; it's their prerogative to assume you can read their minds." Edwin caught himself and smiled crookedly at Lucien. "Ah, well, no offense."

"None taken. I barely have the strength to walk, let alone take offense. What is your plan now?"

"We look for tracks."

They reached the camp and Edwin could barely see anything in great detail because of the darkness. He picked up a large, nearby branch that had probably been intended for the fire.

"Can you light this so we can see?" Edwin passed the branch over to Lucien.

Lucien touched it gently and it ignited in a bold orange flame. "Stay," Edwin commanded. "Rest. I'll call you if I find anything." Edwin took the torch and searched north of the camp. He found their footprints heading south. He then went west and noticed two small sets of footprints leading away from the camp.

Edwin called to him, "Lucien, I found them! They went west!"

"Are you certain?" Lucien steadied himself as he walked to where Edwin knelt by the tracks. He held the guttering torch over the set of fresh tracks pressed into the soft ground. It must have been them. "West...where would they have gone west to?"

"I don't know. Let me see if there are any other prints south or east." Edwin rushed south to look. He checked around the south path and found nothing. He then moved to the eastern path and found two sets of footprints heading west, toward Kate's camp. He returned to where Lucien waited.

Edwin could not guess what they could possibly be doing, but he now knew what direction. "They came from the east, and were headed west. And we know at least where they were two days ago. Roger said they left in the pre-dawn, so they have two days' head start on us."

"We need to let Brian and Elias know," Lucien said resignedly.

"I know. Can you port again?" Edwin's voice was quick and urgent.

"I might just have one more."

Edwin stomped out the torch and grabbed Lucien. Lucien grimaced and they vanished.

Lucien collapsed face first to the floor of the manor bedroom. Edwin quickly rolled him over onto his back, wiping at the blood on his face. "Lucky your nose broke your fall," he said softly.

Edwin moved his legs around and pulled him onto the bed. He propped him up against the pillows so he would not choke on his own blood and hastily threw the covers over him. Sure he had done all he could for his friend, Edwin left the room, slamming the door.

He rushed down the hall and burst into the throne room. Brian and King Elias were there alone. Edwin quickly bowed and ran up to them.

Edwin panted, holding up his hands. "I think we know where they went."

Elias calmly leaned forward on the throne. "Calm yourself. Now, where did they go?"

"Spit it out, boy," Brian growled. "Every moment you waste is a moment spent not searching for them!"

"They went to Kate's camp. Roger saw the fire there two nights ago, and we found footprints heading west. There were no other footprints around, other than those coming to the camp from the east."

"Hmmm...so they went west." Elias stroked his beard.

"What is west that would take a day or more to reach?" Brian scratched his head trying to think of anything.

"Maybe they went to the south road and took it to the Pier," Edwin surmised.

"No, we had a rider from the guard arrive today. He did not see anyone in South Pier that even remotely resembled them, and he saw no one like that on the road either. They had no reason to hide on their way."

"Perhaps she went to my sister's estate, near the mountain? It is a good way west of the south road. It is possible that is where they went." Elias looked to Brian. "I have mentioned it once or twice in stories to Viola. It is abandoned now, but it was something to see in the old times."

"The mountain is treacherous. There are tribesmen everywhere, slavers even. Why on earth take such a risk?" Brian raised his arms and dropped them to his sides in helpless exasperation.

Edwin could only shrug.

Elias added with a chuckle, "For adventure, of course."

CHAPTER 16

KATE AWOKE IN the morning. Only a few fading embers remained of their fire and the sunlight peeked through the windows, spreading shadows like spilled ink across the great room.

Kate raised the corner of her mouth when she saw Viola gone. Her things had been packed to leave, but Viola was nowhere to be seen. "Again?" she muttered under her breath.

She quickly packed her own things and made her way around the maze of barriers until she reached the main entrance. It was unlocked. *Viola must have gone out,* she thought.

Kate went out into the courtyard and headed toward the gate as the sunlight began to stream through the trees. She did not see Viola anywhere. The weather was surprisingly warm after snowfall yesterday, and Kate enjoyed the feel of the sun tracing along her face. *Viola has probably gone out into the woods to gather herbs again.*

Kate sighed as she walked around the palisade, searching the swampy woods for any sign that Viola was nearby. She finally turned north and spotted Viola crouched down, picking something off the ground.

Kate walked over to her. "What are you looking at?"

Viola held up a flat mushroom. "Fly amanita," she said, as if that should be explanation enough.

Kate leaned back, kicking some loose mud from her boots. "What is it for?"

Viola giggled as she stood, putting it in her satchel. "Poison. It will kill you in moments. I need to make some more, just in case. That bandit left me feeling uneasy with just the one vial."

"Kind of creepy, sneaking out in the morning to pick poison ingredients," Kate said.

"Well, I was just enjoying the sunrise when a shaft of sunlight pierced the trees and fell on the grass next to the path. That's how I found it. I am glad I did because this will make a bunch. Let's head back. I can't wait to get to South Pier."

"I admit that I know nothing of potions and tinctures, but shouldn't you at least be wearing a glove when you pick up poisonous things?" Kate asked.

"Oh," Viola said, and giggled. "I was so excited to see a perfect fly amanita specimen, I quite forgot. Next time, I will."

Once back at the estate, Kate waited for Viola on the porch as she gathered the rest of her things, sealed windows, and closed the main door, locking it behind her.

"Ready to head out?"

Viola joined her, taking one last look back at the manor. "I hope I get to come back here. It was fun to see this old place."

Kate looked around at the outbuildings they passed on their way to the gate. "It must have been something in the old days. No reason it couldn't be again, if there was ever enough peace."

Viola and Kate left the gate and turned south, toward the roar of the ocean in the distance. The swampland could get very treacherous the closer to the coast one came. They walked east, keeping the ocean-sound on their right. As long as they could hear it, they would not get lost as they moved east through the dense forest swamps.

It took most of the day to arrive at South Pier. The rays from the setting sun painted the tree tops the color of fool's gold as they reached the palisade.

Kate had been to the town before, but that had been at night. She now gazed upon the rundown port city in the waning light of the day. The horse trader was near the gate. There were three horses in the makeshift stable. Kate shook her head, knowing that was bad. They needed two horses, and it seemed unlikely he would be willing to part with two of his last three.

Kate turned to say something to Viola but she had wandered off near the palisade, picking up some new weed or flower, but at least she was wearing a glove now. Kate walked over to her. "We have to stick together in town. What if someone snatches one of us?"

Viola put the last weed in her satchel and took off her glove. "I can't imagine such a thing. We are not to be trifled with, that I can assure you. Anyone who puts a hand on me will be dead within a moment with the amount of poison I am carrying."

Kate rubbed her tired eyes. "What if they take the satchel first?"

Viola shrugged. "Fine, we can stick together. Do you want to use code names?"

Kate laughed. "I do! I am Karl and you are Catherine."

Viola stuck out her tongue. "Catherine? How do you get a man's name? I want to be Bob."

Kate grabbed her arm and dragged her along the road. "I get a man's name because I am pretending to be a man. You are Catherine, my sweetheart. We are to be married, and I just spent the entire dowry on supplies for our trip to Westfall."

"So you only want me for my dowry?"

"It was a handsome dowry. Anyone would have done the same."

Viola shook her arm free. "Well, in Westfall I want to be the man. It isn't fair you get to pretend and I don't. What fun is it to be some tramp?"

Kate sighed and began, "You don't look…oh, never mind. When we get to Westfall, you can be Bob. Short, busty Bob from Dawnbridge."

Viola giggled as they approached the stables. She looked at the horses, then back to Kate. "I thought the first rule of travel was securing lodging? It will be nighttime soon."

The tradesman stared blankly at them as he put away his buckets and crop. "Well, we need to find out how much the horses are first. That will tell if we can lodge for the night, or if we must share a stall with our four-legged friends," Kate said.

The horse breeder came out of the stalls and stopped in front of them. "Wat uz needz?"

Kate grimaced at his accent. "I need two horses?"

"Nean, two me betz er still ute," the man said, pointing to the stable.

Kate shook her head. The man was impossible to speak with. "How much, two horses?" She asked, over-enunciating, nearly shouting at the man.

Viola grimaced as she spoke. "He is not deaf, but he will be, soon."

The man showed a toothless smile as he held up two fingers. "Hundez, crowzs."

Kate chuffed in frustration, then turned with Viola to walk away. She yelled back over her shoulder, "We don't have the money, but we will be back."

Kate shook her head and waved her arms all the way to the tavern steps, muttering under her breath. Viola had to hurry to keep up with her. "You should never have wasted my dowry," she said amusedly. "We really could have used it back there."

Viola stood on the road as Kate mounted the steps to the tavern door. Kate noticed she did not follow. "What are you doing?"

Viola held out her arms. "We won't get two hundred crowns in there."

Kate sighed, tilting her head to the side. "What are you suggesting? We gamble our money on dice before getting lodging? The first rule of travel is securing lodging, remember?"

Viola clenched her fist at her side as Kate walked into the tavern. "I said that first."

The tavern was empty as she approached the counter. There was a thin man with dark hair and a mustache standing with his back to her. He put scroll papers into the mailboxes on the wall. Viola recognized him from before.

Kate stood with Viola and cleared her throat and, making her voice as deep as she could, asked, "Can I get some service?"

The man behind the counter turned and smiled when he recognized Viola. "Your highness, this is an unexpected pleasure. How are you?"

He completely ignored Kate and was looking at Viola with a besotted grin on his face. Viola smiled, lowering her chin until it touched her chest and looked up at him through her eyelashes. "It is good to see you again, Walter."

Walter laughed and looked at Kate. "Who is this? You're not with Edwin anymore?"

Viola batted her eyes. "No, this is just a good friend. We need a room for the night."

Walter turned and put a key on the counter. "I am fine putting you up, but really, this guy over Edwin? He is dainty enough to be a fairy princess."

Kate scoffed. "How do you know I am not her guard?"

Walter and Viola both laughed. He had tears in his eyes. "Lad, listen, Arnold is her guard. He would pick something like you out of his teeth."

Kate's face was red with embarrassment and anger. Viola took the key from the counter and put two crowns in its place. "Walter, is there any dice being played at the roadhouse next door?"

Walter's eyes widened. "Your highness is going to go throw dice with cutthroats and hoodlums?"

Viola rolled her eyes. "We need to make a couple hundred crowns."

"A couple?" Kate coughed, nearly choking on her words.

Walter leaned forward on his elbows on the counter and answered softly, "They play, but I wouldn't recommend it."

"You're forgetting, I have a bodyguard," she said and jerked her thumb in Kate's direction.

Viola winked as she turned to Kate and then nodded toward the door. Kate looked at her, annoyed, opened her mouth as if she was about to say something, then relented and walked outside to the road.

Kate looked around the town. She didn't know much about it, but even in the fading light she could see it was in horrible disrepair. The buildings all had patchworks of mortar or wood on their sides. Windows that had been broken were still unrepaired or simply covered over with rough wood. The signs were nearly all broken or faded to illegibility. It didn't matter. The people who lived here had lived here long enough to know which buildings were which. It was a town without many choices.

Viola pointed to the rough building next door. "That is the warlord Mitchell's place."

Kate grabbed Viola's arm. "Warlord Mitchell?"

Viola snickered. "He runs the town. He also doesn't pay tax to the king. So someday he is going to be gutted and hung from the palisade. In the meantime, he is our best bet for getting money."

111

Kate wrung her hands and followed Viola to the roadhouse. She clutched her sword handle as they went inside. There was no way something so ill-considered could end without blood being spilled. She meant to see it wasn't theirs.

There were not many people there; two at the bar, and a round table seating a portly man with a beard and funny pointed hat. Kate followed Viola to the round table. The two rough-looking men from the bar turned and stood when they passed by.

The man with the funny hat laughed and coughed with a wheeze, "Your highness, I hope you haven't come to collect taxes."

Viola put her hands on her hips. "Not exactly. I want to play some dice."

The man noticed Kate and stared at her intensely. "Who is this? I have never seen him before. You trade up on that wild man Edwin already?"

Kate jutted her chin defiantly. "I am Karl, her bodyguard. You must be Mitchell."

The man stroked his beard. "I am. I hope you aren't a hot-head like that Edwin fellow. He nearly beat my man to death."

Kate arched an eyebrow in question and turned to Viola.

Viola shrugged. "What? He had it coming. He shouldn't have grabbed me in the tavern. You know I am always well protected, just like now."

Kate didn't like the bluff. She was not well protected at all. The two men at the bar stood behind Mitchell and crossed their arms. The threat was subtle but spoke volumes.

Mitchell stroked his beard and then put two sets of six dice on the table. The dice were all different colors and were heavily worn. Kate noticed right away that Mitchell's dice were blatantly loaded. The metal fillings were sticking out from the face with six dots even though there should have only been one dot.

Assuming she wanted to lose all their money, she had found the perfect way to do it. Kate hoped that Viola knew what she was doing.

Mitchell picked up the dice. "Put the crowns on the table."

Kate put thirty crowns on the table, and Viola put thirty-eight. Viola picked up her set of six dice. "I assume you will throw first."

"Naturally," Mitchell said, and tossed the dice with a practiced flick of his wrist. They landed two, one, one, five, five, and five. The roll brought a smile to his face. "Pass," he said, and sat back in his chair, his stubby fingers laced together across his great belly.

Viola rolled her dice with a strange twisting motion of her wrist. They landed two, three, six, six, six, and six. Viola smiled. "I win! Go again? Double or nothing?"

Mitchell sucked at his teeth and nodded. He rolled again to the hurrah of his team. His dice landed one, three, six, six, six, and six. Viola looked crushed as she motioned to Kate.

Mitchell laughed as he raked in the crowns from the table, "It was a pleasure, your highness. Give thanks to the king for me."

Kate followed Viola as she stomped out of the roadhouse. Kate had to quicken her pace to catch her in the road. "What was that?"

Viola crossed her arms, fuming. "He got lucky."

Kate stomped her foot, growling in frustration. "His dice were clearly loaded. How is that lucky?"

Viola tilted her head back and looked at the moons as if she were about to howl at them. "Gods, what are we going to do now?"

Kate shrugged. "We are going to have a very long walk."

Viola's hands fidgeted as she thought, rejected, and thought again. Deciding, she opened her satchel and looked inside. The satchel hung low on her side now and was bulging with all the fresh plants and fungi she had collected.

Kate watched her curiously. "Do you have something in there we can sell?"

"I don't know, but there is a trader here we should go see."

There was a rundown shop near the stables. Like almost every other building in town, it was almost black with age and soot, and its shingle was broken. What remained of the sign showed half a scale on the side of the building; the other half was lying on the ground, nearly covered by dirt and filthy footprints. They went to the grimy window. Kate wiped a small circle in the dirt, allowing them to see a man holding a candle and shuffling around inside. The interior of the building was nearly as dark as its outside.

Viola pushed the door open and went in. Kate followed, her eyes darting furtively around the place, looking for a concealed threat. There were a lot of wooden stakes, some rock tools, and odd bits of leather strewn about. The wall behind the counter had a few worn weapons hanging there, but the shop seemed safe. She relaxed but remained alert.

The man at the counter was missing an eye and must have been at least eighty. He leaned forward in a hunch. "Here to trade?"

Viola approached the counter. "Do you trade in foodstuff or potions?"

The man looked at her blank-faced. "What are you talking about?"

"Food and alchemical," Viola said, and showed him a ceramic flask.

The man pursed his lips at her. "What did you have to trade?"

Viola dug into her satchel and placed several items in a row on the counter. "These are some mussels, a few oysters, a small pouch of lutea seeds, and I have a potion for sexual virility."

The man took a balance scale from below the counter, set it up and put the mussels in one pan, then added some small, smooth stones to the pan on the other side. "Hmmmm..." He looked at the other mussel and weighed that also. Then he weighed the oysters and lutea seeds.

Kate looked at Viola dumbfounded and whispered in her ear, "Is any of that worth anything?"

Viola said, "Yes, quite a lot, if we were in the city. But here..." She shrugged. "The gods know."

The man took the virility potion and opened it to smell. His nose crinkled and he pulled a face, then smelled it again. He corked it and put it on the scale. He looked at her and asked, "How many doses for the sex potion?"

Viola looked insulted. "It is not a sex potion. It is a virility potion."

"Whatever," the man grumbled.

Viola frowned and said, "Several. At least six."

The man looked at the items and then to her, arms spread wide, leaning on the counter. "What do you want for all of it?"

Viola looked at him defiantly. "Two hundred and fifty."

The man looked again to the items and then back at her. "One hundred and fifty."

Viola shook her head. "Two hundred and thirty."

He pretended to consider. "One hundred and eighty."

Viola sighed, "Two hundred and twenty."

The man looked again at the items and then at her. He paused for a moment, then looked at Viola. "My last offer: two hundred."

Kate looked ready to jump forward and accept but Viola grabbed her arm. "Two hundred and ten."

The man laughed, "You are a right pinch-purse. I will trade." He put a purse of coins together from an iron box below the counter and handed it over.

Kate felt so relieved that she wanted to hug Viola. All that stuff she had collected really paid off.

Viola opened the purse and checked the contents. Convinced the coins were real and all there, she pulled the drawstrings tight and they went outside.

Kate was smiling and hugged Viola as soon as they were out of the shop. "Thank the gods!"

Viola didn't smile. "I want to go back to the roadhouse."

"No!" Kate screamed, eyes widening.

Viola burst out laughing. "I was just trying to get a rise out of you."

They both laughed and went back to the tavern. Walter was busy doing Walter-things around the desk, so they retrieved their belongings from behind the counter and went up the stairs to their room.

Kate was exhausted and grateful to finally unload her satchel and bedroll. Viola set out her items on the bed and sorted them, placing them in neat rows.

Kate watched her, curious about all of the things Viola had gathered on their journey. "So how much were those items worth?"

"The potion was worth maybe three hundred in the city. The rest could be fifty or sixty crowns, maybe more," Viola said without turning to Kate.

"I should learn from you. I could have scavenged for stuff all these years." She paused, looking at Viola for a moment. "What does that potion actually do?"

Viola put her things away and closed the pouch. "Well, it takes a lot of time and reading to find where to get those things. I was collecting them for days. The potion was something that required intricacy. Also, I am sure he knew me; they would never trust someone without a reputation for a potion like that," she carried on before looking at Kate. "Maybe I will give a potion to Lucien and you can find out for yourself."

Kate put her hand up. "No, gods no, absolutely not, no. He is randy enough as it is. I don't want him any more eager." She lay back on the bed; it was lumpy and smelly and the linens were rough and full of holes, but it was the most comfortable bed she could remember lying in. "But I am very grateful we have the money now. I am exhausted and need to sleep after this day." Kate turned over, facing the wall.

Viola put her satchel on the bed table and lay down on her bed.

Kate didn't want to pine for Lucien; she'd done quite enough of that lately, but she did wonder what he was doing. She wanted to tease Viola about Edwin, but when she looked over, Viola was asleep.

"Sweet dreams...short, busty Bob from Dawnbridge," she whispered, and stifled a giggle.

CHAPTER 17

LUCIEN AND EDWIN had been on horseback most of the afternoon. The sun had set in the east as they arrived once more at Kate's abandoned camp. A few night birds began their evening song; soon, there would be an entire chorus of them.

The men were both exhausted as their horses slowed to a trot. Lucien dismounted and took the reins. "I am barely standing. Do you want to stop for the night?"

Edwin dismounted and walked the horse to a level area. "I can continue, but you have had only a few hours' rest. There is not much we can do. I want you at full strength."

Lucien tried to hide his frown; he knew he was a week away from full strength, and if they found Kate he might never be. He tied his horse to a tree and put a bucket of water nearby. Edwin did the same, and they both collected sticks for the fire. There was little said between them. What was there to say? They both knew they needed to rest and get moving again as soon as possible.

Lucien put a bundle of sticks in a small pile by Kate's shelter and ignited it with his hand. He looked up at the sky as he put his bedroll out near the shelter. The two moons were clear overhead. It was getting colder at night since autumn, and the blue moon shone brightly.

Edwin returned and put a pile of sticks on the fire. "Lucien, there is a rather large tree down over there. If you can cut it up with your power, I can collect it."

Lucien looked at the fire, wincing at his fatigue. Just the thought of the amount of energy he would have to expend to break up the tree left him exhausted. "No. We will try to sleep a few hours, then head west. The map Elias had put the estate near the mine gallery by the mountain. I want to head out as soon as we can."

Edwin lay back on his bedroll next to the fire. Lucien sat with his boots toward the fire as he chewed on some dried fish. "I don't sense them, so they could be anywhere by now. They might even have passed us."

Edwin looked up at the moons. "Do you think they are in danger?"

Lucien chewed for a moment, swallowed, and answered, "No, Kate is plenty capable and Viola is smart enough to keep out of trouble."

Edwin rolled to his side, looking at Lucien through the flames of the campfire. "Do you think of Kate much?"

"Yes." Lucien stared down at the ground beside the fire.

Edwin smirked. "Good talk, Lucien. I think of Viola all the time."

Lucien looked up from the ground at Edwin. "I don't want to gush about her all the time. She is older than me, and more mature. So it is not the same as you and Viola. Kate is a woman.

I need to treat her more seriously. She doesn't want some little boy pining for her whenever she is gone."

"You're an idiot. Kate is giddy for you more than Viola is for me. She gets red in the face whenever you're around." Edwin tossed the leftover fish into the fire.

"Let's get some sleep. I think about Kate enough for the both of us."

Edwin let out a laugh and closed his eyes.

Lucien laid back and looked up at the moons, wondering what the hell Kate and Viola had been doing, and if he should blame himself for their disappearance.

CHAPTER 18

KATE WOKE EARLY the next morning and dumped her satchel contents out onto her bed. She carefully and methodically searched through the items, preparing for their trip. Viola was still asleep, and Kate could feel the anxiety of going back to the horse trader. The ritual of sorting gave her purpose and helped calm her nerves while she waited for Viola to wake.

She looked through her bandages, treatments, unguents, and the few coins she still had. When she finished, she put it all back neatly in her satchel to make space for anything new she might find. Viola had split the ten crowns from the trader with her, and if she could find some more lichen or dried meat in Westfall, she would buy all that she could.

Viola stirred on her bed and yawned. "I think now is when I request you fetch me water and breakfast."

Kate turned, pulling her satchel over her shoulder. She was going to say something terse to Viola until she noticed Viola was laughing.

"Kate, for a moment I thought you might yell at me. I am just joking. I lived a pampered existence, yes, but it isn't like they showered me with luxuries. I had to forage to find a decent meal, unless you want to eat fish every day."

Kate rubbed her forehead. Her cheeks were still warm from her momentary flush of anger. "Yeah, sorry. I am just nervous about the horse trader. He has the worst accent I ever heard. That is completely disregarding our trip to Westfall. It is dangerous, all of it."

Viola laughed. "That isn't an accent. He is a toothless simpleton. You just say two horses, and give him the crowns."

Kate nodded and began pacing as Viola gathered her things. "Will it take long for you to be ready?"

Viola ruffled around with her satchel and stood by the bed, pulling on her cloak. "Nope, I am ready. I am done. It is the simple life for me."

They went down to the tavern's dining area but there was no one around. Walter was nowhere to be seen, so Kate left the key on the counter. The sun was just rising in the west when they stepped outside. Viola stopped for a moment to enjoy the sunrise.

Kate grabbed her arm and dragged her along. "No time to dawdle, we need to get the horses and ride north. Even with mounts, it will take a long time to get to Charbel."

The early morning road was empty as they walked to the horse trader. The keeper was not in the stables when they arrived. The horses stirred, and they could hear some buckets being dragged on the floor of the shack nearby.

The trader came outside, carrying the heavy buckets. He saw them and smiled his toothless smile. "Uz gine? Uz haz da crowz?" he asked.

Kate quickly took the coin purse and handed it to the man. He shook it in the air. Then he held it in the palm of his hand, weighing it. "Gudz."

The man led them into the stable and took the reins of two horses. Kate held her hand, palm-up, and he laid the reins in it. With a nod, it was over. Kate wasn't very comfortable on horseback and gingerly climbed into the saddle with a little help from Viola and the trader. She could think back to her father and the donkey cart. When she rode horseback it was the same- she did her best to avoid trees, but was poor in the saddle.

"Gods! Why is it so high off the ground?" she said.

Viola bit her lip as she watched Kate. "Ummm…I have ridden but once in my life."

Kate slapped her leg. "Are you serious? Why didn't you tell me? We could have just purchased one horse and ridden together!"

Viola looked embarrassed and tried to climb the horse. The horse moved in a circle as she tried to mount up, causing Viola to hop along with him, one foot in the stirrup, the other still on the ground. With one final leap and pull, she was finally in the saddle.

Viola laughed, trying to keep the horse steady. "I will give it my best."

Kate shook her head and laughed. "Just use your legs to go forward and back, and pull back on the reins if you want to stop. For the rest, you turn his head in the direction you want him to go with the reins. No sudden commands, just keep it very simple and calm."

Viola giggled as she kicked and the horse went into a trot. Kate had to spur her horse to catch up and they started north. The two of them swooped from one side of the road to the other as they went through the gate.

CHAPTER 19

LUCIEN FELT LIKE a blacksmith was pounding with hammer and anvil in his skull as he woke up, the sun blinking through the trees overhead. He felt strange and empty.

Lucien stood up and the emptiness clung to him like oil. His hands felt numb. *Kate?* He paced the camp, trying to find the direction the feeling came at him from, but it was too vague. "Edwin, I sense them."

Edwin tossed back his blanket and sat up. "Gods, we overslept." Edwin struggled to wake up with a yawn, then realized what Lucien had just told him. "What?"

Lucien continued pacing, a needle unable to find true north. He looked at his hands as his power dimmed and dulled, and he could not see far away like he had before. *She is nearby now, but where, and how near?* The anxiousness and desire to see her flooded him. He wrapped his arms across his stomach and felt loneliness. *Gods, it is crushing me. Where are you?*

Edwin grabbed him. "What the hell is wrong? You look terrible. Where are they? Are they in danger?"

Lucien gasped. "No, but they are close. It is difficult to tell what direction. But they must be coming toward us because it is getting stronger."

Edwin leaned Lucien by a tree and untied the horses. "We need to move south."

Lucien held his stomach. "Why? Do you think they are coming from that direction?"

Edwin helped Lucien into the saddle. "Yes, it makes sense. We will just go slowly west through the swamp. It will take an hour or two, but I see paths in that direction."

Lucien took the horse to the west path and Edwin followed close behind him.

They rode slowly westward, and Lucien felt more and more of his power draining away. It began to return again gradually, and that made him nervous that they were going to miss the girls. If his power was returning, it must have meant they were moving away from Kate and Viola, but what could he do? If he told Edwin, he would know that Kate could dampen his power, and that knowledge could put her in danger.

They eventually reached the south road. Lucien stopped and dismounted to study the road for tracks, but it was so worn he could not make out anything. He picked up a handful of dirt.

Edwin dismounted and followed him. "What is it?"

Lucien felt his power getting stronger and stronger. "They are moving away. I don't know what direction." He let the dirt sift through his fingers.

Edwin paced as he brushed his hand through his short, curly hair, trying to think. "Gods, they had to have been on the road."

Edwin squatted down beside Lucien as they searched for tracks. The road was eaten up by hoof marks and was a mess of dirt and rubble. A few weeds spurted up in random places.

Lucien gazed north, then south. "I think we should go to South Pier," he announced.

"Why?"

"I don't know, but at least someone can tell us if they were there. If they are headed north, then east, they will return to Dawnbridge. If they came from the north going to South Pier, we will catch them."

Edwin watched Lucien as he crossed the road and then back again. Edwin knew he was not looking for anything; he was giving Edwin time to think about what he had said.

Edwin sighed and said, "We might as well saddle up and go south. I hate that South Pier crap hole, but why would they be headed north other than to return home? I agree, South Pier is the best choice."

Lucien smiled as they both mounted their horses. He looked at Edwin. "It is a good plan. I am not sure what will come of it, but the girls must have had horses. We need to see if someone there knows where they would go. It is too confusing to expect them to just return to Dawnbridge.

CHAPTER 20

KATE AND VIOLA had ridden most of the day and it was near sundown when they reached Tallin. They dismounted, and Viola tied their horses to the post outside the gate.

Viola looked nervously at her. "This is a fort full of young boys, you know. Do you think it is safe?"

Kate chewed on her lower lip and shook her head slowly. "I don't know. I know nothing about Westfall and hoped they could tell us of a village near the border we could visit."

The guard in the tower above noticed them and climbed down the ladder to talk to them. "Good day. Is there something you need help with?"

Kate tried to look boyish. She stood proud with her hands on her hips and chin up. "We are headed to Westfall and wanted to know if there are any taverns to stay at near the border. It is our first trip."

The man looked them over. "Well, I couldn't tell you. There will be guard patrols at the border. I doubt you will get far if you take the road. If I were you that is what I would do."

Ugh! Stupid of me! Kate looked down at her feet. She didn't want the man to see how foolish she felt. "Thank you for your time." She waved quickly and took Viola's arm over to the horses.

The man climbed back up into the tower and watched them curiously.

Kate climbed into the saddle as Viola struggled. "Gods, I am so stupid."

Viola finally climbed aboard, lying on her stomach trying to struggle upright. "Well, who knew? We could always camp somewhere. It wasn't a horrible plan."

Kate took the horse to a trot, keeping her head down to avoid looking at the guard because her face burned such a bright red that she was convinced he would be able to see it even from the tower. Viola was finally able to wriggle upright into the saddle and get her horse moving down the road. Kate let her pass and then followed beside her. "I don't know how far the border is, but it could be a long ride."

Viola gritted her teeth as she rode. "My bottom is sore as can be after this ride. I will be happy to never ride a beast like this again."

Kate was sore, but not yet to the point of pain. She never considered being in the woods had kept her fit and in shape, while Viola was in the castle all the time. *The difference between wild game and veal,* she thought, and bit her lip to keep from laughing.

They rode for several hours until they spotted torches ahead. They brought their horses to a slow trot. There was a gate across the road before them, with watchtowers on either side of the entrance.

Kate felt very nervous, unsure what to expect. Viola's eyes shifted and she gripped Kate's arm with her hand. "What will you do?"

Kate pulled her coif and helm tight to her head. "Just don't say anything. I will do the talking."

They slowly approached the gate and the guard called to them. "Halt! Who are you?"

Kate and Viola stopped their horses. "I am Karl and this is my bride, Catherine. We are hoping to travel to Charbel, but would like to find a village near the border where we could stay the night."

The man walked the palisade and climbed down a stairwell on the far side of the gate. As they waited for him, Kate was able to really see more of the border wall. It seemed more like a fortress, with towers farther down on either side in the woods, west and east.

There were two guards who now stood in the gateway as the man approached. "I am Sergeant Heinrich. Dismount your horses. We need to search you if you wish to cross the border."

Kate could feel her pulse quicken. Viola glanced at Kate, her lip trembling as she dismounted. Kate climbed down from her mount as the man approached to look in their satchels and saddle bags. Heinrich came closer. Kate could see now that he was young, probably no more than her age, and good looking-clean-shaven, with short dark hair. He made a cursory search. It was surprisingly gentle and he didn't grab them.

After the search he stood back with his men by the gates. "What business do you have in Westfall?"

Kate approached him, trying to use a strong, firm voice. "There were some women taken from the mountain. They said they were taken as slaves to Westfall. I have met Prince Henry and hoped to inquire about possibly locating these women."

Heinrich looked at her disbelievingly. "You say slavers are taking women to Westfall? That is preposterous. They put you on a fool's errand, boy."

Kate cleared her throat. "Perhaps, but they offered enough reward that I felt I should at least try. The marsh is no place to make a living."

Heinrich looked to his men and scratched his chin, then settled his gaze on the travelers. "I think you're lying."

Kate's sword had cleared its scabbard before Heinrich had finished speaking. The guards were just as quick to draw their weapons. Viola withdrew a potion from her satchel and fumbled with her dagger as they cautiously backed toward the horses.

Heinrich held out his hand, looking over his shoulder to his men, trying to keep his attention on the travelers. "Don't attack. Wait." He looked back at his guards until they lowered their weapons. He turned back to Kate and took a step forward. "We do not wish to fight you. I just was going to say that you didn't need to lie."

Kate and Viola looked at each other nervously and lowered their weapons. Kate's heart was pounding and she didn't want to get into another fight after the mountain. "Why would it matter? We just wanted to travel to Charbel."

Heinrich smiled and laughed. "I have been on this gate for nearly a year. Do you know how many travelers have come through here?"

Viola and Kate both shrugged, looking at each other.

Heinrich came another step closer. "Just the delegation for the gala, not another soul. They came from Westfall and then returned back through. No one travels this gate. It is the only border in Westfall that hasn't been attacked in the last month."

Kate's eyes widened. "I didn't know. We just wanted to save those girls. We never have traveled to Westfall."

Heinrich looked them over again. "Who are you...really?"

Viola put her dagger and potion away. She held out a small circular seal of metal coated over with wax. "I am Princess Viola. This is Lady Aela O'Neill. We are trying to save those girls, not because of money, but because we made a promise."

Heinrich furrowed his brow as he studied the seal. Satisfied, he nodded and handed it back to her. He then reached into his armor through the collar and held out a seal from his necklace. Viola looked at Kate, who nodded, and then leaned closer to Heinrich. "I am Lord Heinrich Franz," he announced as Viola studied the seal. "My cousin is Prince Henry. I am very grateful that you were finally truthful." He put his seal away and then waved his hand to the gate. "If you wish, you can stay here for the night. It will take you a long time to get to Gera, which is midway from here to Charbel."

Kate looked at Viola, willing herself to stay calm. These men could still attack them, but Heinrich was at least trying to be forthcoming.

They followed Heinrich through the fort. The towers on the front were connected to guard shacks, and there was another larger building behind, and a smaller building next to that. Heinrich walked them to the door of the small building. "This usually serves as a jail. There are two bunks and the key works from both sides. Hope you sleep well. In the morning I will tell you how to get to Gera. I don't want you leaving before sunrise, on account of all the troubles in Westfall."

Kate took the key from Heinrich. He gave a friendly nod to Kate and they went into the small room. There was a candle on the table between the two beds.

Viola placed her satchel on a shelf on the wall. Kate put hers on the small table between the beds.

"Well, this worked out." Viola proclaimed and sat on the bed facing Kate.

Kate was still trembling from the encounter. "Just barely. They could have killed us, or worse. They could still," her voice trailed off.

Viola kicked her legs off the side of the bed. "You have to look at the bright side, it is a great adventure. We can tell stories for months to people in Dawnbridge."

Kate sat on the edge of the bed with her hands clasped between her legs. "If we survive. So far we haven't exactly made much progress. We are in Westfall, but still have a long way to go till we find the girls."

Viola smiled broadly. "I have lived more in these past few days than in my whole life. I am certain we will be hunted by now. There are probably soldiers searching everywhere. It might be wise to leave a message with Heinrich."

Kate tried to suppress her excitement at the thought of someone coming to get them, and so much the better if that someone turned out to be Lucien, with Edwin beside him. It made her warm and happy and calm. "I think you might be exaggerating. We are not important. We are practically expendable. I doubt anyone will come for us."

Viola frowned. "Wow, you have a low opinion of yourself. Lucien will come for you, no matter how far you go. Edwin said he would cross the world for you."

Kate stood up and paced, crossing her arms. Her face was brick red thinking of Lucien and his desire for her. She felt the same way, but how would it ever work out? "I don't think he is quite that smitten. I just think he has a lot that he has to deal with and I am just one more problem."

Viola lay on the bed looking at her. "That must be it. He has girls from all over that want to be with him, or like me, have to wait till he is gone before they can marry. Yet, he picks you and it is just a side nuance?"

Kate removed her weapons, placed them on the table, and lay down on the bed. "I just think he has a lot to deal with. You don't know everything."

Viola studied the ceiling for a few quiet moments, then looked over at Kate. "I know there is something strange about him. Elias and Martin always whisper when he is brought up. I wish people would trust me with the truth."

Kate yawned and rubbed her eyes. They felt like they'd seen enough for one day. "They are doing you a favor, I promise."

"It doesn't feel like it." Viola turned to the wall to sleep.

Kate stared at the ceiling, her heart aching. It was never that simple, and she doubted Lucien and Edwin would come looking for them.

CHAPTER 21

LUCIEN HUNG HIS head and rubbed his eyes as he rode into South Pier. They took their horses to the stable by the tavern. Edwin's arms hung low at his side as he stumbled and slumped from his horse to the ground.

Lucien looked around with a yawn as he put his horse into one of the stalls. "The town seems quiet."

Edwin splashed some water from one of the horse's buckets on his face. "Yeah, it usually is. If there aren't any Elnoran ships in port there is not much going on. This place is a cesspool of criminals and cutthroats. Where do you want to ask about Viola?"

Lucien walked out of the stables with Edwin. "We will get a room at the tavern and see if the innkeeper knows anything."

Edwin grimaced and huffed as they walked into the tavern.

Walter was wiping down one of the tables and quickly went behind the counter, pretending to clean it as they approached.

Lucien paused a moment to look him over, but Edwin slammed his fist on the counter with a growl.

"Ed…win, my good friend Edwin, what brings you to town? It is nice of you to visit," Walter stammered and felt around his shirt collar as if it was too tight.

Edwin's right eye twitched and narrowed. "Where did Viola go?"

Walter was trembling. "Viola, oh, I haven't seen her. I have no guests, so you can have any room you want."

Edwin grabbed the man by the shirt, and Lucien put his arm between them, pushing Edwin back. "Enough! What the hell? Are you going to beat everyone we encounter? You didn't even give him a chance."

Edwin seethed at Walter. "This guy is scum. He let one of Mitchell's men get his hands on her. I had to nearly beat the thug to death. He is a weasel."

Lucien snapped his head quickly to look at Edwin. "When was this?" he asked with great surprise.

Edwin shook his head. "Viola and I snuck away here after the gala. It is a long story."

"Edwin, I told her it was a mistake. That man she was with, he is nothing compared to you," Walter whined in a panic.

Edwin's fist clenched at his side. He fantasized about smashing Walter's face as he stared intensely at his chin. He drew back his fist, preparing to turn the fantasy into a reality. "What man?" Edwin grabbed Walter's neck and pulled his face to his. "Tell me what this piece of feces looked like!"

Walter was covered in sweat and nearly in tears. "I swear, he was so feminine I thought he was a dandy. He could not possibly have stolen Viola. They rented a room and then played dice with Mitchell."

Edwin slowly released him and relaxed his fist. Lucien looked sternly at Walter. He raised the corner of his mouth, patting

Edwin on the chest with a sigh. "What was this man's name? Was it Karl?"

Walter nodded nervously. "Karl, yes, Karl. He did all the talking. That sword on his belt was pretty sinister for such a small man."

Edwin stood back, his face a mess of dejection. "Walter, those are our friends. Any idea where they went?"

Walter put a key on the counter. "I have no idea. They lost all their money to Mitchell, and somehow still ended up with two horses. The only way out of here is north. I am surprised you didn't see them on the road. They left this morning."

Lucien opened his coin purse as Edwin tried to make sense of what he'd just heard. "All right, they went north, but probably not to Dawnbridge. Where would they go in the north?"

Lucien stepped up and put two crowns on the counter. "Can we get a couple plates of fish in our room?" Walter nodded, pocketed the crowns, and headed into the back room.

Edwin folded his arms. "Do you want to talk to Mitchell? I think we would have trouble trying to get anything from him. He is a warlord in this town, not to mention a complete ass."

Lucien considered for a moment and said, "He doesn't pay taxes. Maybe we shake him down for Elias, and then in-between we can make him tell us what we want."

Lucien started for the door but Edwin grabbed his arm. "Do you plan on killing him?"

Lucien looked back at him over his shoulder, his face like stone. "Only if I have to."

"Gods, Lucien, just killing people isn't going to go over well, criminal scum or not." Lucien shook off Edwin's arm and stepped out of the tavern. Edwin quickly followed. Lucien stood outside the roadhouse but didn't see any guards. He nodded with certainty and they went in. There were two guards at the bar and Mitchell was sitting at a round table with a woman.

He saw Edwin and motioned to his men. The woman hurriedly left the table. "Edwin, coming to beat one of my men again?"

Edwin sneered at him. "If you don't give me the information I want, I may beat you."

Mitchell's men approached Edwin. He stood face-to-face with them, not yielding any ground. Edwin stared past them to Mitchell. "Pull your maggots back into your pus-pocket before I kill them both."

Lucien stood watching this display, fascinated. It would be worth the weakness that would follow if he used his power to make Edwin wipe the floor with the men, but he would rather just get the information and leave.

Mitchell stood, enraged. "You can't come into my place and disrespect me!"

Edwin's right fist shot out and struck the first man on the nose. He grunted and went down. The second man lunged at him, but Edwin stepped lightly aside and pushed him into the wall.

Lucien used his power to give the man an extra push, smashing him through the wall. He dropped to the floor, unconscious. The first man was already shrugging off Edwin's punch and getting up, but a force like unseen hands grabbed him and threw him face-first to the floor.

Lucien dabbed at the blood on his nose and coughed. Even this slight effort took a toll on him; Kate's earlier nearness had stifled his regeneration, and it felt almost as if she drained him and took with her all of his strength as she went.

Mitchell pulled his sword and Edwin drew his. Mitchell's face was as red as the odd pointed hat he wore. "You sick bastards. I will run you through for that."

Edwin took a step back over the body on the floor into a more open area. Mitchell slowly stalked him, his sword held with one hand before him. Lucien leaned at the bar, thirstily downing a flagon of ale one of the guards had abandoned. The barkeep looked as if he was about to reach for something under the counter. Lucien slammed the flagon down on the barkeep's hand, making him forget about whatever he might have been planning. He nursed his injured fingers, wrapping his other hand around them and holding them tightly to his chest, looking petulantly at Lucien.

"Watch," Lucien instructed him. "This is going to be entertaining."

Edwin took a tentative swipe at Mitchell, only for him to slice across Edwin's chest and miss. Edwin stepped to the side and thrust his blade at Mitchell. He parried, striking the foible of Edwin's sword with the forte of his own. Edwin looked at Lucien, worried. Lucien smiled and held up a fresh flagon of ale in a cheers salute. Mitchell swung wild in an overhand chop. Edwin dodged it. Mitchell's blade buried itself deep in the tabletop. Edwin smashed his hilt into Mitchell's face. He fell with a grunt to his back on the ground.

Mitchell's hands were cupped across his nose, and blood spurted between his fingers with each breath he took. Edwin held him up, their faces close together. "Your money or your life?"

Mitchell laughed. "You are going to rob me? You have more money than any man on this continent. What a petty man you are, to take from me."

Edwin pushed the tip of his blade to Mitchell's jugular. "I just want your fair share of taxes. I was not going to take it all. The king needs that money to run this province. Your lack of payment is an affront to his power. Viola is part of that power. I hope you understand."

Mitchell spat blood on the floor and looked to the barkeeper. "Give them the large purse from under the floorboard."

The barkeeper started to kneel, stopped, and looked at Lucien like a whipped cur. Lucien nodded once, and the barkeeper knelt and took a large purse from beneath a false board in the floor. He handed it to Lucien and stepped back.

Lucien held it up and searched it with his mind. He smiled, raising an eyebrow. "This is most generous, over eight hundred crowns. You have been doing rather well. Now for what I came for," Lucien pulled the black sword from his waist and rested its tip against Mitchell's groin. "I will know if you're lying. Trust me when I tell you if you answer with a lie, you will forever regret it."

Mitchell tried to scoot away nervously, his eyes wide. "Gods, Edwin, your friend is a bigger psycho than you."

Edwin sheathed his sword and crossed his arms. "I suggest you tell him the truth."

Lucien could feel every part of Mitchell's emotions as they were completely opened by the fear coursing through his veins. "Where did Viola and her friend go?"

Mitchell tried to swallow, but his throat was dry and he could only manage a strained gulp. "I have no idea. I cheated them at dice, and then they left. The trader said they sold some things to get crowns for horses. That is all I know."

Lucien smiled and sheathed his sword. "It has been a pleasure. If you see either of them again, I suggest that you leave them be, or the two of us won't be such pleasant company when we visit next time."

Lucien jerked his head in the direction of the door, and Edwin moved toward it. Outside, Edwin was exasperated. "Damn pointless, all of it."

Lucien looked around the town. Somehow, it looked even older and drearier than just a few hours ago. "Yes, I doubt they told anyone. There isn't anyone here to confide in. All we can do is continue north to Tallin and see if anyone saw them ride in their direction. There is a good chance if they didn't pass Tallin they went to Dawnbridge, and all this was for nothing."

Edwin walked with Lucien to the tavern. "That is a solid plan. I think we can make Tallin before nightfall tomorrow. I just hope we get some information. I am worried they have gotten themselves into trouble."

CHAPTER 22

KATE WAS ALREADY awake and prepared, just resting on the bed when Viola awoke. "Get ready," she said. "I want to leave as soon as possible."

"Gods, Kate, it's barely sunup and you are ready." Viola yawned, slowly waking. She rubbed her eyes and stretched.

Viola took a flask from the block of wood and drank some. She became sharper almost instantly with a burst of energy. She smiled at Kate, dangling the flask between her thumb and pointer finger and waggled it. "Want some?"

Kate shifted herself, took the flask, and then took a drink. She could feel herself gain more energy, feel the potion flowing through her bloodstream. "I think those potions are dangerous. They seem to be able to kill, heal, and alter people's behavior."

Viola smelled the top of the potion wistfully. "I know! Isn't it great?"

Kate shook her head as she opened the door to go outside. Viola followed behind and there was a campfire nearby. Heinrich was sitting with one other soldier. Kate looked around the fort. The road went through the center and it was a large circle, but she could see, further west in the woods, that the other tower was connected by a walkway along the palisade. There were perhaps a dozen soldiers who patrolled the camp, and half were on the walls.

Viola sipped her potion as they walked to the campfire. There were four blocks placed in a circle around it, and Heinrich waved them over.

A battered pan sat on a rock near the fire. Heinrich held a ladle, taking a scoop from the pan. "Do you want to take some breakfast? It is porridge, mostly wheat with some berries thrown in to cut the taste."

Kate took the bowl from him. "Thank you. This would be a luxury in the marsh."

Heinrich smiled and handed a bowl to Viola. She held her hands up, palms toward Heinrich, and shook her head. "I already had breakfast, thanks."

Heinrich placed the bowl in his lap. "I am glad you decided to stay the night. There have been daily attacks in the west and in the north. It has everyone on edge here."

Kate took a spoonful of the porridge. It was good, better than she'd expected. She nodded to Heinrich. "I have a hard time being sympathetic. Didn't Westfall start this by raiding those areas?"

Heinrich laughed. "Overzealous commanders with promises of resources started it, yes. The king has ended all offensive attacks. The Vale is moving soldiers around near the imperial city to the east of Charbel. War seems almost certain."

Kate put the bowl on her lap. "What has happened? Why would the Vale be moving soldiers?"

Heinrich said with a sigh, "There was trouble in Elgin. The Fire-Demon Prince of Elnora destroyed their entire army. Many fled north to the Vale. We think the extra men have emboldened the Valdivians. King Harold is no fool- If he sees an opening, he will use it."

Kate's stomach sank. The porridge no longer tasted good to her. She felt sick. She put her bowl on the rock in front of her. *Was it really Lucien?* "Was there a description of the demon?" she asked, her voice soft because she could barely breathe. The porridge sat like a stone in her belly.

Heinrich frowned, looking at the fire. "They said he had horns and was enormous, with twisted black armor. His eyes were red and he could appear anywhere on the battlefield. Elgin is all but destroyed."

Kate trembled as her heart twisted and she held her hands to her chest.

Viola was shocked and could see Kate's face had lost all its color. She looked at Heinrich, puzzled. "'Destroyed' sounds a bit extreme. I am sure the king will…"

Heinrich cut Viola's thought off before she could finish. "The king is dead. The demon burned him alive in his bed. His mistress was also burned with him. Elgin is likely in the middle of a civil war as Lord Commander Rabin has taken control of most of the country. Queen Elena is in prison in the Free Marshes."

Kate was moving closer to tears and despair the more she heard. *Please let it be a lie, because if the story he just told is true, Lucien is a mass murderer.* She looked at Viola and she put her flask away. Kate tried to speak, but all that came out was air and vowel sounds.

Viola shifted on the wood block. She was worried, thinking of what might be going through Kate's mind. She was going to say something when Kate spoke curtly, nearly in tears, "Lies."

Heinrich paused, his spoon halfway between bowl and lips. "What do you mean?"

Gods, Lucien, what have you done? Kate smeared a tear from her cheek. She was enraged that anyone could believe that story could possibly be true, but more enraged that she wasn't sure. Not completely. "I know this demon you speak of and he would never have done those things. These are all lies."

Heinrich looked away, as if to think. He then looked to Viola. "I only know the story they tell. It is impossible to verify, other than the Vale having moved east."

Kate stood and paced near the campfire. "Why would the Vale move east if Elgin is destroyed? Do you seriously think they would try to move south to attack? That would be quite foolish with a demon running around. No, I think they are moving east to protect themselves, fully aware that Elgin may attack them after something has happened with this demon you speak of."

Heinrich stood and rubbed his hand down his chin. "I have no idea. It is plausible, but you bring up something interesting. If Elgin is so weak, why move knights from our border? Surely we are the stronger opponent if the story is true."

Kate felt relief hearing that Heinrich was also skeptical. She looked at Viola and noticed she was sitting silently, staring at the fire, not moving. "What's wrong?"

Viola looked up, fighting tears. "Edwin could be dead. Lucien might have gone mad and killed all those people if something happened to Edwin."

Kate knelt and hugged her. "It is nonsense. That would never have happened. This story is just that: a story to scare Westfall. I think the Vale has moved east and spread this lie to keep Westfall from threatening them."

Heinrich clasped his hands behind his back. "You both should leave for Charbel. I would not stop at Gera. It is halfway, but if you leave now and ride late into the night or early morning, you can make the city. It will be a very long ride, but you can make it if you run the horses and rest them in intervals."

Kate and Viola both seemed confused. "Why? Why do you want us to hurry?"

Heinrich moved closer and fixed them with a penetrating look. "Something is happening. If Elgin is going to attack, they won't attack the Vale, they will attack Dulimore. If Dulimore falls, so does the marsh. It will be a disaster for us, one more front for us to have to defend, and the Valdivians will overrun us."

Kate could tell by Heinrich's expression and tone of voice that there was serious trouble in Westfall. The kidnapping must have been part of what was going on, and this trouble in Elgin was inevitable. Kate realized she was still embracing Viola and released her. "We have to go now," she told Viola. "There must be someone in the city that can help us."

Kate and Viola went to mount their horses. The soldier Heinrich had been sitting with had fetched their bags and pouches and secured them to their steeds' saddles. It seemed it had already been decided that they would leave immediately. Heinrich helped Viola into the saddle, then held the horses' reins to guide them to the north gate. "There is a college in Charbel. If you go there, they will put you up. It is for the nobility, and as soon as you arrive, the king will be told. It is the Altar College. It used to be for the clergy but since the empire collapsed, they use it to educate everyone, and the nobility are heavily involved there. Go quickly, and tell them I sent you."

Viola was still upset and kicked her horse into a gallop. Kate waved to Heinrich as she kicked her horse to catch up to Viola.

Kate was numb at the thought that Lucien had gone mad and killed all those people. It was impossible to imagine him killing King Richter in his bed. Viola was right to worry because

it could only mean someone close to him had been hurt. Kate
began to cry as she rode with Viola.

They would need to take the road north to the cross with the
King's Highway, then turn eastward. Neither of them had any
idea what to expect the farther north they went. When they came
north through the gate it was as if they entered another world.
The land was rolling hills and fields for miles in all directions, and
to the west they could see the mountains. It was an odd feeling,
as if they were on the tip of the world and could touch the sky.

CHAPTER 23

LUCIEN AND EDWIN had ridden north for most of the day. The Tallin fort was just now coming into view and they could see the guard in the tower wave to the men below.

Edwin and Lucien took their horses to a trot as they approached the gate. There were several guards now on the stands near the palisade.

A young man approached them. "How can we help? It seems we are getting a lot more travelers lately." The man smiled, looking to the other soldiers.

Edwin nodded and responded with a tired, weak smile. "We are in a hurry. Did you see two people come through here on horseback?"

The man cocked his head to the side. "We did, they asked about Westfall. Who are you?"

Edwin presented his seal. "I am Lord Edwin Ulbrich of Elnora. This is my servant. We are to meet up with the two people who passed through here. It is urgent."

The man looked from Edwin to Lucien. Lucien could feel the guard's fear rising as he looked at him. "I am not a servant. I am Lord Lucien of Elnora. The two people who passed through here were Princess Viola and her guard. They are truant from the castle. King Elias has sent us to make sure they are all right. We mean them no harm."

The man's eyes widened as he took a step back. "Princess Viola, here?" He looked nervously at the young men around him. They all seemed to share his nervous expression. "Gods yes, they went north. They were looking for a place to stay the night in Westfall."

Edwin looked to Lucien. "Did they say where they were going or why?"

The man stammered, "No, gods no. We just told them the gate north will have Westfall guards that could give them information."

Edwin nodded to the men. "Thank you. We are in a hurry; we must catch up to them. Send a rider to Dawnbridge to inform the King." Edwin handed the man a large coin purse. "This is tax from South Pier. Make sure you remember to tell him about the princess." Edwin moved his horse back onto the road, and Lucien followed as they galloped north.

Lucien glanced over his shoulder as the Tallin tower passed out of view. They both pulled the reins, taking their horses to a trot.

"What do you think?" Edwin shifted in the saddle to look at Lucien.

Lucien shook his head. "I don't know. They must be up to something. I can't figure out why they would go to Westfall after going so far south as the pier."

Edwin patted his horse's head. "We need to make the gate tonight. They might have a day's lead on us, but we will be close soon."

"Agreed." Lucien kicked his horse into a gallop, and Edwin followed.

CHAPTER 24

IT WAS NEARLY midnight when Edwin and Lucien saw the torches on the gatehouse fort. They brought their horses to a stop as Lucien held his hand out to the side.

Edwin walked his horse in a half-circle to face Lucien. "What is it?"

Lucien felt something strange. "There is something going on. The men are alert and very anxious. There must be trouble in Westfall. I suggest you don't provoke them."

Edwin chafed. "I never provoke anyone. You know that better than anyone. We need to know where they went and I don't have time for platitudes."

Lucien sighed, letting his hand drop. "Exactly. These men are on edge. It is best to find out what is going on and not antagonize them before we get any information."

Edwin scoffed at Lucien as they slowly rode toward the gate. Closer now, they could see the men running into position, and they looked prepared to fight.

Lucien glanced over at Edwin and could tell he now understood. There were twelve men in heavy armor on the walls, and the gate was sealed closed.

Lucien and Edwin approached and saw a man in heavy armor with red laurels on his helm gesture to them. "Who are you?"

Edwin pursed his lips and looked to Lucien. Lucien drew back his hood, revealing his face. "I am Lord Lucien and this is Lord Edwin, we are from Elnora. King Elias has sent us north to find Princess Viola. We believe she is in the company of one other person."

The men on the wall had fear in their eyes as they held their shields and spears tight. Lucien could tell they knew who he was and were terrified. The man in red laurels was afraid, but tried to stay calm. He must have been the commander. Lucien held up his hands. "I mean you no harm. I speak the truth."

The man with the red laurels on his helm looked to his men and back to Lucien. "I am Lord Commander Heinrich Franz, cousin to the king of Westfall. Your reputation is that of a mass murdered and you are wanted for regicide. What do you say to these charges?"

Edwin swallowed hard, looking to Lucien. As he did, he moved his horse to the side as if preparing to run, but Lucien held up his hand and said, "Don't run. It only makes us look guilty." To Heinrich he said, "I have killed no one, and certainly not a king." Lucien took off his sword and approached the gate. "Edwin, get off your horse and lay down your sword."

Edwin dismounted and pulled his sword, holding it before him almost as an offering as he approached the gate. "You are out of your damned mind. These men mean to kill us."

Lucien looked at him. "Don't you think we should find out what is going on? Unless you remember killing a king, and we don't even know what king they are talking about."

Lucien looked up at Heinrich. "I am not sure what story you have been told, but I want to listen. If they said I killed many people, this might not be much of a gesture, but we will surrender our weapons in order to speak to you."

Heinrich waved to his men who pulled out their bows. The gate opened and four guards with spears approached to take their swords. Lucien handed over his bow as well. Heinrich stood behind his men as they searched Lucien and Edwin. "Lady Aela said you didn't kill those men. I want to believe her."

Kate? Gods, what must she have thought? Lucien looked into Heinrich's eyes and could feel he was being honest, but no matter how much honesty Lucien could feel, snakes of jealousy writhed in the pit of his stomach. It was unfair that this man should be able to talk to Kate when he himself had not seen her in several days.

Heinrich led them to the campfire. "Sit with me. My men are only here for defensive reasons."

Edwin gritted his teeth as he stared at Lucien. Lucien could tell he didn't like being disarmed, and definitely didn't like that this lord had talked with Viola any more than he cared for his talking to Kate.

Lucien sat at the campfire and Edwin joined him. Heinrich filled a bowl with something from a pan that hung on a trivet over a small fire and handed it to Edwin. "It is porridge, if you want it." Edwin took the bowl and passed it to Lucien, trying to suppress the scowl on his face.

Heinrich filled another bowl and handed it to Edwin. "There must have been a rumor about something in Elgin. I will tell you what happened and you can tell me what is being said."

Heinrich nodded. "That is fair," he said, and sat down.

Lucien swirled the berries in his porridge around and ate a spoonful. "The Elnoran army is stationed at Port Porin in southern Dulimore. Lord Jan is worried, as many are, about invasion. Edwin and I went north to observe and…dissuade the

Elgin army. I have obsidian armor made to resemble a demon that I wore to frighten the men away, but I killed no one. The army scattered and we left. The scouts who went north so far had said nothing strange had happened afterwards, other than the army had left its position."

Lucien could feel Heinrich didn't completely believe the story, but neither did he think it was a lie. Heinrich watched Lucien intensely as he spoke, and when he finished, put his bowl down on the rocks around the fire. Heinrich looked from Edwin to Lucien. "Scouts have reported the Valdivians have moved their forces from the imperial city east. We sent scouts and there are rumors that King Richter is dead, burned alive in his bed. They say Lord Rabin has taken control of the army and there is a civil war, all this at the same time that the Elgin army was burned to cinders outside the castle by the Demon Prince of Elnora."

Edwin scratched the back of his head. "Quite the story."

Heinrich smiled. "It is sounding more and more like a fairy-tale for our benefit. There is something going on and they want Westfall to be afraid. We have had attacks on our north and west borders daily for the past week. They are trying to make sure we don't react to whatever is being planned."

"Agreed." Lucien clasped his hands together and rested his chin on them. "Did Viola and Kate say where they were going?"

"They said something about freeing two girls who were kidnapped from the mountain. I did not fully understand, but I told them to visit the Altar College in Charbel. They thought maybe Prince Henry could help them."

Edwin clenched his fists in frustration. "Prince Henry? What does he have to do with anything?"

Heinrich raised an eyebrow warily. "It was their idea. You will need to catch up to them and ask them."

Lucien blew out an irritated breath and closed his eyes. The more he heard, the more confused he became. He needed to find out what happened in Elgin. It could be dangerous if they killed Richter and decided to march into Dulimore anyway.

Edwin was still fuming at the idea of Henry helping Viola, but when he looked at Lucien to try to get some sort of perspective, he was gone. Heinrich turned to see what had upset Edwin.

Alarmed, Heinrich jumped to his feet, sword drawn. His men fanned out, searching. "Where the hell did your friend go?"

Edwin gritted his teeth, seething in rage. "He does that, the bastard."

CHAPTER 25

LUCIEN APPEARED AT the castle manor in Porin. His bedroom was just as he had left it. He wiped the blood from his mouth and quietly opened the door. There were no guards in the hallway. He moved as silently as a shadow down the hallway to Alaric's room. He tried the handle, but the door was locked. He held his hand near the keyhole and flicked his wrist.

The click of the lock disengaging was louder than Lucien expected, but he opened the door silently, closed it behind him, and went quickly to the bed. Alaric was not disturbed. Lucien lit a candle by the bed and gently put his hand over Alaric's mouth.

Just as he sealed his hand, Alaric's eyes opened and Lucien felt a blade stab into his side and push him to the floor. Alaric stood over him. "Gods, Lucien, I might need to change my trousers after that."

Lucien held the gash on his side where blood dripped through the leather armor. "Damn you Alaric, didn't you see it was me? I was trying to be quiet."

"How bad is it?" Alaric helped Lucien up to the bed.

Lucien grimaced. "Not bad. It will heal quickly. What is going on in Elgin? The men in Westfall think that Richter is dead and the Elgin army was destroyed, all by a fire demon?"

Alaric furrowed his brow. "What? Richter is dead? How?"

Lucien shrugged. "They said he was burned alive in his bed...by me. I also apparently wiped out the Elgin army. Lord Commander Rabin is now leading a rebellion against Queen Elena."

Alaric grabbed some clothes from his armoire and started to dress. "Where did you come from?"

Lucien winced in pain. "I was sitting with the guards at the Westfall gate. Edwin is there, by the way."

Alaric couldn't help but laugh. "Edwin is probably cursing you, you jackass, and who could blame him? You left him there alone."

"We need to find out what is going on. There is a reason that story is spreading in Westfall," Lucien said pointedly.

Alaric went to the door and Lucien followed. "Where are you going?"

"I need to wake Jan immediately. Elgin is going to do something and we need to be ready, no matter what happens." Alaric stepped into the hall.

Lucien followed. "So you have not heard anything?"

"Nothing. Nothing has changed. The last report was that the army had gone back to the castle. There has been no movement reported since then, but we pulled the scouts back two days ago." Alaric's pace quickened and Lucien fell behind.

Alaric turned to Lucien but he was gone. He shook his head. "What were you doing in Westfall?"

CHAPTER 26

EDWIN STOOD DUMBFOUNDED as the guards surrounded him. "Listen, he has the power to teleport. He will be back shortly."

Heinrich looked uneasily around the area. "Where would he go?"

Edwin shook his head. "I have no idea. He does this a lot without telling me. It is getting to be more annoying lately."

Heinrich paced the area. "Don't be offended that I will be putting you under arrest if he does not return."

Edwin put his hands on his hips. "Yes, yes, I expected as much. He really is such an ass, you know."

Lucien appeared at the campfire, falling to his knees. Blood covered his lips and chin. He spat it out and clutched his side. There was blood smeared from his side to his thigh. "That didn't work out," he told them.

Edwin grabbed him. "You bastard! I hope whatever you did, you paid for it." But then concern for his friend overtook him and Edwin asked, "How bad is it?"

Heinrich and his men approached, weapons drawn. "Where did you go?"

"Port Porin, I had to find out what the Elnoran army was doing. Alaric stabbed me when I tried to wake him." Lucien panted as blood dripped from his nose, and he grimaced in pain.

Heinrich stood by Lucien as Edwin tended to his wound. "What did they say?"

Lucien winced at Edwin's less-than-tender ministrations. "Nothing, they had not sent scouts in two days. Alaric was worried. He raised the men and is planning to send out scouts to find out what is happening. They have heard nothing; Elgin was as you and I left it. The army scattered and the castle was on the defensive."

Heinrich's jaw clicked and he scowled as he paced by Lucien. "There is something going on. Those lies about Elgin are being spread for a reason. You two better get to Charbel and find your lady friends. If you don't, they might be walking into something they don't even understand."

Edwin watched Lucien with growing concern. "You look terrible. Can you make it further tonight?"

Lucien panted and wiped the blood from his nose. He coughed into his sleeve. "How far is the next town?"

Heinrich pointed. "It is several hours north. I suggest you stay here 'til you get your strength back and then head out in the morning. I told your friends if they left early they could make Charbel in a single day, but it is a long ride. It would not surprise me if they arrived past midnight."

Lucien sighed. "Then I guess we stay. I just hope those two don't get into any trouble before we get there."

CHAPTER 27

KATE COULD BARELY keep her eyes open by the time they saw the light from the fires in Charbel. The city was massive and had come into view hours ago, but they continued to ride on for what seemed like forever before they finally arrived.

Charbel was a citadel fortress city. It was the capital of Westfall and the second largest city on the continent. It had huge outer walls and the castle town was on the outer ring, followed by two more sets of walls before the castle bailey. There were over three hundred houses and buildings in the castle town alone. It stood tall, guarding the entire Westfall fields, and was built near the center of the province and on the main river that traveled to the imperial city. It was the most strategic point in the western half of Amor. Its position this close to the imperial city was at times a great boon for commerce. Since the fall of the empire it stood at odds, as the Vale had control over the eastern border and the imperial city.

Kate became more awake as her nerves started to rise with every step closer she took to the city walls. They soared overhead like a steep cliff, and there were several guards stationed near the gate. Viola was slumped forward on her mount, her forehead resting against the horse's thick mane.

A guard in full steel armor carrying a bill hook approached and raised his hand. "Halt! he commanded. "Who are you, and what business do you have in the city?"

Kate had neither the time nor patience for pretense. "I am Lady Aela O'Neill, and this is Princess Viola. We have ridden all the way from the border with the Free Marshes. We need somewhere to sleep for the night."

The guard looked to his men and back to her. "We will put you at the Tavern on the Wall. It is just inside the gate. In the morning the bailiff will see you about entrance into the city. I don't have to tell you, it is an odd thing that a Princess should arrive here in the night."

"We are in a hurry," Kate snapped, struggling to keep her head up.

Kate dismounted and nudged Viola. "We are here," she said. Viola opened her sleep-heavy eyelids just enough to see as she slid off the side of her horse.

The drawbridge lowered and the portcullis rose. They took the reins as they walked across the drawbridge and into the city. The tavern inside was small but still had lanterns giving off an inviting glow at the open door. The guard followed and led their horses to the stables.

They went inside where a skinny young man in his night clothes was talking to a guard. The guard turned to them and said, "Up the stairs, first door on the left. The room has two bunks."

Kate and Viola went up to the room and did not even take off their weapons before they collapsed into their beds.

CHAPTER 28

KATE AWOKE TO a knock at the door. It was bright, and she guessed it must have been mid-morning. She groaned, pushing her helm and coif off to the floor, making a thud when they landed. Kate looked over to Viola but she had slept through it. In fact, it looked like Viola had not moved at all since lying down. Kate's backside was screaming in pain, and she doubted Viola would be able to sit on a chair for a couple days after the riding they had done.

Kate sat on the bed and there was another knock at the door. She let out a groan. "Who is it?"

"I am squire Esch to the bailiff. I need to check you into the city. Do you know when you will be ready?" The man spoke through the door.

Kate heard his voice and he sounded very young. She stood up with a groan and opened the door. He was barely a boy. He might have been fourteen or younger. Kate smiled wryly. "Does your mother know where you are? How old are you?"

Esch stood proud. "I am sixteen, my lady. I know I look young."

Kate yawned and rubbed her eyes. "What do you need from us?"

Esch cleared his throat. "Do you have a seal that I can review and make a mark with?"

Kate went over to Viola and reached into her cloak pocket. She took her seal and handed it to the boy.

He took it and pressed it in ink onto a scroll he held. "Does the lady have her seal?"

Kate had a seal, but never took it with her. She was so impoverished it wasn't going to get any respect wherever she went, but for the first time in her life, she realized she probably should have brought it with her. "No, my house is -- or rather, was -- so impoverished I never have carried it. I am sure her highness will vouchsafe for me, and that should be enough. I am also acquainted with Prince Henry. If her highness's word is not good enough, perhaps Prince Henry's will be."

"Her highness." Esch blushed and looked down at the seal he had just stamped. "Gods, princess, I am very sorry for waking you. The innkeeper said there is food if you wish, down in the dining room. I...I...I only have one other thing. Can you tell me where you are planning to travel for the record?"

Kate took Viola's seal and put it back in her pocket and turned to the boy. "We are going to the Altar College. It is a place for nobility or something?"

The boy nodded and left abruptly, not even closing the door.

Kate brushed her hair up and sat on the bed. She could tell Viola was not going to wake for at least for an hour. She put the hair at the top of her head in a bun, the hair at the back in a tail, and went to get food.

The dining area had several people at the tables, eating. She was taken aback by the sight of so many. She felt her clothes and wondered how bad she must look to the others. She rubbed the patchwork on her side where she had sewn three tears from Omskov. Fidgeting, she stood in front of the teller. "I was told there was food here?"

The teller bowed. "Yes, my lady." He handed her two plates of eggs, cheese, and a small piece of cooked meat.

Kate looked down at the plate with a gasp as her face reddened in embarrassment. It was the best meal she had ever seen. "I really can't pay for this."

The man laughed. "Compliments of the crown. They are expecting you at the castle."

Kate looked suspiciously at the food. She didn't think it was possible to have such a meal without some kind of bill to come due. "Thank you." She didn't like them knowing where she or Viola were. *Everything has a price.* She went up to the room and saw Viola had rolled to her back, but was still asleep.

Kate barely tasted the food as she wolfed it down in just a few huge bites. These were the first eggs she'd had in a very long time, and the cheese was excellent. She watched Viola sleep, trying to keep from devouring the contents of the plate she had brought for her. Impatient, she pushed Viola with her hand. "Wake up, I have breakfast."

Viola groaned, "My bottom hurts terribly. I hope I never see another horse as long as I live."

She rolled to her side, looking at Kate, and then the plate of food on the counter. Her eyes grew wide. "Are those eggs?"

Kate laughed. "Yes, and if you don't get them soon, I will eat them."

Viola tried to sit up but had to settle on her hip. It was uncomfortable, but not as much as her bottom was after her long ride. She reached for the plate. "Gods, they must live like kings here."

"You could say that," Kate said, and smiled. "The food came from the castle. They want us to go there after we get up."

Viola ate vigorously and didn't stop chewing to speak: "Mummrfe memr, mi mermum."

Kate let out a laugh. "I can't understand you when your mouth is full of food. I wish Edwin could see his dainty lady eating like this."

Viola swallowed. "Would it be poisoned, my meal?"

Kate shrugged. "Probably could have just killed us in the night in that case. I am not sure who or why anyone would want you dead, but I am sure there is a reason for someone."

"How comforting," Viola scoffed, shoving the last of the food in her mouth.

Kate put her coif and helm on. She pulled her cloak and bow over her shoulders as Viola finished eating. Viola had a potion from her satchel out and took a drink. "Did you want some? It will help with digestion."

Kate took it from her and had a sip. "Does it do anything else?"

Viola laughed. "Nope, it just calms your stomach if you eat too fast."

Kate stood and smiled at Viola. "Sounds like a potion you would make after watching yourself eat that plate."

Viola stood with her satchel over her shoulder and picked up Kate's plate. "I think I see saliva on this. Did you lick the plate clean?"

Kate looked away and went to the stairs. Smiling, Viola put the plate down and jogged after her. They both shifted themselves and lowered their heads as they walked through the crowded tavern. Outside there were a few people wandering the street. The city was far healthier and more vibrant than Dawnbridge.

Kate and Viola walked the market street toward the inner walls. There were dozens of stall vendors and shops along the road, and many had goods for sale. There were also abandoned shops and many beggars. The town was not as rich as it might first appear. There were homeless camps along the side streets and human waste ran in the gutters along the road. The stench would have been overwhelming if not for the flowers that were placed around the buildings to help improve the odor.

Viola pulled up her dress and skirt as she looked at Kate. "The streets are filthier than Dawnbridge."

Kate continued to survey the area as they walked toward the castle gate. "They are fighting on two fronts and may have a third and fourth soon. These people must be refugees from all the conflicts on their borders."

Kate and Viola approached the gate. The drawbridge ramp went up over a canal below. The gutters on the inner wall side drained to the canal and it was a good ten-foot drop on all sides.

A guard approached them as they stood on the bridge. "Halt, identify yourselves."

Kate stood with her hands on her hips. "Lady Aela O'Neill and Princess Viola."

Viola wiped her shoes on the side of the bridge as the man approached. He looked them over. "Very well, you may pass. The steward will see you at the castle. Ask for Liam."

Kate and Viola continued through the gate and were stunned by what they found inside. The entire area was luxury homes, and the streets were stone-paved. It was a city within a city, with many very fine shops lining the street that wrapped around the wall to the keep.

Viola looked in awe, almost gaping. "It must be the high quarter. It is incredible. There is more wealth here than in all of the Free Marshes."

Kate rubbed her worn-out armor and pulled her cloak tight. It was like a different world to her. There were a few people on the street that simply smiled and gave them a nod as they walked. There was a circle walkway near the keep entrance and a large statue of Saint Charbel. He held a book with his head turned to the sky, hand raised out to his side as if trying to steady himself.

Viola stood near the statue and looked around the area. There was a very large collection of fine buildings. Viola approached a sign and looked back to Kate. "The Altar College is here. It makes sense being in the high quarter. We should stop by before we leave. I heard in imperial times, every clergyman in the empire was educated here."

Kate looked at Viola without an expression. Viola looked back at her with narrowed eyes.

"What?"

Kate rubbed her shoulders. "This place. I don't belong here."

Viola smiled and linked arms with her. "Come on, we will be in the castle soon enough. Just imagine it is King's Port and you are here to meet your father-in-law, the god-king himself, Delvin."

Kate shuddered. "That is definitely not helping."

They approached the gate to the inner castle. A man with just a helmet and fine patterned clothes approached, blocking them. "What business do you have in the castle?"

Viola pulled her hood back and looked at him haughtily. "Princess Viola to see Steward Liam. We are expected."

The man rubbed his chin as he opened a ledger and ran his finger down a list of names. "Very well, make your way to the main entrance. His office is just to the right of it."

Kate and Viola made their way through the gate and up a wide stairway. There were large double doors at the top and a single door to the right. Kate went over to open the door. It was unlocked and Viola went in as Kate held it open.

Inside, a young man of scarcely twenty sat at a desk stacked with scrolls and paperwork and a small pot of ink and several quills. He had a round, orange hat with upturned felt around the brim. Viola was quite sure this was Liam and watched as he sorted through a pile of scrolls. "Yes?" he said without looking up. He continued to scribble on a scroll at his desk.

Viola frowned. "Princess Viola, I was told to see you."

He kicked his chair back and jumped to his feet and rolled his scrolls together. "Your highness, I am very sorry. I did not expect you so soon. They said your trip brought you in late in the night."

Viola brushed her hair back with a wink at Kate. "I hope there is somewhere to bathe, the trip was very long."

Liam gestured toward a door at the back of the room. "Please, let me show you to the manor quarters. The king has you near the outer windows. It is a beautiful view of the countryside."

Kate still felt uneasy as he led them to the doorway. Inside, there was a stairwell that took them up two floors. It opened into a long, wide hallway with doors on either side. It seemed quiet and they did not see any people wandering about the corridors.

Two guards stood at attention outside their room. Liam nodded, and they opened the door and went inside. Two large, four-poster canopied beds stood at opposite ends of the large room, facing each other. There was a water basin and a cabinet made of rich cherry wood standing in the middle between the beds. Ornate gold leaf filigree decorated the cabinet. Fresh water pitchers stood nearby on a desk that was nearly as elegant as the cabinet.

Viola brushed her elbow into Kate's side, managing to raise a weak smile from her. They were both amazed by the accommodations. Liam stood in the room, smiling. "I hope it is satisfactory."

Viola nodded, trying not to smile. "Yes, this will do."

As soon as Liam left, Viola jumped up on the bed, giggling and kicking her feet as she bounded about on the overstuffed mattress. "It is amazing, isn't it? I may have to consider Henry as a suitor after all. You might want to consider Heinrich. I think he had eyes for you."

Kate laughed, "I have serious doubts about that. I think he was too busy keeping his eyes trained on your backside. Besides, I would rather live in rags in the woods with Lucien then live in a place like this. This wealth in a continent filled with misery makes me feel gross all over."

Viola jumped and bounced from the bed to her feet. "You just remember this when you are an old lady trying to use the privy in the winter. I can tell you a basin in your room like this is high society."

Kate laughed. "There is more to life than comfort; that, I promise you."

Viola tilted her head, smiling. "You're right. I wouldn't give Edwin up for this. I am sure his vineyard is paradise anyway."

Kate walked around the room trying not to seem happy. It was very nice, but she knew it wasn't to be. She could feel it all around her that something bad was going to happen, no matter how nice everything might seem.

CHAPTER 29

KATE HAD JUST finished bathing after Viola when a
knock came at the door. A voice called through, "It is
Liam, and I am here to take you to the king."

Kate quickly donned her clothes. She left her weapons and
armor behind and just wore her leather armor over her under-
shirt and a pair of trousers. Viola tried to make herself pretty
and more like a princess. She put on a gemstone necklace and a
gold bracelet that held the seal of her family. Kate worried she
looked too plain to meet the king. When she visited the castle
in Dawnbridge, Elias was never dressed formally.

Viola opened the door and met Liam with a smile. "We
are ready."

Viola gestured to Kate to hurry as she followed Liam. He
took them down the hall to another stairwell and then down to
the lower level. They walked through what seemed like a maze
of corridors, then through a heavily-guarded doorway into the
throne room. It was enormous. There was a gallery above and
fire pits on both sides of the room with several grazing tables.
It was at least twice the size of Elias's.

Kate tried to keep her eyes on the floor to stay calm. Her hair was down and she held her left arm straight at her side, cupping her elbow with her right hand. She didn't know what to do with her hands and she was trying not to panic. Viola was fidgeting with her dress, but kept her wits about her as they both had generous bows at the king.

King William sat on a raised level of four steps, with Queen Priscilla sitting to his left, and William's commander standing next to the king's throne. Priscilla was older; her hair had mostly turned white. William had a medium-length gray beard and wore patterned clothing in red with yellow. It was similar to the pattern they had seen on the guard at the gate. Liam approached the throne quietly and deferentially, clutching one of his many scrolls.

William did not seem fair-tempered and looked annoyed. His lips were crimped and he tapped his index finger to his mouth. Kate tried to not make eye contact as Viola approached him. "Your majesty," she said, and bowed deeply.

William stared down at them as he took the scroll from Liam. His duty discharged, Liam bowed and silently backed from the room. "Why have you come to Charbel, Lady Viola?"

Viola raised her head from her bow. "We are searching for two girls who were taken from the mountain. A tribal warlord named Tel-son said they were taken to Westfall, and we hoped someone in the city would know where they are."

William scowled upon hearing the name Tel-son. "I have heard of the man, but know nothing of any kidnapping. My men have been only defending for the past year or more after my commanders blundered into a war with the mountain warlords."

Viola wrung her hands and stammered, "We did not plan to trouble you. We just wanted to visit the Altar College and see if there might be anyone there who knows anything."

William stood and descended the four steps. He stood with his hands behind his back, looking at Kate, who looked up just long enough to see he was there and then back down at the floor. William studied her curiously. "I have heard of the exploits of Lady O'Neill. I daresay we are in your debt."

Kate curtsied. "It was no trouble, my lord."

William laughed. "You gave my people their first true victory in five years. Or perhaps I should say you and his lordship. How is Lord Lucien? I have heard rumors that you are very good friends."

Kate felt more at ease after hearing William compliment her. She released her arm and clasped her hands together at her waist. She looked up at the king. "We are a couple. He has yet to make it formal with his father, so we cannot be married."

William showed no emotion as he continued, "I am grateful for your honesty. I am sure you know about the trouble in Elgin. It is difficult news for my people. We are at war with the Boreal and the tribal men from the mountain. Meanwhile, our mortal enemies are removing soldiers from our border. It has everyone uneasy. If Elgin or the Valdivians take the Free Marshes, it may spell our doom."

Viola looked to speak but Kate already started: "The Elnorans will never allow the Free Marshes to fall. They need the port for access to trade."

William paced as he nodded his agreement. "I have heard that before, yet King Delvin does not formalize any relations. I simply see treatises passed around talking of cooperation. It is hard not to think Delvin and Elias are just waiting for us to weaken and, with their combined forces, conquer Westfall."

William turned to Viola and Kate. He inspected them as he paced.

Viola did not know what to say. It was possible that Elias and Delvin secretly wanted to get rid of Westfall. It would stop the conflict with the Boreal and tribes. Viola could not say for certain what they were thinking.

William arched an eyebrow. "I take it from your silence that you feel that is a possibility as well."

Viola said, "I don't think King Delvin would ever support any conquests on the continent. He is far too cautious."

William laughed nearly to tears. He was still chuckling when he answered her: "You are so very young and sweet, Viola. King Delvin used to bathe in blood during the imperial wars. He killed thousands with his violence. I promise you, he is capable of anything."

Kate felt her heart rate rise hearing stories such as that. Lucien never spoke well of Delvin, but she was not certain of anything with him. She looked at Viola and immediately knew that even Viola was frightened at such talk.

"I would not know. Elias rarely lets me sit in on any strategy meetings. I just know the Elnoran army is formidable and they have helped defend the marshlands," Viola answered meekly.

King William turned to face Viola. He was at least two heads taller than she. He was an imposing sight that made Viola want to step back, but he leaned in close to her. "You both realize that I had to have you here because if anything were to happen to you, that it would create a pretext for war?"

Viola swallowed dryly, looking to Kate and then back to William. "Yes, I realize that. I would assure you we are capable of taking care of ourselves. You should also know that Lord Lucien will be here shortly. If anything were to happen to us, I doubt there would be much of a war, if you follow my meaning."

William seemed puzzled and absently twisted the ring on his finger. "Why would Lord Lucien come here?"

Kate took a step back, trembling. Viola said, "Did you not hear Lady Kate? They are together and we left without telling anyone. The first two people to come looking for us will be Lucien and Edwin. They were both in Elgin, apparently making some sort of trouble. Lucien moves far faster than you could possibly imagine."

Kate nodded quickly in an attempt to support Viola's blind embellishment. She hoped William didn't realize that was all it was, but it was all they could do to throw him out of sorts.

William looked to his guards and then to his wife. A look of momentary concern crossed her face, but was almost immediately replaced by one of polite interest. William waved his hand dismissively to his commander. He left the room without a word and William took a step back from them. "You are guests, but I do not want you freely wandering the city. It is safe, but there are many desperate refugees here. If they were to find out who either of you are, you could be in danger. I will send spies to gather information about this kidnapping. It sounds like stuff and nonsense to me, but it is difficult to tell truth from fiction with Elgin conspiring against us."

Viola and Kate both sighed quietly in relief.

William laughed. "I would never have harmed you. I am just fearful of something happening. I do not want you to even return to the marshes. If Elgin were to get his hands on either of you, it would be catastrophic."

Kate slowly shook her head in confusion. "Why would Eglin care about either of us?"

William said, "If you are close to Lucien, they would use you to get to him. Viola would be a way of putting legitimacy to a false claim on the marshes. I am sure Richter has some cousin he could marry her to and claim Elias's throne. With Elias's sons dead, Martin has no more of a claim to the throne than Viola."

Viola clutched her hand to her chest. Until she heard him talk so plainly about it, she had not fully understood the pressure they were under, but she felt it now. All of it.

Kate's breath came in little gasps and hiccups. She looked sidewise at Viola, who was trying to look stoic.

William stood before them as more guards entered the room. "I am sure by now you realize I am confining you to your quarters for the time being. Once I have news of Elgin and this kidnapping, I will have Liam visit you, but until such time, you are my honored guests and will be treated well."

Kate's heart pounded in her chest. *Confined to quarters, for how long?* She looked to Viola with a frown on her face. The two of them did not resist as the guards surrounded them, front and rear, and led them back to their room. It was getting harder by the moment to feel like honored guests.

Kate walked with her head down the whole way, but Viola was studying every detail of the hallways and how they linked together. She even "mistakenly" entered a wrong doorway just to see what was inside. It was a stairwell leading down. She looked back over her shoulder at Kate with a wry grin. To the guards, she said: "I am so very sorry. I thought that was our room." The guards paid no attention as they continued to the correct room.

There were four guards at the doorway now, and Kate and Viola were locked inside.

Viola went to the desk and took out a paper and charcoal. She quickly scribbled on it.

Kate lay on the bed with the crushing realization she may never see Lucien again. They would keep her here to make him do whatever they wished. Lucien would never find her if his powers could not function correctly.

The more Kate thought about it, the more afraid she became that Lucien would destroy this city trying to find her. He would take days peeling away the walls and burning the houses. It would be horrific. Tears formed in her eyes as she gasped, trying to compose herself.

Viola was keenly focused and mixed ingredients on the desk. She had her flasks and vials scattered about as she worked. Finished, she placed several of the small ceramic flasks in the fireplace to warm them.

Viola went to the bed and sat by Kate. "Don't worry, I have a plan."

Kate sniffled and wiped at her tears. "I hope it is quite cunning because right now, I don't know what Lucien will do if he even does come."

Viola smiled and rubbed her shoulder. "Lucien is coming, that is for certain. I am sure he was the first person summoned when we went missing. My plan is quite cunning; however, I am not sure if you will get to see most of it."

Kate sat up in bed. "What do you mean?"

"I just have an uneasy feeling that William has a very bad character. I am even more worried that he may be quite the fool as well," Viola said with a frown.

CHAPTER 30

LUCIEN AND EDWIN had ridden the entire day, stopping only to rest the horses. They both yawned and rubbed their backsides. The wound on Lucien's stomach had healed, but his power did not replenish anything else while it did. The closer they came to Charbel, the weaker he felt. Kate's presence took from him and he felt exhausted already.

The massive city glowed in the night as they approached the gate. They came to a stop; guards milled about on the bridge.

Edwin moved his horse closer to Lucien and asked softly, "What do you think?"

Lucien studied the guards ahead. "I feel almost nothing, but I am certain she is here. I can feel that much."

Edwin nodded. "The guards, do you want to move past, or should we play it straight and announce ourselves?"

Lucien had already decided. The guards would know soon enough, and hiding would only make them look guilty. He looked at Edwin with a frown. "We have to announce ourselves and just deal with what comes. They will be suspicious already, and I just want to make sure Kate and Viola are safe. We can leave after that."

Edwin sighed, looking ahead. The plan did not sit well with him but they needed to know what was going on before making conclusions. He took his horse to a trot as Lucien followed toward the guards. It was past midnight and strangers would make anyone uneasy.

They stood on the drawbridge as several guards now appeared above on the ramparts. There were at least thirty that Lucien could see, and several more he could sense. A man with a bill hook approached and raised his hand. "Halt and identify yourselves."

Edwin looked at the man and spoke plainly and commandingly: "Lords Edwin and Lucien of Elnora."

The guard nodded. "We expected you. There is a tavern just inside the gate. The king has arranged for you to stay there for the night. We do not want any trouble, and you may keep your weapons if you follow our rules."

Lucien could feel his pulse rise. *They knew they were coming? It is a trap.* Edwin gritted his teeth, knowing this was going to be trouble as soon as he saw the look on Lucien's face. "Very well, lead the way."

Edwin and Lucien rode to the tavern and dismounted, and the guard took their horses to the stables. Lucien followed and noticed there were two horses with odd brandings in the stalls already. They had to have been Kate and Viola's horses. His stomach tightened. *Where did they take them that they do not need their horses?* he thought. *It could just be a coincidence. Try to stay calm.*

Edwin watched Lucien follow the guard with mounting fury. He could count nearly a hundred guards in the streets and along the walls. They all had easy access to attack the tavern from every direction. They had willingly walked into a trap and Lucien had said nothing.

CHAPTER 31

VIOLA WAS STILL working on her potions at the fire when the door behind her suddenly opened. She jumped from the fireplace and quickly turned to face the door. Three guards stormed into the room and grabbed Kate on the bed. "What?! No, don't do this!" She tried to punch and kick but they held her down as they put a gag around her mouth and a bag over her head. William stood observing from the doorway.

The guards took her weapons and then searched Viola. They held the dagger they found up to the king. He nodded and turned to face Viola.

"She will not be harmed."

Viola stiffened her lip and stared at King William, clenching and unclenching her fists at her sides in helpless fury. "You're making a terrible mistake."

He sighed resignedly. "I have made so many. What is one more?"

Viola sneered. "Fatal."

The three guards took Kate from the room. William lingered long enough to smirk at Viola before leaving. He slammed the door behind him.

Viola held her hand to her chest as she heard the click of the door. She threw herself onto the bed and buried her face in the pillow and sobbed uncontrollably. She didn't want the guards to hear and the pillow stifled her wailing. It was the nightmare she expected, but it still overwhelmed her. Expecting the worst didn't change the fact that when it happened, it was still the worst.

Viola cried for a long while before calming herself. She drank a sip from one of her potions and set it back on the table. She looked for something – anything – the guards might have overlooked that could help her rescue Kate. She opened the desk drawer and a sinister smile twisted the corners of her mouth as she held up a metal-tipped quill.

Viola packed up her satchel and set some vials on the desk next to the quill. She dipped the quill in a vial and placed it on the bed stand. She went to the window and gently pushed it open. It was just large enough for someone as small as her to fit through. She looked down at the nearly twenty-foot drop to the battlements.

Viola held her cloak sleeve to her mouth to suppress her giddy laugh. Then she went to Kate's bed, stripped it, and began to roll and tie the ends of the sheets. She took the under sheets from her bed and tied them in sequence with Kate's and then covered them all with the top level of blankets, careful to hide any suspicious lumps in the bed.

Viola took off her dress and shirt. She had only her underwear and a wrap around her chest under her cloak. She slipped beneath the covers on her bed and waited.

It was not a long wait, for there was soon a knock at the door. "Who is it?"

A weak voice replied: "Zara."

Viola rubbed her hand over her face in frustration. "You may enter."

The door unlatched and slowly opened. Princess Zara entered, wearing only her night clothes. She gently closed the door, trying to find Viola in the darkness. The small candle holder she carried gave off little light. She was a fit girl with silky brown hair down past her shoulders. She was nearly as tall as Kate, but not as pretty as Viola.

Viola tried to mask her frustration. "I am here. I have to be here, but why are you?"

Zara approached the bed slowly, shielding the dancing candle flame with her free hand. "I wanted to talk to you. It is about Lady Kate."

Viola sat up in bed with her cloak tightly wrapped around her. "What about her? Your mad father has taken her away. She could be dead for all I know."

Zara sat so softly on the edge of the bed that it made Viola think of a bird lightly perching. Zara studied her free hand lying across her lap. "I do not know where she was taken, but you must save her somehow."

"How am I supposed to save her? What about you? You could at least find where she is." Viola was incensed and growing more furious.

Zara looked up from her hand. "I am nothing here. I am like a ghost. My mother does not even care for me anymore since I will be married off to some foreign land as soon as Lucien is married. I fear it, but welcome it at the same time. That is why it is important to find Kate. Lucien has to marry her so I can hope for some kind of freedom from this place."

Viola had to fight to keep from shouting. "You're pathetic. You can leave whenever you want. I live in a hovel of poverty and have less than nothing. You have means, if you would get off your ass and do something about it."

Zara had tears in her eyes. "I was never taught anything other than to be proper and polite. You see it as so great, but I would rather have affection than wealth or luxury."

Viola threw up her arms in mock defeat and fell back into bed in a huff. She grumbled, "I don't know where my friend is and I don't know what happened to those girls from the mountain. If you can answer those questions, I will consider it. I suspect that she is far enough from here as to not bring the Lord of Darkness to destroy this place."

Zara stood to leave. Her standing had no more effect on the mattress than her sitting had. "I will try to help you any way I can." She moved to the door and looked back at Viola. "Lord Lucien is already here. That is why they took your friend. Edwin is with him too. I don't know what my father is planning, but it involves them."

Viola wrapped her arms around herself, squeezing tightly so she would not cry until Zara was gone. As soon as the door latched, she released her sadness once more into the pillow. They both had come after her and Kate. It was incredible to think they were in the city and there was no way to find them.

Viola was startled out of her reverie by voices in the hallway. The guards were talking to someone else. She couldn't make out the words but the tone of the guards was deferential. She sat up in bed, wiping at her tears when a knock came again at the door.

"Who is it?"

"Henry. Can I come in?"

Viola had an otherworldly wicked grin as she took off the wrap from her chest. She tossed it to the floor and held the cloak around her. "You may." She quickly moved under the covers in the center of the bed and wrapped them around her so that her breasts were visible above them.

Henry opened the door and entered. He looked around the room, letting his eyes adjust to the darkness as he closed the door. "I hope you are not upset?" Crown Prince Henry was devilishly handsome with his hair cropped tight to his temples and his medium-length blonde hair on top. Taller than even King William, his chiseled features were shadowed by the candle in the room as he searched for Viola.

Viola giggled coyly. "A little, but I am sure you can kiss it and make it better."

Henry stumbled as he slipped on the chest wrap on the floor. He picked it up, fumbling and stammering, "Well, I suppose I may be able to. That is, what did you have in mind?" He dropped the wrap, approached the bed, and sat on the edge, facing her.

Viola yawned and stretched, allowing the covers to slip from her enough to reveal the perfect curve of her breasts. "Maybe you could cuddle with me so you can heal my broken heart." Viola licked and pouted her lips.

Even in the candlelight Viola could see Henry's face had turned a ruddy red. He swallowed twice and said, "If you are trying to seduce me, it is.....ah, working." He slid next to her, putting his hand under the covers to stroke her leg. As he moved closer, Viola's lips slicked away from her teeth in a feral snarl. She moved fast, faster than he could react, and struck him on the side of the neck. He reared back, slapping at his wound. "Ouch, what the hell was..." His eyes grew wide and unfocused and he toppled face-first into Viola's lap.

She pushed his head off of her and rolled him to his side. She checked the door to see if anyone had raised an alarm, but she had struck quickly and silently, and the effects of her potions were instantaneous. No one had heard. She quickly put on her clothes.

Henry's dazed eyes were all he could move, and he whispered, "What did you do to me?"

Viola studied her reflection in the mirror as she fixed her hair. "Sleep paralysis, it should wear off in time."

Henry tried to struggle and shout, "Help." It sounded like he was whispering to himself as he lay alone on the bed.

Viola laughed, straddling his chest. "Don't bother. Another strike and you will be dead. Don't make it easy for me."

Henry managed to reach his hand up, and she stabbed him again in the neck. He winced in pain and his hand dropped limply to the bed. "Oooh..."

Viola held the quill over his head in her fist. "I meant another strike and you're dead, I, ah...think." She shifted herself, dabbing the quill in another vial from her satchel on the bed. She held the metal tip in her fingers over his eye, close enough he could see the bolos of poison quivering at the end of a ropy thread of liquid. "Now, you're going to tell me where Kate was taken, or I am going to learn how to perform surgery on your nethers. I haven't decided if you will be awake or not. Your answers – and how much I believe them – will help me make my decision."

Henry's breath was shallow and he struggled to talk. "If you kill me, they will kill you slowly."

Viola leaned close enough to smell the fear on his breath, like curdled milk. "Gods, you are weak. I can barely hear you. Try again."

"I will kill you."

Viola smiled and shook her head. "I don't have time for this. Tell me where she is." She drove her knee into his crotch. His eyes grew large as he groaned out in pain. "I should probably have told you: just because you can't move doesn't mean you can't feel pain. In fact, I understand the pain is made even... more intense by the potion."

"I...I...there is a passage north of the circle by the college. It goes beneath the city, north beyond the walls. If you go there and walk the corridor deep underground, beyond the city, there is a dungeon at the first right. It is down another level of stairs before you reach the cells. There might be guards. I don't know."

Viola leaned close to Henry. "I never wanted to do this. Why did your father have to attack us? We came here to help people."

Henry tried to see what she was doing. Viola went and dipped the quill into another vial and came back to him. He gasped, trying to move. "We are desperate. Why can't you see that?"

Viola looked at him disdainfully. "If you are desperate, you ask for help. You don't keep making more and more enemies. You are prideful, paranoid assholes. It will be your undoing." She stabbed him again.

Viola watched Henry's look of growing terror and a tear slowly tracked down the side of his face. "I just put you to sleep so I can escape, so you shouldn't worry." She could tell by his eyes that he understood, but he still looked very sad. She waited until his eyes closed to warn him, "You might piss and shit yourself though." She moved to the other bed to retrieve her rope of tied sheets.

She fastened the rope to the leg of the bed, made sure the guards below were not looking up, and tossed it out the open window. She grunted, pushing a small dresser against the doorway, careful not to make too much noise.

Viola stood at the window looking down. It was the moment of truth. There was but a single guard below in the darkness.

carrying a torch. He had passed under the window, walking north. It would be awhile before he would circle the battlement.

Viola tied the sheet under her arm and set her legs out. She paused before beginning to scale down. "Kate, you had better pay me back for this," she said, and slipped off of the ledge.

CHAPTER 32

KATE TRIED TO stay calm as they carried her out of the room and down several flights of stairs. She was crying and tried to fight back the tears, but she was so frightened. Viola would have to save her a second time, and that was looking more unlikely if they locked her up so far away no one could find her. Her chest was beginning to hurt from being slung over the guard's heavily-muscled shoulder.

"Lady Aela, it will be all right. We are not going to harm you," the voice of William reassured her from somewhere just near her head. Her current situation made it difficult to believe his words of comfort. Why would he do this? They were no threat, and making Lucien angry was dangerous. He was unpredictable already, and she never had seen him truly mad when he was with her. If he were to lose control, there was no telling what he might do.

The men had walked another long hallway and then taken more steps. She could hear others talking as they passed. "They are at the tavern. What shall I do?" a man groveled.

"Just bring them here in the morning. I want every man in the city at the castle when they arrive," William spat.

Kate could only imagine that they planned to kill Lucien or force him into a bargain for her life. It was sickening they would choose to do this; they were friends. If they had just asked, Lucien may have helped. She was not sure if those poor girls who were taken would ever be saved if she could not get free.

Kate's legs and feet were growing numb. It felt like a very long time since she had touched the ground. There was a horrible smell around them that grew worse as they continued to go deeper underground. She was startled by a large clang and a grinding squeal as a door opened, and they put her down on her feet. She stumbled and leaned against what must have been a wall.

They took off her hood and blindfold. The light was dim but still bright enough that it made her blink. When she could focus, she saw she was in a stone cell just big enough for her to stand up or lie in. Her heart ached in her chest from pounding so hard and she felt lightheaded. One of the guards removed the cloth from her mouth. There were six guards in total in the small room. It would have been impossible to leave. They slowly backed out of the cell, leaving Kate's hands bound in front of her.

The last guard to leave gestured to her. "Hold your hands to the window on the door, and I will cut them free," he said, his tone almost apologetic. He closed the door with a loud creak and bang.

The only thing she could see besides stone was the door, and a tiny square window set into it. It had two bars through it, and a door flap on the far side. She held her hands up to it and the man cut her bindings. The guard closed the flap.

Kate rubbed her shoulders as she paced the room. There was a hole no bigger than her fist in the middle of the floor, covered by a rusty grate. In the corner was a bucket with water, and a blanket. She picked up the blanket and wrapped it around herself. The room, so far underground, was cold, but it wasn't just the chill that caused her to shudder: it was the fear of being in the small room. No matter where she walked she could feel it getting smaller. She crouched in the corner with her knees under her chin as she cried.

Kate sniffed and trembled as she spoke quietly under her breath: "Gods, Lucien, I hope you find me before you massacre the entire city."

CHAPTER 33

KATE LAY ON the floor for what felt like hours, but she knew it was much less. She heard a conversation outside the door. The guards were arguing with someone.

Kate stood near the square window in the door and tried to hear. There was a woman's voice. It was faint, but it might be Viola. Kate struggled with hope. She clasped her hands to her chest, leaning against the wall near the door, praying that Viola had come for her.

She jumped as the flap on the door opened and a note was shoved through. It fluttered to the floor. Kate frantically picked it up and read it:

Lady Aela, the girls you are looking for are at Crosshill – Zara

Zara? Why would she help her? Kate held the note and kept reading it, wondering what was going on. What good would this note be in here? Kate folded the note and put it in her pocket. She returned to pacing the small room. She could not fathom why on earth Zara would help her, and did it even matter if she went to Crosshill at this point to save the girls?

The girls she had saved before were there. *It was not a coincidence, something more was going on. It had to have significance that they took them to the same village.*

Kate sat down to rest. If there was a rescue, and this note was the point, she needed to be ready just in case it happened. She was startled to hear the men in commotion, followed by a yell that grew faint, then faded away altogether.

Kate went to listen by the door. It was quiet until she heard a woman's voice, very smooth and seductive sounding. She thought it had to be Viola, or the guard had taken his girl down to the dungeon for a rendezvous. What a disgusting thought. Kate jumped back after hearing a loud thud on the door.

The latch screeched as the bar was lifted, and the door opened.

CHAPTER 34

VIOLA HELD THE sheet tight around her arm as she slowly descended the face of the castle. She was careful to not look down, and grimaced in pain as the sheet felt like it was going to tear her arm off.

The farther down she went, the more excited she became. When her feet touched down on the stone, she nearly cheered with delight. She shook her arm free of the sheet and moved close to the wall, using her cloak to cover everything but her eyes. She came to a doorway and carefully leaned into it. It opened onto a long hallway. She slid the quill up her sleeve and held the metal tip just off her fingers. Using a vial from her satchel, she soaked the tip, then pressed her back tight against the wall and moved down the corridor.

She looked each way at the hallway's junction but there was no one else. She stepped quickly around the corner, found a doorway, and pushed it open. She listened for sounds from above and below as she softly descended the steps and stopped one level down. She cracked the door enough to see and listened. She heard footsteps and the door was jerked open.

It was a guard standing right in front of her. He had a bemused expression on his face. "You're small for an assassin." In a panic, Viola launched herself at him and nicked his left hand as he brought it up to shield himself.

He stood back, looking at his hand. He watched the single drop of blood slowly roll across his palm and drop to the floor. "Gods, you could put an eye out with that," he admonished lightly. "You're coming…" He collapsed to the ground.

Viola had to hurry now. She quickly ran the length of the hallway to another door. It opened into a corridor, and she followed that into another hallway. She listened and, hearing nothing, ran down to the door at the end.

She pressed her ear to the door and then gently pushed it open. It was the room they had first arrived in. Liam was asleep on his bunk. She crossed the room silently, placed her hand over his mouth, and stabbed him with the quill as he slept.

His eyes snapped open as he sat up and grabbed her arm. "Who...how did…?"

Viola smiled as he slumped back on the bed. She blew the candle out and slowly opened the outside door. The guards at the main entrance were up several steps to the right. She stayed in the shadows as she traced around the courtyard to the large archway at the college circle.

She passed under the arch quickly and then crouched by the walkway north. It had to be what Henry had described. She opened the door at the end and ran down the corridor. It was very long, and at the end there was a cross-hallway. She went to the right and soon heard voices. She slowly walked down toward them. She leaned against the wall outside an adjacent room. It was a barracks of some kind. There were men inside, talking. She listened and counted at least four separate voices.

Viola couldn't think of a way to get past without being seen. She leaned against the wall and felt inside her satchel for her flasks, wondering if there was a combination of potions she could quickly cobble together that would paralyze all the guards at once. Just as she thought that, she heard a voice whispering to her from nearby, "I knew you would come."

Viola held her hand up to strike but froze, watching in amazement as what she first thought was a shadow detached itself from the shadows on the opposite side of the doorway where she stood. She could see now it was Zara, and she marveled at how much like an assassin she looked. Zara looked at her and held up her finger, glanced in the guards' quarters, and waved her hand for Viola to come to her.

Viola made it and the men did not see her pass by. They hurried farther down the corridor so the men might not hear them. Viola shook her head at Zara, uncertain whether she should smile, but she did. Zara smiled and embraced her.

"What are you doing here?" Viola whispered.

Zara leaned close and answered with a whisper, "I want you to take me with you."

Viola rolled her eyes. "You can't be serious? We will be hunted as kidnappers, and maybe even murderers. Why would you want that?"

Zara's expression was frozen. "The girls are at Crosshill. I just dropped a note into Kate's cell. There is just one guard. I will be quiet, and help however I can, but in return, you must promise to take me with you."

Viola studied her. "How do you plan on getting out of here?"

Zara looked giddily at her. "There is a sewer grate just down this hall and to the left. It is where they dump refuse from the college. We can navigate it north to the river. There is an old farm there, and stables. We can steal some horses and go west."

Viola thought about it for a moment. It wasn't a terrible plan. In fact, it was sound. "But won't they just chase after us and catch us?" she asked.

Zara shifted her back to the wall, blending into the shadows. "Maybe, but we will have a head start, and if Lucien is powerful, he might give us cover to escape."

Viola looked again down the hall, then back to Zara. "How do we get Kate out of the room?"

Zara said, "That is your problem. I will go open the grate. You take care of the guard and get Kate out."

Viola nodded. "Fine, let's go."

Viola followed Zara down the dungeon passage, amazed by how Zara would vanish if she fell too far behind.

Zara disappeared into the small inlet off the hallway and Viola walked farther along, led by the glow of a torch ahead. There was a guard standing beneath it, his back resting against the wall. He seemed to be dozing on his feet. She opened her cloak, dabbed some red paint on her lips, and then pushed up her breasts.

She shook her hair down and teased it into a mane around her face. *This is going to be difficult, but not impossible.* She slowly approached the guard, hips swaying, lips pouted. "Hello, I think I am lost, but maybe you can help me."

The guard snorted awake and held out his spear. "What the hell?"

Just as he did, Viola pushed his spear aside with her left hand and lunged, stabbing him in the neck. He grabbed her wrist and struggled, then whisper-yelled, "Ass..." He collapsed, striking the cell door as he went down. Viola put the quill in her pocket, rolled the guard onto his back, found his keys, pushed him aside, and opened the door.

CHAPTER 35

KATE STOOD BACK as the door opened and Viola ran in. She swept Kate into her arms and hugged her. Tears bloomed in her eyes as they held each other tight.

Viola released Kate and grabbed her hand, dragging her out the door. "We have to hurry."

Kate followed Viola as they ran to the inlet for the sewer grate. Zara had already climbed in and was waving her hand at them. Kate grabbed Viola from behind. "Who is that?"

Viola pulled Kate into the sewer. "Zara; she wants to come with us. Come on, we don't have time to argue."

The three of them crawled on their hands and knees through the sewer. Viola coughed at the stench. "I want to complain, but it is worth it just to get out of this place." At the end, there was a six-foot drop into a ditch. They jumped one after the other into the drainage pond.

They all shivered in the morning cold as they stood beside the pond. The sun had risen over the plains to the west and Kate could not stop smiling, despite feeling half-frozen and reeking of sewage.

Kate looked at Zara with a laugh. "I hope you are prepared for this. If we don't freeze to death, we will have them chasing us soon."

Zara smiled, trembling from the cold. "There is a stable just west, and we can rest there if you want."

Viola's teeth chattered as she said, "Let's go. I want to get out of the open."

The three of them quickly ran across the field to the barn. They did not see anyone and they sneaked through the door inside.

Kate, Viola, and Zara all looked on in despair at the empty barn. A barn swallow, disturbed by the commotion, flew from the rafters with a flutter of wings.

Viola gritted her teeth. "Horses, there are supposed to be horses!"

Kate looked confused, and Zara buried her face in her hands. "Gods, they must have sold them or moved them. What will we do?"

Viola shrugged. "I am out of ideas. Zara and I got us this far."

Kate chewed her lower lip as she thought, rejected, thought again. She said, "What about the tavern by the gate? We left our horses there. It is possible they are still there."

Viola considered Kate's suggestion. "That is a terrible idea. There are guards on the drawbridge."

Zara looked up quickly. "There should be just one after mid-morning. They ordered all the guards to the castle for when Lord Lucien arrives."

Kate looked anxious at the thought. If they could meet up with Edwin and Lucien they could escape together. "Maybe --"

Viola cut Kate off mid-sentence. "No, we can't go to them. We will do it ourselves. The best they can do is give us cover. If Lucien knows you have escaped, he might help us with a diversion."

Zara nodded and put her hand on Kate's arm. "They will be fine. My father is bluster, and if Lucien does anything, he will give in. I don't think there will be bloodshed. We need to get as far from the city as we can, though."

Kate stood quietly, looking at the city walls from the barn door. It was a good distance, but perhaps still not far enough. "We need to go farther away for Lucien to know I am gone. It might need to happen around the same time they are being questioned."

Zara said in an hour they should be brought to the castle, but Viola still looked worried. "What is it?" Kate asked.

"I am not sure how long my poison will work. I knocked out Prince Henry in my bed, and a guard in one of the halls. They could be out for days, or just till mid-morning." Viola looked to Kate and Zara with a shrug.

"Your bed," Zara said timidly, her face reddening.

Viola smiled. "I had to find out where Kate was being held."

Zara snickered. "He was just going to tell you. I don't think you had to knock him unconscious."

Viola grunted. "Gods, he will be furious."

Zara shook her head. "I doubt it. He is fond of you. It will just be embarrassment that you were able to get one over on him."

Kate laughed. "Well, at least we have some time. If we go to the western gate, it might be just far enough for Lucien to notice I am gone. It would be on the opposite side of town. Then, we grab the horses and leave."

Zara held her hand to her mouth. "The guard, how do we get past without harming him?"

Kate shook her head. "We have to accept there might be casualties."

Viola winked at Zara. "It will be a cinch."

CHAPTER 36

LUCIEN AND EDWIN sat across from each other on their beds. The tavern below was completely silent, and the hallway beyond their door was equally still.

Lucien had felt strange ever since waking. He felt some of his power return. Kate might be moving farther away, but he did not know for sure.

"Gods," Edwin said, standing.

Just as he stood, there was a knock at the door. Edwin opened it to find a soldier in heavy armor decorated with heraldry. He stood proud, a man of advanced age, bald with a white mustache. "My name is Lord Commander Berg. My apologies to your lord-ships about the wait, but the steward has taken ill this morning."

Edwin turned to Lucien, the corner of his mouth turned up wryly, and then back to the commander. "Well, let's get on with it."

"Yes my lord, this way." Berg held out his hand as Lucien and Edwin walked down the stairs to the street below.

Edwin's eyes widened when he saw there were over a hundred soldiers surrounding them. Lucien looked on emotionlessly as they walked through the city. There were no people on the streets, nor did anyone gawk at them from the windows. It seemed unnatural.

They walked through the market and up to the high quarter. It was a parade of soldiers all around them and on the ramparts above, crossbowmen and archers kept their weapons trained on them as they walked past.

Edwin said sharply, "Quite the welcome."

Lucien was stoic. "It should be expected."

In the courtyard, there were easily a thousand men all around them, on every level of the battlements and on the grounds nearby. Edwin studied them with mouth open and eyes wide. "It must be the entire army here to greet you, Lucien."

They were led through the main gateway to the castle, through the foyer, and down the hallway to the throne room.

The king sat upon the throne in heavy steel armor adorned with golden laurels on his head, and a cape of heraldry. The queen sat to his left in a patterned yellow and gold dress. The king rose as they entered. "Your lordships, I must apologize for the delay. There has been a bout of illness in the castle and it delayed my men. Please accept my apology."

Crossbowmen lined the sides of the room and full-armored pikemen filed in behind Lucien as they approached the throne.

Edwin was no longer surprised and smiled amusedly. "It has been quite the welcome. I hope you have left at least a few soldiers to guard your porous borders, your majesty."

Lucien suddenly felt very strange. His power was slowly coming back. He could feel the fear of the men in the room, and the king was filled with anxiety. Lucien looked at Edwin and held his hand out to him. Edwin narrowed his eyes trying to judge what he was thinking, and then quickly nodded.

Lucien bowed gracefully and said, "Your majesty, no apology is necessary as our arrival was unannounced. It is we who should be apologizing for the intrusion. Judging by the response, we should have followed better etiquette."

King William tapped his gauntleted finger on the arm of the throne, shifting back and forth in the seat as if unsure whether to slouch or sit up straight. "Sometimes in urgent situations, we must act with haste. I am sure you have good reason."

Lucien rose from his bow. "I have, and am grateful for the audience. Princess Viola and Lady Aela O'Neill are missing. They left Dawnbridge without word and King Elias has listed them as truant. We have tracked them to Charbel and hoped that you would aid us in our search."

King William worked his fingers together in front of his face. "They have arrived, but they may not leave. They are here on house arrest."

Edwin looked at Lucien, incredulous, and then burst out laughing. "You must be joking. Do you know who he is?"

Lucien held his finger up to Edwin. "Edwin, please. I will handle this."

Edwin's lips compressed in a thin line and the vein in his neck throbbed.

Lucien nodded to him with his hand raised. "Why? What benefit do you gain from kidnapping them?"

The king rose from the throne, stepping down to stand before Lucien. The soldiers moved around the room as he approached, keeping a wary eye on the king's visitors. "I had dreamed the rumors of the destruction of the Elgin army were true. I was foolish to believe such a tale. The truth is their army, as we stand here bickering, is descending on Drommer castle."

Lucien narrowed his gaze on the king. "What of it? Drommer can hold for decades with their stockpiles and access to resources. The Elnoran army is stationed south in Porin, and Elgin would never be allowed to camp there for that long."

The king lifted his chin. "Perhaps, but there is a delicate balance of power in Amor. If the Vale was to take over Elgin's lands, or Elgin is allowed to capture the south provinces, it would be the end of Westfall."

Lucien tilted his head and cocked an eyebrow. "The Vale is reclusive and would never attack Elgin. They moved their forces to defend the massive army that marches along the southern border. Elnora will never allow the conquest of the southern provinces either, and Elgin is our sworn enemy."

William stood defiant. "Richter Elgin must be killed. You will bring me his head or you will never see Kate O'Neill again."

Edwin was incensed. "You're mad. You want us to commit regicide for your blackmail."

Lucien turned to Edwin with a withering stare. "Let me handle it. I am the one they are blackmailing, not you." He turned back to William. "I won't kill Richter Elgin. If you harm Kate, your kingdom will cease to exist."

Lucien stroked his chin as he paced and thought. The spearmen followed as he turned and walked back to William. "I offer a compromise. Let Edwin visit Lady Viola to make sure she is in good care, and turn over Lady O'Neill's weapons and armor you confiscated. You do these things and we can talk about strategies to eliminate the Elgin threat."

William turned and raised his hand to Commander Berg, who nodded and left the room. William held his elbow on his forearm as he thought. "I am willing to comply with your demands, for now. Berg will return with the confiscated items, but I will not allow you to see Princess Viola. It is too dangerous for you to pass information to her."

Edwin crossed his arms and hoped his contempt for William wasn't too obvious.

Lucien held his hands out to his sides. "I accept your offer, and will make a bargain: the Elgin army will withdraw back to their territory, and in exchange, you will release Kate and Viola."

William nodded and looked to the queen who also seemed to agree. "This is fair. The Elgin threat will be neutralized for the time being. It will aid us with our conflicts on the rest of our borders."

Lucien turned to Edwin with a nod, then back to William. "Can we take quarters to bathe, eat, and rest for our journey? We plan to leave immediately."

William held his hand out. "Sergeant, take them to the guest house to recuperate for their journey." Commander Berg had just returned to the throne room with Kate's items. He handed them over to Lucien.

Lucien inspected Kate's bow, then held out her armor to make sure it was everything. He nodded. "Thank you, it is very much appreciated."

The sergeant held out his hand and led them to the adjacent hallway and then down some stairs where they crossed the courtyard to a four-level building. There were soldiers all around as they were led inside. The guard held the door. "Please do not leave, and when you are ready, we will escort you from the city."

Edwin said nothing as he entered, still pouting from the conversation in the throne room with King William.

Lucien nodded to the sergeant as he entered the guest house. The door closed behind him.

"You should have trusted me in there." Edwin looked around the first floor. There was a wash basin, drinks, and several plates of food set out. Edwin took an apple, juggling it from hand to hand as he looked at their meal. "This won't be half-bad, I suppose."

Lucien frowned as he carried Kate's things. He could smell her scent on them. It was a tortured feeling, being so close to her but not be able to see her. "Get cleaned up. We need to get out of this place soon, and I mean very soon."

Edwin was already seated at the table and demolishing his plate of food. "Well, I sure hope you have a good plan, because I am not leaving here without Viola."

Edwin laughed, but when he looked up, Lucien was gone. "Of course," he muttered, and reached for a drink.

CHAPTER 37

THE GUARD STOOD at attention on the gate bridge. The main drawbridge had been raised, leaving only the narrow pedestrian bridge with which to enter the castle. He stood tall with pride, rotating his bill hook from arm to arm as he blocked the single access point to the city. The day had warmed as the sun crossed the sky and heliographed off his well-polished armor. He lifted his visor and closed his eyes, letting the sun warm his face.

It was all very pleasant, and he smiled, happy to be a small part of this perfect moment. And then the sound of a woman screaming made his eyes snap open. She was wearing all black and covered in blood. "Help me!" she cried as she stumble-ran toward him. He reached his arms out to steady her and was stabbed with a quill on his cheek.

His eyes widened as he fell to his back, already unconscious by the time he struck the ground. Princess Zara turned to Kate and Viola as they ran toward her across the bridge.

Zara looked down at the man. "I am sorry if you piss yourself. I am led to believe it's one of the unfortunate side-effects."

B.E. Scott

They stepped over his body and through the doorway.

Kate ran to the stables at the tavern. Viola tried to turn the gear to lower the drawbridge. "Zara, you have to help me," she grunted. "It is too hard to turn."

Together, they were able to overcome the gear's inertia, and it began to turn more easily. The chains holding the drawbridge rattled along the stone wall as the bridge slowly lowered.

Kate threw open the first stall, and the second. She reached for the third stall but froze when she saw her armor hanging from the horse's saddle bags.

Terror flowed through her as she turned the horse to see her quiver, bow, and scabbard. And now she could feel someone watching her. She turned to look behind her.

Kate's entire body trembled as the terror left her in a rush, replaced by more emotions than she would have thought possible. She gasped, "Gods, Lucien!" and ran to him. She threw her arms around him, letting the tears fall freely.

He held her close. "I'm sorry, but I can't stay. I just wanted to return your weapons and armor, hoping to see you before you left."

Kate wiped at the tears on her face. "Where will you go?"

Lucien frowned at her. "We have to stop the Elgin army. Where are you going?"

Kate placed the palms of her hands on his chest, feeling his heart pounding through the leather armor. It was a small thing, but she had not felt so close to him in longer than she cared to think. "It is horrible to find you, only to see you go again. William is a desperate fool. We have to go to Crosshill. I made a promise to Tel-son on the mountain. His daughters were taken and I don't think it was a coincidence."

Lucien's expression grew stony. "Be careful. I am certain it is a trap you're going to. I will return if I can, but you need to get back to Dawnbridge where you are safe. Do not return to Charbel and cross the border south to the marshes."

Kate pulled Lucien's face closer and kissed him. "Be careful, and try not to massacre them. I know you will try, but it will just make things worse."

Will you marry me? I love you. Lucien could feel the sadness as he let her go. He looked at her, fighting back tears. "Return to Dawnbridge as soon as you can. I will look for you there. Tell Viola that Edwin is as angry and wild as ever for her."

Kate watched as he disappeared, and it felt as if he was taking the biggest part of her heart with him. She grabbed her armor and weapons, quickly getting them equipped. She could hear the drawbridge strike the stone base and took the reins of the three horses. She pulled the horses to the gate as Viola and Zara turned to find her. Kate held out the reins to them.

"Quickly."

Kate helped Viola into her saddle and struck the horse on its flank. Several people in the city had noticed them and came running to see what was going on. Kate climbed into the saddle and rode out last behind Zara.

CHAPTER 38

EDWIN HAD JUST taken off his shirt and washed his face when he turned to see Lucien sitting at the table, wiping at the blood from his mouth. He jumped momentarily, then gritted his teeth and began to seethe. "Where the hell did you go?"

Lucien cut an apple slice and chewed it. "I had to return Kate's things," he said, and coughed. "Otherwise, she wouldn't be prepared for travel."

"What the hell?!" Edwin flailed his arms, almost screaming. He stormed across the room, slammed a palm down on the tabletop and leaned into Lucien's face. "You knew where she was the whole time?"

"No." Lucien trembled as he took some bread and cheese. "I suspected they would go back for their horses. I could feel her moving farther away. When William said we couldn't see Viola, I assumed they had escaped."

Edwin noticed blood from Lucien's nostrils and handed him a linen napkin. "Well, what did you find out? Did you find her or not?"

Lucien dabbed at the blood from his nose. "Quite a lot, actually. They are headed to Crosshill. There was trouble in the mountains. She has some plan to rescue Tel-son's daughters."

Edwin raised an eyebrow, becoming more docile. "Tel-son, he has several tribes that support him. It is possible he is the one who was raiding the western border with Westfall."

Lucien held a piece of cheese in his unsteady hand. "I was thinking the same thing, although it is more likely that it's a trap to lure them there."

"What, you still let them go?" Edwin screamed again, his face a twisted red mess.

Lucien chewed on a piece of bread and washed it down with a large draught of wine. "You don't trust that Viola and Kate can handle a rescue? It will matter nothing if the marsh is overrun—or worse, Dulimore is. We have to stop Elgin first, and then we can worry about them. I am confident that Kate can take care of herself." *Gods, I hope so.*

Edwin was furious and snatched Lucien's apple and threw it across the room. He went back to the wash basin, splashed water on his face, and toweled himself dry. The mirror on the wall showed a shadow glide across the window. There was a brief commotion outside the door, followed by an authoritative knock.

Edwin pulled his sword, but Lucien stood from the table and held his palm toward him. "Calm down," he advised. Lucien turned to the door. "Who is it?"

"Prince Henry."

"Enter," Lucien said.

Prince Henry opened the door. He had on a cuirass with a lion on the chest, and was wearing leather armor throughout. "Gentlemen."

Edwin approached, his scowl turning into a smirk as he bowed. "Your highness."

Lucien crossed his arms. "What do you want?" he asked with a weary sigh.

Henry looked apologetic. "I know my father has wronged you, but I want to help. My sister left with Viola. I tried to help comfort her, but she refused."

Edwin jabbed his finger at Henry's chest. "You are scum, is why. Why would she ever get help from someone like you? You and your father are traitors. You turn on your only friends in this gods-forsaken continent."

Henry preened and said, "She invited me into her bed, at least. Can you say the same?"

Edwin's face nearly touched Henry's. "What did you say?"

"That woman of yours left me in a puddle of my own piss after -- " Edwin's fist smashed into Henry's mouth before he could finish. He stumbled and pulled his sword. "You ungrateful bastard, I could have you hanged for that."

Edwin held his sword forward with both hands. "You're too much of a pretty boy coward to strike me down."

Lucien returned his attention to the food on the table. He popped a grape into his mouth. "You two fools are wasting time. If you want to fight, though, no wounds; it would be nice to have someone in decent shape to fight the Elgin menace."

Henry tilted his head, backing to the door. "In the courtyard, first strike wins."

Lucien sighed and spit out a seed. "Henry, I think you should reconsider and talk with us. We can forget this. Edwin is a master swordsman. Do you want to be embarrassed in front of your men?"

Henry smiled. "I have used a sword my entire life. I have no fear of him."

Edwin followed Henry outside. The guards raised their spears, backing up. Henry waved his arm at them. "We are to duel for honor. No man is to touch either of us, do you hear me?"

The guards moved back in a loose circle. Henry stood with his sword in one hand, and Edwin stood with his raised over his head in both hands. Henry lunged and Edwin stepped to the side.

Lucien leaned against the door frame, chewing on bread and cheese.

Saliva hissed and bubbled between Edwin's teeth as he swung wild over the top at Henry. He was able to just parry and make a stab toward Edwin. Edwin shifted and the strike missed. They circled around again.

Edwin could tell that Henry fought well, but had never fought someone of his skill. This would be over shortly.

Henry swung across into a stab; Edwin moved back to avoid the slice and parried the stab to the side. In a single motion of the parry, he used his hilt to strike Henry in the face. Henry stumbled back, and before he could regain his footing, Edwin struck him across the face with the flat of his blade.

Henry fell to the ground, his sword tumbling from his hand. The guards looked on, stunned. Henry was dazed as he pushed himself into a sitting position.

"You will never speak the words of Princess Viola and your piss in the same sentence again." Edwin stood tall over Henry.

Lucien tossed an apple core to the street. "That's a shame. It is over, men. We will take his highness back in the house so he can be cleaned up." Lucien waved as Henry slowly climbed to his feet, and they all walked into the house.

Henry sat next to Lucien at the table. Edwin closed the door and put his shirt on. He still studied Henry with narrowed eyes.

Henry rubbed at the side of his head; it was already starting to bruise. "Gods, you are fast. I feel humbled indeed. What a mess it all is."

Lucien looked to Edwin. "You said something about aiding us. How did you plan to do that?"

Henry tilted his head side to side. "I need to come with you. I am sure by now you know my sister went with Kate and Viola."

"Absolutely not, we can rescue them by ourselves," Edwin said firmly.

Lucien glanced over at Henry. "We are going to Porin, I am not sure you are up for it."

Henry shook his head. "I want to go with you. I need to do something to actually help my people rather than watch my father make one blunder after another."

Edwin sat opposite Lucien at the table. He reached across to get a piece of bread. As he did, Lucien grabbed Edwin's wrist, hooking arms with Henry at the same time. "Why not?"

With that, the three of them were gone.

CHAPTER 39

PORTING FROM A seated position, Lucien knew to quickly put his feet down to catch his fall. Unluckily for Edwin and Henry, they did not share such knowledge and dropped hard to the floor when they reappeared.

"Lucien! You ass! Why can't you tell me before you do that?" Edwin flailed on the ground, yelling.

Henry looked around his new surroundings in wonderment. "What the hell just happened?"

Edwin stood and brushed his pants off. "We need to see what Alaric has found out before we decide what to do next," Lucien said. He dabbed at his bleeding mouth with the napkin from the table. He walked gingerly, as if his bones were made of spun glass, down the hallway, leaning unsteadily against the wall.

Edwin helped Henry to his feet. "We are in Port Porin. Lucien has the ability to teleport. You should probably be aware he does it without warning."

Henry rubbed his head, still throbbing from the blow Edwin's sword hilt had dealt him. The sudden trip did nothing to help. "Gods."

The two of them followed Lucien down the hallway.

Lucien walked into the dining room where Jan and Alaric sat eating lunch. "Well, I wish I could say I am surprised to see you, but from what Alaric tells me, you come and go rather at ease."

Alaric pointed at Henry and Edwin with the squab's leg he had been nibbling as they entered the room "Gods, you are multiplying. If I didn't know better I would say that looks like Prince Henry of Westfall."

Jan stood rather abruptly. "Your highness, I did not know."

Henry shook his head. "It is just Henry for the time being. There should be no formalities."

Alaric laughed and took a bite out of his squab. "What brings you three to Port Porin?"

Lucien stood next to Alaric. He leaned on the table, short of breath. "What did your spies find out in Elgin?"

Alaric put down his food and leaned forward. "Elgin moved its army to Drommer. We don't know what the plan is, but from the looks of it, it's a siege."

Lucien shook his head. "It makes no sense. Have they made camp? When did they arrive?"

Alaric thought for a moment. "The report said they were headed north. We won't know more till tomorrow morning from the next messenger."

Henry looked uneasy standing in the dining room. "I think we should rest. I know I could use some."

Jan gestured Henry to the door. "I will get you some quarters, your highness."

Henry nodded. "Thank you," he said, and followed Jan out of the room.

Edwin poured a cup of wine and sat down at the table. "What should we do, Alaric?"

Alaric cleared his throat. "The king told us to stay put and wait it out. He suspects a trap."

Lucien said, "It makes no sense to attack Drommer unless Richter was just annoyed by my stunt and wanted to bring me out in the open again. His daughter knows I can only do so much."

"Precisely," Edwin said, and nodded in agreement. "They want you dead and are trying to draw you out."

Lucien found it hard to believe Richter would be so cunning. The whole plan seemed wrong. "We will rest tonight and see what the messenger brings in the morning. I want to go to Saints and find out what is left of his army."

Edwin scoffed. "That is insane. You want us three to go to the capital to search for soldiers?"

"He had to have left some behind, but how many?" Lucien asked Edwin rhetorically.

Edwin just shrugged. "We should send the army north and smash the Elgin forces in the open. We have to fight them eventually."

Alaric laughed without humor. "I will not throw men away on someone else's war. Elgin's men will be wary at Drommer. The siege will tire them out and they will desert with time. If Lucien hounds them it will wear them down even more, and I doubt they make the walls at Dawnbridge. They would be surrounded when Dulimore sends soldiers to help."

Edwin drank some wine as he pondered what to do. "It is almost as if they are desperate. They send their forces on a suicide mission to Drommer."

Lucien sighed tiredly. "We will find out from the capital what is going on. If we go north to Drommer it might draw them out into the open. Do you want me to hound the army now, or investigate more in Saints?"

Alaric scratched his beard stubble. "I don't know. Saints is a good plan. If the king is gone, there has to be something big happening. It just doesn't make any sense."

Lucien rose unsteadily from the table. "I have to rest. I am worn out from all the traveling. I feel terribly weak."

Edwin shook his head in frustration. "You're worn out? You at least you got to see Kate."

"What are you talking about?" Alaric asked, his brow knitted.

Edwin watched Lucien make his unsteady way out of the room. "We went to Charbel," he told Alaric. "Kate and Viola went there to find two of Tel-son's daughters. They made some kind of bargain with him."

Alaric leaned forward on his elbows. "That is strange. Someone from Westfall kidnapped the warlord's daughters."

Edwin nodded. "Sure. Why is that so surprising? They have been fighting on the border for a month or more."

Alaric laced his fingers together and rested his chin on his knuckles. "That makes even less sense than what Elgin is doing."

Edwin leaned back in his chair, absently swirling the last of his wine around in the glass. "It makes perfect sense. They wanted revenge for the other kidnappings."

"Don't be stupid. It would only make the attacks worse," Alaric growled.

Edwin finished his wine. It was clear that Alaric was worried about this news. It was not sitting well with him.

Lucien undressed and washed himself as best he could before weariness overtook him. He did not so much climb into bed as collapse across it. He drifted off to sleep almost instantly.

He did not hear the door open and close as someone approached the bed. Lucien was startled awake by arms wrapping around his waist.

He gestured and ignited the candle on the bed stand.

Anne smiled at him. "I was stunned to hear you'd arrived."

Lucien turned in bed to face her. "You can't be in here."

Anne frowned. "Why not? You afraid Kate will get jealous?"

Lucien's mouth twisted as he held up his hand to her. "She means a lot. You understand, right?"

"I do, but what does it matter? I'm not interested in you anyway. Can we not just spend the night together?" Anne asked, and made a pouty face.

Lucien sighed wearily. "I am exhausted. I haven't the strength to argue. How did you find out so quickly about Kate? Spies?"

Anne laughed gently. "Of course! They are everywhere. That army in Dulimore has set the continent on fire. The Vale is upset, Westfall is in a panic, and I hear even Cirimar is worried, although communication seems to be spotty."

Lucien rolled over to look up at the ceiling. He folded his arms behind his head in the shape of a "V". "Do you know what they are planning?"

Anne paused to think, studying Lucien's profile. "No, but it is not out of desperation. They have a plan; I am not sure we will like the results."

Lucien stared at the ceiling, working his jaw. He could not imagine what was going on. It pained him to think he would need to attack the Dulimore army to get rid of it.

"What is it? You look stressed out. Birthdays are always stressful, but you will get over it." Anne laughed.

Lucien grimaced. "I saw Kate and couldn't ask her to marry me. It was just a brief moment, but I wanted to so badly."

Anne rubbed his shoulder. "Don't worry, you will get a chance again."

Lucien turned his head to face her. "What happened with Melissa?"

Sadness fell like a curtain across Anne's face, and she was close to tears. "Let us just enjoy the evening. My spies will be back in the morning, and you can worry about what to do then."

Lucien nodded and closed his eyes. Anne pulled herself closer to him, and he couldn't help but be aroused by her. If only it was Kate. He fought back sadness, and even as tired as he was, sleep eluded him for a long while.

CHAPTER 40

KATE, VIOLA, AND Zara had ridden well past nightfall. The crossroads with the south road was over an hour behind them and there was no sign of any pursuers. The horses were tired and so were they.

"We can stop there," Zara said, pointing to a spot just beyond a row of trees. "It is a shallow creek that runs between two hills. It is a good place to rest for the night."

Kate was relieved to finally slow the horse to a trot. The past few days' riding had worn her backside numb, and Viola stood in the stirrups for at least the past hour because of the same thing. Kate saw Viola had her eyes closed as they brought the horses to a stop.

Kate dismounted and tied off her and Viola's horse. Zara brushed the head of her horse with her hand to calm it. "I am not much good at making fires. I only have a blanket for warmth."

Kate began to gather sticks along the creek while Viola used three flasks to gather water. There were several large tree limbs along the bank. Kate broke a few over her knee and made a pile mixed with some brush.

217

Viola had already found a dry and abandoned bird's nest and used it to start a small fire. She added some of the larger sticks and the fire grew larger and warmer. Zara sat on her blanket close to Kate. "You two are very skilled. I could not make a fire like that."

Viola barely noticed her comment. "I am so tired, I feel like I am sleepwalking."

Viola had the three flasks standing upright near the fire and was adding ingredients. She went back to the creek and began digging with her dagger in the ground. She stopped and sat staring at the water, then suddenly grabbed at something below the surface.

Kate lay on the ground. She and Viola were lucky to have bedrolls. She glanced over at Zara and saw she was shaking in the cold. "Zara, we will make a bed and you can lie here." Kate moved Viola's and her bedrolls together and put Zara's blanket with theirs. The three of them would be able to keep warm in the night if they huddled together.

Zara watched, curious, as Kate made a makeshift bed for them. "Have you two ever done this before?"

"We've never had to," Kate said and smiled. "It has only recently become so cold at night."

Zara carefully sat next to her, admiring how effortlessly they worked together.

Viola returned with her hands shaking from the cold creek water and mixed some things into the flasks. Her hands were wet and she held them up to the fire for warmth. "We can have some soup in a moment. I just want it to boil for a few more minutes."

"Soup," Zara repeated. Her eyes widened and she raised her eyebrows as she watched Viola.

Viola wrapped her hands in her cloak and pulled the three flasks from the fire. She set them aside. "Let them cool and you can eat," she cautioned. "I cannot keep my eyes open. I need to rest." Viola lay down next to Zara on the bed. She pulled her cloak over her, and Kate drew the blankets over Viola.

Kate stared at the fire as Zara sat quietly next to her. Zara pointed to Kate's helm on the ground. "Did you leave your armor with the horses?"

Kate turned her face away, biting her lip, suddenly uncomfortable. "No, Lucien brought them to me in the stables."

Zara held her hands out to the fire. "How is that possible? He should have been at the castle."

Kate fed another stick to the fire, consciously trying not to look at Zara. "He teleports. I wish things could be different. I wanted him to come with us; Edwin also."

Zara drew her knees up to her chest and wrapped her arms around them. "Well, I am glad he can do that. I was afraid they might try to imprison him. I doubt any prison could hold him with such a power."

Kate lay back on her side. It was painful to think of him. They were together for only a moment, but it felt incredible to see him again. He had looked at her with such longing. It felt good to be wanted. *I love you, Lucien.*

Zara watched Kate quietly. She lay down beside Viola and pulled the cover over herself. "Crosshill is just southwest of here. It will take us 'til midday. I think we should approach carefully."

Kate nodded. "We will. You are able to move about quickly; I hope you can scout."

Zara said she could. "I need to sleep as badly as Viola."

Kate closed her eyes to sleep as well.

CHAPTER 41

LUCIEN SAT UP in bed with a groan. He felt miserable and sore all over. The sun had just risen in the west and he could see shadows below his window. He realized he was alone. Anne had left early to check the reports from the spies. He hadn't even felt her get out of bed.

Lucien dressed as quickly as his aching body would allow and went to the dining hall. Henry was sitting at the table with Alaric and Jan. They were so silent as he entered that Lucien was not sure they were awake.

Lucien approached Alaric. "What news is there?"

Alaric relaxed and leaned back in his chair. "Elgin knights are camped outside of Drommer. They are several hundred yards from the wall. It does not appear they are building siege equipment, but they have made some ladders."

"It is utter nonsense." Jan sat with his hands in his lap.

Alaric shook his head. "I do not understand it either."

Lucien gave a nod to Henry. "Did you sleep well?"

Henry smiled. "I traveled three days in a moment. I slept well. What are you planning? This Drommer attack seems half-hearted, at best."

Lucien considered as he sat at the table between them. He said, at length, "I think we should go to the City of Saints. We need to investigate the city and what is going on. I think Richter is there, or he is dead. Either way, we need to find out what we can about the political situation."

Edwin entered the room. "What news is there?"

Henry stood from the table. "It sounds like we are going to the City of Saints."

"What of Drommer?" Edwin looked at Lucien and tipped his head to the side like a dog that's just heard a strange noise.

Alaric laughed. "Elgin knights are camped, building a few ladders. Certainly nothing that won't take them a month and ten thousand men to take the outer walls with."

Edwin was no less confused and he beetled his brows together. "The walls are over thirty feet at Drommer," Alaric explained. "They couldn't possibly take the city with ladders."

"Madness," Jan muttered, and shook head.

Lucien stood and laid his hands on Henry and Edwin's shoulders. "We have to find out what is going on in Elgin. We will not get anywhere speculating about Drommer in the meantime. This is why we are going east."

Henry's eyes widened and Edwin reached for Lucien's hand. "Wa....."

The three of them vanished.

Jan raised his goblet and looked over the rim to where the trio had been just a moment before. "To the demon boy, and his many talents."

Alaric gave a slow nod and raised his own goblet. "Cheers."

CHAPTER 42

"**— AIT A minute!**" Edwin finished the exclamation he had begun in another room far away. "Gods! I hoped to never see this damn place again."

Henry rubbed his head, looking around. "Where are we?"

"This, Henry, is where I fell, unconscious, leaving Lady Kate to be tortured by Elena." Lucien held his arms out expansively. "It is a very easy place to port to because of the powerful memory." He wiped the blood from his nose and mouth.

Edwin had already disengaged from the little band and climbed the hill on the eastern slope. Lucien and Henry followed. They stood atop the hill studying the valley below that led to the city walls far in the distance.

"It appears they are gone, after all." Edwin shaded his eyes from the sun with his hand.

Lucien looked out over the valley. He could just barely see the castle in the distance. "Looks like we have some walking to do."

Lucien, still recovering from this port, stumbled down the hill to the flatland at its base. Henry gave Edwin a worried look, and then they followed Lucien down the slope.

222

Edwin caught up to Lucien and grabbed his arm. "What, we're just going to walk up to the gate and ask to enter?"

Lucien glanced over at him. "Good idea. We will try that."

Edwin released Lucien's arm and stood watching him, trying to decide if he was joking or serious. He blew out an exasperated breath and hurried to catch up.

The three of them walked for several hours toward the seemingly giant city. There was a single guard standing in the open as they approached from the west. The main gate to the city faced south. The city consisted of at least two hundred houses, and the keep was on the far north side. The towers were easily visible from Dulimore.

Edwin held his arm out to Henry and Lucien. "Let me handle this."

Henry looked uneasily at Lucien, but he just smiled and made a little clucking sound with his tongue.

The drawbridge was up but the pedestrian plank was still down and a single spearman in leather armor stood watch. He held up his spear, ready for trouble. "Halt, identify yourself!"

Edwin laughed freely and smiled his brightest smile. "My good sir, we are traveling bards requested for his majesty's amusement."

The guard looked suspiciously at them and took a step back. "What are your names?"

Still smiling, Edwin bowed and said, "I am Aramis." He held his hand out to indicate Henry. "This is Athos, and this is Porthos. He is the blind one."

The guard squinted as Edwin pointed at Lucien. Satisfied, he lifted his spear to his shoulder. "Well, you seem all right, come on in."

Lucien had to stifle a laugh at Edwin's confident grin while Henry looked on, dumbfounded.

The guard opened the gate door, and the three of them walked through. They looked around but the streets were empty. The city was very old and the streets were cobblestone.

Edwin could not wait to gloat. "I told you I would get us in." Lucien had no response, but Henry scoffed, "It just so happens the dumbest guard in the province was on watch today."

Edwin waggled his finger at Henry. "As the son of a vintner, I have to say 'sour grapes.'"

Lucien felt unease inside the city. There was sickening dread growing from the walls and houses. Lucien looked around as if he could see it hanging in the air like a fog.

They walked down the street 'til they rounded the corner and stopped. Lucien stood looking at the statues of the saints standing alone at the city circle. The city named for the six saints of Amor had once been the religious center of the empire, but now the statues were corroded and covered with thick vines. The city looked run down and Lucien might have thought it nearly abandoned if not for a few candles they could see burning in the windows.

Edwin swallowed when he saw the statue circle in such a condition. "Gods, it is as if they all but abandoned them."

Henry looked up at the vines wrapped about Charbel. The statues all were twenty feet high or more. The book that Charbel held was covered in brown moss, and vines wrapped around his neck, obscuring his face. Henry stared up at him emotionlessly. "No," he said. "They abandoned us."

Lucien understood the significance and rubbed his chest. The dread pressed against him as he stood looking up at blindfolded Valdivia. He shuddered as they walked past the statues to the market street. They could see the gates of the castle in the distance. The three of them rested their hands lightly on their sword handles as they slowly approached the castle.

There was a young soldier there in full armor. He looked quickly from side to side with bird-like movements and shifted his weapon on his shoulder as he paced. Lucien could feel the fear dripping from him. Lucien held his hand up to Henry and Edwin. "I will deal with this."

Edwin shrugged and Henry smiled at him. Edwin leaned over to Henry and whispered, "Watch this."

The guard lowered his spear and held it at Lucien. "Stop. What are you doing here? Who are you?"

Lucien approached him, lowering his hood. "I am here to see Richter. You will take me to him."

The soldier backed away, stammering. "What? No one is to see the king."

Lucien stepped forward. "No one but us." He held out his hand and the guard's spear flew out of his grip and into Lucien's open palm. He broke it over his knee. The guard was momentarily stunned and confused, but then his training took over and he reached for his sword. As soon as it cleared the scabbard, it flew out of his grip and struck the castle wall with a clang.

"Demon!" the guard screamed, and turned to run. Lucien held his hand out once more and the guard fell face-forward to the ground. He kicked and screamed as Lucien dragged him up to his feet.

Henry looked on in horror and Edwin was nearly giddy with laughter. Henry reached for his sword but Edwin placed his hand on his arm and shook his head.

Lucien held the boy by his cuirass and shook him. "I won't ask again."

The soldier was in tears and snot bubbled at the end of his nose. "I will do whatever you say. Do not hurt me, please!"

"Just take me to Richter." Lucien released him.

The soldier wiped his hands on his grieves and turned to walk toward the castle. Edwin grabbed his arm. "Not too quickly now."

The soldier opened the gate and they went into the courtyard. There were no soldiers stationed anywhere inside. It was disturbing that the castle seemed abandoned as well. The guard took them to a side door that opened onto a stairwell leading down.

Edwin held the guard's arm tight. "Where are you taking us?"

He trembled in fear. "To Richter, like you asked. He is in the dungeon." The three of them all looked at one another in disbelief.

Edwin let the soldier's arm free. "All right, lead the way."

They followed him down the circular stairwell and into a long corridor. There was a hallway they turned into, and then another stairwell leading still farther down. At the bottom, they came to a door that had a large steel plate across it. The guard unlocked and opened it. Inside was a hall with several cell doors on either side, and at the end was a large caged cell.

Edwin and Henry's eyes widened to see Richter Elgin in the cage. He stood and his chains rattled on the floor. Lucien could feel his fear, and that fear suddenly turned to pity.

There was maddening laughter from Richter. It echoed off the walls as the three of them approached. Henry pulled his sword from his scabbard. "He is completely mad."

Edwin pulled his sword as he followed Lucien. Lucien glared at the unshaven and unkempt man in the cell. Richter could have easily passed for a beggar. "He hasn't gone mad, but we have been made fools."

Richter gripped the steel bars and growled at them. "The demon lord himself. Your father must be so proud." His voice was guttural and thick.

226

Lucien removed his blindfold and Richter took an involuntary step back from the bars. "What has happened? How are you down here in the dungeon?"

Richter came forward once more and Henry's sword stabbed at him through the bars. "I will see you dead." Edwin grabbed Henry's arm, pulling him away.

"Stop."

Richter was faster than Henry expected and moved to the side just in time. His laughter was a wild, tittering whine. He cocked his head and watched Edwin struggle with Henry.

Lucien pushed Henry back. "We haven't found out what is going on."

Henry struggled until Edwin released him. "My people have lived in fear of that man their entire lives. We cannot leave here until he is dead."

Richter laughed, waving his finger in the air. "Cut off the serpent's head and it shall grow another."

"You are pure evil," Henry said, his nostrils flaring.

Lucien stood in front of Henry with his hand on his chest. "It should be obvious that Richter is no longer a threat. I am starting to feel like he never was."

Richter stepped close to the cell bars. "You should have killed her while you had the chance. I shudder to think of how many you will kill once she captures your friend. She said she would skin her alive with her bare hands."

Lucien could feel his stomach tighten. "Elena?" Lucien passed through the bars like a phantom and grabbed Richter by the throat. He lifted him from the ground. "Where is she?"

Richter struggled as his feet kicked helplessly in the air. "I think by now she has already captured her. It is far too late. She might even be dead."

Lucien threw Richter against the wall. "How did she get free?"

Richter coughed and squirmed on the cell floor, trying to sit upright. "I wish I knew. You scattered my men and when Rabin came back, he had me arrested. Then he came to me in my cell. He told me my daughter had betrayed us. I refused to believe him, but he told me that it was the truth. He took command of the army. He claimed there was no other option for him and he had to obey her or join me in the dungeon."

Lucien stood over him, his eyes glowing red. "Why did she attack Drommer?"

Richter stood against the wall, shaking his head. "I have no idea. She has less than half my men. She could never take the walls, no matter how capable Rabin is."

Lucien could not control himself; his clothes began to sizzle and smolder as his body warmed. The straw beneath his feet burst into flames and quickly burned out. The temperature in the cell began to climb and Richter whimpered.

Edwin held the bars. "Get out of there. We have to get back to Charbel to find Kate."

Lucien appeared outside the bars beside Edwin. Henry stood by the cell, staring at Richter. "Are we going to just leave him?"

Lucien looked at Henry, his eyes returning to normal. "What good is killing him? If Elena has started this, killing him will not solve anything." Lucien put his hand on Henry's shoulder. "That army at Drommer is our pressing concern for the moment. We must find out what they are actually doing, and we have to find Zara."

Edwin grabbed Lucien's arm. "How close can we get to Crosshill?"

Lucien said, "The closest I can get is to the gate on the south road."

Richter stood at the bars, screaming, "You will fail, she will die! My daughter will take everything, and her lap dog Rabin will destroy you all!"

Lucien held his hand with his palm toward Richter, pushing him hard to the wall. Richter's head struck the stone and he dropped into an unconscious heap.

Henry sighed. "I wish you had killed him. Crosshill is west of the gate, but it is close to the border with the marshes. It would take us a few hours by horseback. I don't know if it will be in time."

Lucien grimaced. "I will be useless if I port that far. You two will have to leave me behind."

Edwin stood between him and Henry. "We won't leave you."

Lucien wiped at the blood from his nose. "You have to save Kate and the others. If you don't, nothing else will matter."

Edwin leaned close, embracing him. "You have to come with us."

"I'm sorry," Lucien said. He released him and grabbed Henry's arm. Edwin and Henry vanished.

Lucien fell to the floor, his mouth and nose dripping blood. He gasped for air as he stumbled to stand.

Richter regained consciousness and slowly crawled to his feet. His sinister laugh echoed from the walls of his cell. "You look as if you're at your end."

Lucien smiled, and his teeth were smeared with blood. "On the contrary, I think this is just going to hurt."

Richter backed away in horror as Lucien's red eyes stared at him through the cage bars and burned through the shadows.

CHAPTER 43

KATE WOKE IN the morning and Viola was gone. She frowned, knowing Viola did not realize how dangerous their position was. Nor was Kate surprised that Viola had gone off searching for lichen or fungi or some impossibly rare plant. Kate shook her head as she stood and scanned the area. The campfire was covered in vials and flasks. She knelt down to look at them and reached to turn one to see if there were any markings.

"Don't touch that," Viola said and grabbed her hand. Kate jumped.

"Gods, Viola, you are like a pinch-purse in the night. I did not hear you." Kate wiped her hands on her pants with a nervous laugh. Her heart still raced from the surprise.

Zara groaned and rolled to her back, squinting up at the sky. "It is morning already. This must be the earliest I have ever awakened."

Kate and Viola shared a quiet laugh at her.

Viola gathered up some of the flasks and placed them in her satchel. There were five medium ceramic bottles left on the ground. Viola gave Kate a bottle. "This is breakfast, drink it all for strength." She handed another to Zara and then sat on the bedroll with her legs crossed.

Kate drank the contents in a single motion. Zara looked uneasy and smelled the liquid inside. She took a tentative sip, swallowed, smiled broadly, and drank it all down.

Viola finished and licked her lips. "All right, these flasks go in your satchel for an emergency. You will know what to do." She gave one of the remaining flasks to Zara, another to Kate, and put one in her own satchel.

Zara put it in her coat pocket. "I am not sure I want to know what it is."

Viola said seriously, "Only use it in a severe emergency."

Kate laughed. "Do we throw it or pour it on the ground?"

Viola shook her hands wildly and followed it with a hop. "No, you drink it, dummy."

Kate and Zara both enjoyed Viola's vigor. "Gods, I hope I am not jumping around like a lunatic after that breakfast," Kate said.

Zara let out a belch. "Sorry, that was very good. I am going to avoid asking what was in it." Zara rolled up her blanket and stood.

Kate and Viola both cleaned up the camp. Kate secured the blankets and bedrolls on the horses, and Viola picked up her vials and some more herbs she had left drying on a flat stone beside the fire.

The three of them led their horses by their reins to the top of the hill on the other side of their campsite. They could not see anything to the west except the sun peeking out above the mountains.

"We are close?" Kate asked anxiously.

"Yes, we will see it in an hour or two. I suggest we ride along the base of that nearby hill. There is tall grass there." Zara told them, and climbed into the saddle.

Kate helped Viola onto her horse and then climbed aboard hers. The three of them rode west until they came to a shallow pass in the creek, and they crossed south.

They rode for another hour until the village of Crosshill came into view. It was sitting on a raised plateau of land bordering the marshland woods. It was strategically located at the base of the mountain and the corner of the two provinces. The three of them rode down into a valley between the hills and dismounted their horses.

They tied their horses to some large rocks, and Zara climbed on her stomach to the top of the hill, perhaps a hundred yards or so from the village. She could see the palisade. There were around forty houses inside the walls and some farms scattered north. A thick column of black smoke rose from the center of the village.

Zara looked down the slope at her companions. "There is something wrong."

Viola and Kate climbed up and lay next to her on their bellies. Viola had to squint her eyes. "I can barely see the place," she admitted.

Kate said, "Your vision is awful. There are no people. That is the problem. It must be some sort of trap."

Viola laughed. "Well, I suggest we turn around and call it a day, then."

Kate looked angrily to her and noticed that Viola was smiling. "I thought you were serious."

Zara seemed focused. "I can go up and scout the interior. I know this village. I used to travel around with my mother, paying platitudes to the local elders."

Kate chewed the inside of her cheek. If Zara were to get hurt, it would make things much worse for them. But they were unlikely to learn anything more by staying here or being too cautious. "Be careful."

Zara pulled her hood over her head and slid down the other side of the hill, then climbed the smaller hill across from their position. She stayed low to the ground until she reached the palisade. The smell of something burning grew stronger the closer she got to the village.

Zara knelt beside the wooden wall and peeked through the gaps in the stakes. She saw a pyre in the center of the village. It was made of furniture and other random items stacked high and set alight, as if people had emptied their homes to make it. She could hear voices of men, but could not understand their words.

Zara waved for Viola and Kate to approach. Kate pulled her bow and put an arrow across. Viola's stomach churned as she drew her dagger and took a soot-stained vial from her satchel. She held her thumb against the vial's cap, ready to open it and douse her blade in its deadly contents. Viola followed Kate as they crept and ran to the village.

Kate's heart was pounding by the time they reached the stake wall. Viola ran up ahead in a panic, and Kate was just a few yards behind when she noticed movement in the corner of her eye. She turned and saw a throwing axe flying toward her. She wasn't fast enough and the axe struck her in the hip.

Kate screamed out and fell to her side. Her leg was numb and she levered herself up on her elbow to see how badly she was injured. She couldn't immediately process the fact that the axe had not buried itself in her leg, but had apparently struck her handle-first and fallen harmlessly to the ground. She started to laugh with relief but stopped as she saw a man dressed in furs charging toward them, blades drawn.

Viola cried, "There he is!"

Kate stood and fired her arrows one after another. The first two missed but the third struck squarely in the center of the man's chest. He stumbled and dropped to the ground. Kate charged to finish him. Her victory cry died in her throat, replaced by horror and sickness when she saw the man's face.

She wanted so desperately to be wrong, but the man lying on the ground coughing blood had a very recognizable scar on his face. It was Tel-son. He smiled a bloody grimace. "I am sorry, but I took their trade: this village for my daughters. I die, knowing they are safe."

Kate held his hand. His grip grew weaker with each rattling breath. "No, gods no. Why? I told you I would save them."

Tel-son had tears in his eyes. "It is war, and my family must be safe. I could never trust a flatlander." His pupils widened, and he lay still and quiet.

Tears fell from Kate's eyes. It was all a trick. An evil trick. They had killed him for the village. She stood just as four men circled the village wall, running towards them.

Zara and Viola ran to her as Kate raised her bow. Her hands were still shaking with rage and fear and heartbreak as she fired her arrow. It missed its target but she immediately nocked another, aimed, fired, and struck the first man in the shoulder. The impact drove him back but a step. He regained his footing and raced on.

"Go!" Kate ordered. "I can handle this!"

Viola and Zara climbed the hill to the east and Kate pulled another arrow. She aimed for the wounded man and struck him in the upper leg and he dropped. The other three were less than thirty yards and closing fast.

Zara threw rocks at the men, trying to draw their attention. One stone pinged off the helm of the biggest. He broke away from the others and ran up the hill after Zara. Fear made her trip over her own feet and she fell and tumbled down the slope to the man. She tried to scramble to her feet but the grass was slippery and the slope too steep. He raised his leg and stomped his boot down on her leg, smashing it against a rock. Zara screamed in agony as the bone broke and tore through her flesh with a wet, pulpy sound.

Viola ran down the hill and launched herself at the man. She stabbed with her dagger, but the man grabbed her wrist and twisted it until the knife dropped from her grip. She desperately searched her satchel, and the man casually pulled his sword and swiped at her. Viola jumped back as far as she could, but the tip of the blade slashed the flesh above her left eye. Blood ran down her face and blinded her. The man pushed her down and raised his sword overhead with both hands, preparing to stab down on her. An arrow punched through his throat from behind. He dropped the sword and grabbed at the arrowhead as blood filled his mouth. He fell to his knees and toppled backwards, drowning in his own blood.

Kate paused but a moment to make certain he was no longer a threat to Zara, then turned to fire again at the two men charging her. They were too close to try another shot, so she threw aside her bow and drew her sword. The first man stabbed with his sword, but Kate stepped aside and drove the tip of her blade up into his armpit. He cried out in pain and pulled away from her. The other man swung his blade in a vicious downward arc that Kate just barely blocked with her sword. He kept hammering at her with his blade and the savagery of his attack drove her back until she lost her balance.

She fell to the ground, and the man kicked the blade from her. She struggled until they put a rope around her legs and drew it tight. They ran, pulling her behind them. Her arms and back tore open to raw flesh on the jagged rocks. Kate was frozen in pain and could not even scream. Her head struck a rock, knocking her unconscious and splitting open her skull.

Voila cried as she rubbed the blood from her eyes. She could barely make out the weeping of Zara. She tore the sleeve of her cloak, tying it around her head. Her eye had swollen shut now, and she could only make out shadows through the blood and tears in her other. "Zara, please tell me you're alive?"

Zara cried out, "I am dying. I can't feel anything and everything is white."

Viola stumbled on the rocks. "I am coming. Did you see what happened to Kate?"

Zara could not compose herself and wailed, "She is dead!"

"No," Viola whispered. The air left her lungs in a rush. She fell to her knees. "Do you see her body?"

Zara sniffled and shook her head. "No, but she stopped moving as they dragged her along the ground. She was covered in blood."

Viola tried to steady herself. Kate could still be alive. She found a vial in her satchel, opened it, tipped her head back, and poured the contents into her eye. The first order of business was for her to regain her sight. Her vision came back, and she looked down at the gruesome wound on Zara's leg. The bone had meat stretched around where it protruded.

Viola fought down the contents of her stomach at the sight. Zara had stopped crying now and was writhing on the ground. Viola held her leg up as gently as she could, even though what followed would not be gentle at all. "This is going to hurt," she warned, and twisted and pushed the bone back inside.

Zara screamed, then stopped moving completely. Her face was pale and waxy, covered with a film of cold sweat. Viola lifted and tilted Zara's head and poured the contents of a flask into her mouth.

Zara coughed, looking up at her. Her eyes were half-lidded and watery. "It tastes awful. Gods, I hope it heals me."

Viola took a sip from the flask and spit it out. "Gods, I am sorry, that was my lunch from yesterday. It has gone off. Here," Viola said, and poured another flask of liquid into Zara's mouth.

It was just a quarter or less, since most of it spilled from Zara's mouth as she slipped down into the dark, icy waters of shock and unconsciousness.

Viola tried to lift her, but small as Zara was, Viola was even smaller. Instead, she wrapped their cloaks together and huddled at the base of the hill.

Viola struggled with complete despair at the thought of Kate being dead. She held tight to Zara, but held even tighter to hope.

CHAPTER 44

E DWIN AND HENRY appeared north of the gate in Westfall. They both immediately looked around, and then at each other. Henry was dumbfounded. "He can send people away like that?"

The corner of Edwin's mouth curled down. "He can do almost anything, but it probably nearly killed him."

The men inside the gate had not noticed their arrival, but tried to jump to attention when Henry approached them. "Men, we need two of your fastest horses, and that is an order."

Heinrich yelled sternly to his men: "Two horses, now! And hurry."

The men scattered to the stables to fetch the horses. They returned within moments with fresh horses, saddled and ready to ride.

Heinrich bowed to Henry and looked at Edwin. "Your highness, I hope you are not in any danger."

"I think the men who attacked Crosshill are in far more danger, sergeant. Send word to Charbel of casualties, and that they need to send guards to the village as soon as they can." Henry mounted his horse and rode out.

Edwin rode behind Henry as they turned north past the gate. They rode the horses hard along the tree-lined road.

A couple hours' ride brought the village into view. They reined their horses to a stop and sat looking at the village.

Henry shifted on his horse. "I don't see any people. That is not normal."

Edwin gritted his teeth. "We better hurry then. There may -- " A scream cut off the rest of whatever Edwin was about to say. One quick glance at each other and, without a word, they kicked their horses into a gallop.

They stayed high on the hill as they raced toward the village and then down the slope. As they got nearer the village, they could see a man's body on the side of another hill. There was an arrow jutting from his throat. And then Edwin spotted two bodies lying wrapped in blankets at the foot of the hill. He jumped from his horse before he brought it to a stop and ran to them.

With shaking hands, he pulled back the blanket to see the battered face of Viola. "Gods, what have they done to you?" he asked, his voice hoarse with emotion.

Viola shook and blinked with her one good eye. She tried to smile, but it looked more like a grimace. "Edwin, you have to find Kate. They took her. She was being dragged and was badly wounded."

Henry grabbed his sister, trying to wake her. "Gods, is she dead?"

Viola held his arm. "No, I gave her a potion to heal. She will wake, but it will take awhile."

Henry turned to Edwin. "Go, find Kate. I will take them to the village and on to Charbel. Hurry, before you're too late."

Edwin lightly placed his palm against Viola's cheek and kissed her tenderly. "I will find you again, I promise."

Edwin scrambled back to his horse and screamed to get it to speed. He pushed the horse as hard as he could, following the tracks along the ground where Kate was dragged. The tracks soon led off into the swamp, and he stuck to the paths as best he could. The ground was soft, and her body left a muddy smear. He continued at a trot, dodging fallen trees and low-hanging branches.

The density of the woods and the gloom made it impossible to see if there was anyone ahead of him. He stopped to listen, but heard nothing. He pushed his horse back into a trot and followed the path, but it soon winnowed away to nothing. He looked around for other tracks and froze: there was a body leaning against a tree. He was just about to dismount when an arrow struck him in the leg. He fell from his horse, biting back a cry of pain. The arrow was deep in his right thigh. He wrapped the horse's reins around his arm and used them to haul himself to his feet.

Edwin heard someone splashing through the shallow water, racing toward him. He pulled his sword, but he was too slow. The blade struck his shoulder. He dropped to one knee, screaming in rage. He swung across twice, and then in a stab. His attacker stumbled back and fell into the water. Edwin drove the blade into his throat, twisting it.

Edwin assumed the threat had ended and crawled back to Kate. A moment later, he realized the danger was just beginning as an arrow slammed into his left side. It drove the air from his lungs. He grabbed at the shaft and collapsed. It was unbearably painful. His body was going numb. The archer smiled as he watched Edwin writhe on the ground. He lowered his bow and approached slowly, like a wolf stalking injured prey.

He pulled his dagger and stood over Edwin, ready to finish him.

Edwin had lost all feeling in his arms but he could tell he still held the sword. He swung his body just as the man knelt down. The blade slashed across the man's face, flaying his cheek open, exposing rotted teeth. He screamed and dropped to his knees. Edwin leaned forward, dragging himself toward his attacker. The man clutched his ruined face with one hand, but his other hand still held the dagger. He stabbed at him and the blade stuck deep into Edwin's shoulder.

The dagger locked Edwin's shoulder and he could barely move his arm. He launched himself forward with his good leg, tackling the kneeling man and knocking him onto his back. The man clawed and raked at Edwin's face as he screamed. Edwin roared in rage and sank his teeth into the man's neck, biting as hard as he could. He bit and chewed until a hot jet of blood sprayed all over his face.

The man lay twitching on the ground as Edwin rolled off of him and onto his side, facing Kate. He spat out a red wad of flesh and stringy vein and muscle. His hands and arms trembled as he lay next to her. He could not even recognize her from the wounds all over her body. Her mud-covered body sat in a puddle of blood. He felt her face and it felt cold, but a coldness was creeping through him, so he could not be sure. Her satchel was tangled around her body and soaked with her blood.

Edwin could barely breathe and his vision went white. He did not have the strength to go on as he clutched the satchel.

CHAPTER 45

LUCIEN LEANED BACK against the wall of the dungeon. He coughed blood down his chest. His latest port had taken all of his energy, and he sat panting in front of Richter's cell like a dog on a hot day.

Richter sat on the floor on the other side of the bars. "Where have you taken me?"

Lucien answered with more bravado than he felt: "Where you will face justice."

Richter stared at him from behind the bars. There were voices in the hallway, growing closer. Blood continued to drip down Lucien's chin as he turned to stare with his red eyes at Richter. It was more than he could manage to keep them open. He smiled weakly and let his eyes slide shut. A guard walked into the block of cells.

He looked at Richter, confused. "Who are you?" he asked.

Then he looked down to see Lucien, and screamed, "Guards! To me, guards!"

CHAPTER 46

ALARIC'S MEN GATHERED in full gear and with wagonloads of supplies. Jan rode his horse up beside him. Alaric shifted in the saddle. "Are you certain?"

Jan looked concerned. "Yes, they have lifted the siege at Drommer and around five hundred men are marching south to the crossroad. They might be headed back to the City of Saints."

Alaric shook his head. "No, I think you know they would not have come all this way to return. They are going to Dawnbridge. The report said they are carrying ladders."

Jan frowned. "Yes, it is likely they will attack Dawnbridge, and I still have no idea why."

"Because they know something we don't." Alaric said. He held up his hand and waved. His men began to march north.

Alaric said, "I hope you can hold if they come. They may send more soldiers west from Elgin and attack here."

Jan watched his columns of soldiers move out. "We will hold as long as we can. Do you know if reinforcements will arrive from Elnora?"

Alaric sighed and said, "I have no idea. If you cannot hold, sail south to Elnora with everyone you can."

Jan nodded. "Good luck." He pulled his horse away and rode back to the castle.

Alaric looked on as the sergeant passed him with a nod. He turned to look back at Porin one last time, then kicked his horse to join up with his men.

Alaric had not ridden far when three horses approached from behind.

Lady Anne sat upon the lead horse, and she rode up beside him. "I have news. The army reached the crossroad and turned west."

Alaric laughed. "I already knew that. There was no other place for them to go."

Lady Anne looked crossly at him. "There was a messenger from the west gate in the marshes. He said Edwin and Henry went west alone to Crosshill. Do you know where Lucien went?"

Alaric shook his head. "He went to Saints with those two; after that, I have no idea. I didn't think he had enough strength left in him to send Edwin and Henry so far. He might still be trapped in the city."

Lady Anne frowned. "I will send a spy to the city. How long will you march before resting?" she asked.

"It will be night soon. We will march until midnight, and rest. In the morning we will attack with whatever we have."

"Elias will be ready to help however he can. He has but a hundred old men and boys. There are a handful of archers on the walls. I suspect you will be heavily outnumbered," Lady Anne warned him.

Alaric gazed over his men. "We have to stop them from taking the city. If there are gods in the heavens above, they'd better send Lucien, and soon."

Lady Anne said nothing. She simply pulled the reins and galloped in the opposite direction.

Alaric looked up and watched the two moons, cold sailors of the sky, begin their endless night voyage once more.

CHAPTER 47

ALARIC AWOKE IN the morning to the sounds of horses nickering and voices in the camp. He sat up to put his armor on over his shoulders. The commander's tent was always lonely at night. It was four times the size of the normal tents and was held high enough to stand. The planning table sat at the center with four empty chairs surrounding it.

He raised his head as he fastened the loops under his neck and shoulders. He stood and put his scabbard around his waist.

The tent flap lifted and the dour face of Anne peered through. He motioned her in. "I have urgent news," she said.

Alaric checked that his buckles and straps were secure. "They have set up siege at Dawnbridge?"

Anne frowned. "Yes, but Dulimore has levies out. They must have a hundred or so men. They left in the night, and you might encounter them on the way to Dawnbridge."

Alaric clasped his hands together behind his back. "Where are they going? I do not believe they would leave the province."

"They are going to Porin to crush Jan. This is the perfect opportunity."

Alaric looked at her pointedly. "How many men, exactly, did your spies see?"

"Thirty cavalry, a hundred and fifty men or more, and twenty archers," she recited.

Alaric shrugged his great shoulders. "I don't know. If they do, Jan will have to try and hold. I gave him the option to sail to Elnora."

Anne laughed without humor. "He would never leave. His father died for that city, he will die too."

"So be it. We march to Dawnbridge. We must stand against the Elgin forces before they take the city. There is not but a few days' supply of goods there. Elias will be starved within a fortnight. Let Dulimore have their battle, we are to focus on solidifying a front with Elgin."

Anne followed Alaric as he went to Sergeant Dalen. "Raise the men," he ordered. "We march." The word carried quickly and others around began to strike the tents and hurried to load the wagons.

"Emery, get the horses ready and prepare the men for battle," Alaric called and waved to a young man. He watched as the camp quickly folded itself and was loaded up. The ghostly remains of extinguished campfires and earth rutted by horses' hooves were all that was left behind.

Anne stood watching with Alaric. "Your men know how to prepare."

"They are good men, and we will fight hard. They volunteered for this, even if we are outnumbered four- or five-to-one." Alaric turned to her, and his tone was kindly when he said, "You should go wherever you are planning. I know your schemes. If we survive the battle we will be in Dawnbridge. If you can get word to Lucien, do so."

Anne left the tent and mounted her horse, pulling it to ride with her two companions. They rode east until they were out of view. Alaric climbed to his horse and surveyed his men as they prepared for battle.

Under his breath, he said a prayer.

CHAPTER 48

JAN'S ARMOR CHAFED as he paced the throne room. He rubbed at his chin and then rubbed his hands together.

Petric sat at one of the feasting tables with his arms crossed. "Do not worry yourself, my lord. My scouts are everywhere in the area. If any soldiers approach, we will be ready."

Jan stopped next to the throne and rested his hand on it. His shoulders sagged and his head sank until his chin nearly touched his chest. "I would feel a lot better if we had word on Alaric's advance. I hate not knowing."

Jan looked up to his right as a man opened the door and entered with a bow. "What is it, Haim?" he asked without enthusiasm.

"My lord, Lady Anne has arrived at the castle. She wishes to see you." Haim rose from his bow.

Jan tried to stifle his smile. "Things are looking up." Petric shook his head as Jan straightened his posture. "Send the good lady in."

Lady Anne entered with a quick curtsy. Jan could hardly contain his wild grin. "My lady, to what do I owe such an honor?"

Anne shook her head. "War," she said simply. "Alaric will soon be at Dawnbridge. The Dulimore army is marching south to this location."

Jan turned to Petric urgently. The smile was gone. "Gather everyone inside the walls. Go to the farms and get everyone. No one is to be left out."

Petric turned to two guards and they followed him as he hurried out of the room.

"How many men?" Jan's mood had changed completely and his words were now sharp and authoritative.

"I am not certain. They were mustering south of Drommer, around a hundred."

Jan's face pulled down in a scowl. "Treacherous bastards. They would attack just as the marshes are desperate for their help. Did you actually see the men on the road north?"

Anne said, "No, my spies did not. They reported they were moving south, and they broke off contact to return as quickly as they could."

Jan took her arm and led her into the hallway. "I must prepare. If they are to siege the castle, I can hold for a long time, but you must leave immediately."

Anne twisted her arm loose and said sharply, "I am not going anywhere. The only source of what is going on is me. Do you think you can win? You should flee to Elnora and take your sister with you."

"I will not leave this place while I live. They have wanted it all my life and I will not live with it in their hands. I have no need of you here in a siege. You could leave and report to Alaric we can hold as long as a week unless we are overrun."

Anne crossed her arms defiantly. "Prepare your men, but I stay."

"You beautiful, stubborn cow!" Jan yelled back at her as he stormed down the hallway.

Anne wrinkled her nose. "Beautiful?"

CHAPTER 49

KING DELVIN ADJUSTED the collar on his combat jacket. The two patterns of blue matched those that adorned the tapestries and rugs of the castle. He paced the bedchambers, rubbing his hands, looking at the guards in the doorway as they shifted about. "How bad is it, Vesper?"

A bald man in a monk's habit rubbed Lucien's body with ointment until it nearly glistened in the candlelight. He lay naked and unconscious on his bed. "My lord, I am unsure. He is in a much-weakened state, and more likely the result of overexertion than illness. Perhaps in your life you have experienced such a state."

Delvin listened intently to the man's very calm and methodical voice. His voice was reassuring, but his face could not hide the strain he felt as he struggled to help Lucien. "Do what you can. I have experienced many bouts in my life of such a thing, but often there is evidence of it. So far, we have just a prisoner in our dungeon to show for this. I expect much more violence and signs of it on him."

Delvin walked into the hallway and over to a guard. He stood at attention, but a slight tremble betrayed his nervousness.

"This is how you found him?" Delvin asked in a tone that was almost an accusation.

The man swallowed. "Yes, my lord. The prisoner was in the cell and the prince lay motionless on the ground. I summoned the guard straight away to aid him."

"You did very well. This prisoner did not say much to you?" Delvin stroked his beard.

"No, he asked only where he was and who we were." The boy dropped his gaze to the floor.

"Come with me to question this prisoner." Delvin said. He was already walking away before the young man processed his command. He had to hurry to catch up.

They navigated several hallways and stairwells before they reached their destination. Another man opened the large, gated door he was guarding. It led to a group of six caged cells.

Richter rose from the wooden bench in his cell as Delvin entered. "I should have known. Only you would have the courage to butcher my sons but leave me alive in your dungeon."

Delvin stared at him without emotion. "What happened to my son?"

Richter laughed, but it sounded like a mad dog barking. "How should I know? He was bleeding from his mouth when he found me. I have no idea where I am, even now, and he was unconscious on the floor when I arrived."

Delvin's mouth narrowed until it was little more than a slit. His bright blue eyes glowed. Brown sewer water rose from the drain in the floor like a slithering snake and wrapped around Richter's leg. He screamed, "No, I will tell you anything!" The liquid pulled him down to the floor, wrapping around his body, squeezing the breath from him.

Delvin waved his hand and the water lost its cohesiveness and fell to the floor with a splash. It drained into the floor grate and dripped into the sewer far below. Delvin placed his left hand on the cell bars. "I will not repeat my questions. You will answer what I want to know."

Richter sat on his knees with a look of unbridled horror on his face. "I will tell you everything," he said, his eyes wide and fixed on the sewer grate. "Everything."

CHAPTER 50

THE WALLS OF Dawnbridge could be seen at the end of the road. The gate was closed, and the torches of the Elgin camps were visible north of the east gate.

Alaric brought his horse to a halt and waved to his men. "Form a line, spears in the back." He dismounted and went to stand by Dalen. "Shields ready, two deep. We need to turn them north and put our backs to the castle if we can. It will help us keep their numbers from encircling us."

Dalen nodded nervously and Alaric patted him reassuringly on the shoulder. Alaric stood in the center of the road and placed his helm upon his head. It was evening, and the sun still shone on his armor as if he were glowing.

He drew his sword and held it high. "Men, we have a single objective: to scatter this band of Elgin scum. We move to put the walls at our backs, and kill as many as we can. They will break and run. We must hold the ground. If King Elias can aid us, he will."

Alaric lowered his sword. "You are the finest men I have ever known. If they take Dawnbridge, they take the marshes. We

255

will be cut off from our island once and for all. It will be the end of our hopes for a better future, and we fight for that now."

Alaric paused to look at the faces of the men and once more raised his sword. "On me, advance."

The men followed behind Alaric, their shields raised. He set a marching pace in the center of the road and the men followed two paces behind. The closer to the walls they advanced, the more Elgin soldiers swarmed to block the road.

A man with a red cape upon a black horse held his sword over his head. The Elgin army filled the road less than a hundred yards ahead of Alaric's advance. Alaric's rage rose upon seeing the man sitting on the black mare. "Rabin," he said in an angry whisper.

Alaric could feel his pulse throbbing in his neck as he raised his sword, "Spears forward and charge!"

The shield line slowed and the spearman passed between them. They linked arms and ran forward with their long spears held before them. The Elgin army was a patchwork of knights and they held their shields up as the spear line closed on them.

The spear line smashed into the Elgin foot knights. The entire Elgin line buckled. Rabin screamed to them, "Hold the line!"

Alaric stood on the southern flank with his feet in the swamp, slashing and cutting down men as he tried to turn the enemy line. His men dropped their spears and unsheathed their swords, cutting into the Elgin center.

Sergeant Dalen led the men in the center, pushing them forward. "Kill them and push them back! Use your shields to make a wall!" The line converged in the center, and Alaric moved farther into the marshes, dueling with two knights at once.

He slashed the first man across the chest and legs and stabbed the other through the neck. Blood jetted into Alaric's face and eyes. He turned and drove the tip of his sword through the first knight's heart, then lifted his leg and kicked the still-standing body free of the blade. The Elgin southern flank began to give as Alaric and the Elnora shield knights killed men and pushed them back.

Alaric stabbed at the sides of the Elgin soldiers, cutting open their stomachs; their intestines unspooled and steamed when they hit the cool swamp water. In a near-berserker rage, he cut down through the shoulder and ribs of another knight, almost splitting him in half.

Rabin looked to the southern flank from astride his horse. "Move men to the south!" he roared. "They are trying to turn the line!"

Alaric could hear the Elgin commander and he pushed himself harder. Two soldiers stood knee-deep in the swamp, trying to push Alaric farther south and away from his men. He stabbed one through his eye and parried with the second. The soldier would not give, and one of his wild swings opened a horrible wound on Alaric's face. Alaric charged him, pushing him backwards into the water. He held the face of his sword across the soldier's throat with two hands, crushing his windpipe.

Two more men tried to charge Alaric and from his knees he turned and stabbed upward, gutting the first. He deflected the second knight's blow with the bracers on his arm. The man stumbled and Alaric stood quickly, striking him across the back of his head. The blow split his neck open and nearly decapitated him.

Alaric frantically climbed to the line as more Elgin men pushed to the swamp, trying to keep them from getting behind. Just as Alaric reached dry land, rocks and stones rained from the walls of Dawnbridge. The men reflexively held their shields up, but they were no protection. The crack and crunch of the heads and bodies of Elgin soldiers being broken and crushed filled the air. Some were blinded from the rock dust thrown down. Several had horrific bloody dents in their heads. They begged for death to take them. The rocks continued to batter them from the high walls.

The Elgin soldiers wavered. "Push them, they are breaking!" screamed Alaric, stabbing his way forward through two more men on the southern flank. He slashed and chopped as the Elgin soldiers tried to cover their heads.

Commander Rabin fell from his horse. He held his shield over his head and ran north to the trees for protection. The Elgin line had fallen back closer to the city. Suddenly from above, cauldrons of boiling tar dumped from the walls. Their screams of terror and anguish mingled with the moans of the crushed and dying.

Alaric laughed as he heard their screams. He stabbed two more soldiers, and hacked the arm off another as he pushed with the men on the flank.

The back of the Elgin line was in disarray as thirty or more men tried to wipe the boiling tar from their faces and clothes. Alaric looked to the walls above, and through the blood and sweat filling his eyes he watched with unspeakable joy as burning torches were thrown from the ramparts into the midst of the Elgin soldiers.

The pools of tar covering the ground burst into flames, forming a fiery wall, stalling the Elnoran advance. The Elgin men doused in tar or unfortunate to be near enough the inferno found themselves suddenly engulfed in flames. They screamed and ran, flames leaping from them and igniting even more soldiers they passed in the line. The Elgin soldiers broke and ran.

Alaric smiled at the victory so close at hand. The men held their shields tight and pushed hard into the line. He raised his arms high in a cheer when he felt something strike his back, followed by white-hot pain. He'd been struck by an arrow.

Alaric stumbled and turned in time to see the Dulimore cavalry smash into the rear of the Elnora line.

It was a betrayal. He stared in disbelief and tried to reach the arrow in his back. He watched as the Elnorans screamed and tried to take cover south in the swamp. The Dulimore archers fired, picking them off one by one as the army broke.

Alaric's right arm was numb. He dropped his shield and took his sword into his left hand. He slashed at the horses' legs and throats and cut two of them down before being knocked off his feet. He scrambled on the ground as the Elnorans dropped, bloody and beaten, around him.

The rest of the Dulimore army advanced on their position and he knew it was over. "Retreat, south to the marshes, every man!" Alaric commanded as he struggled to his feet.

Alaric slashed the throat of one of the dismounted cavalry, and chopped off the sword-hand of another as he made his way back into the marsh. The archers fired after him and an arrow buried itself deep in his shoulder. The pain slowed him and Alaric took cover behind a tree. He could hear men crashing through the marsh after him. They couldn't help but find him, but he would not sell his life cheaply. As he was thinking that, someone grabbed him around the waist. "Come on, we can make the south wall."

Dalen dropped his sword and lifted Alaric to his feet. They struggled through the waist-deep water as arrows dropped around them. Blood ran from Alaric's wounds, and when he looked at Dalen, he could see he had suffered a terrible cut under his eye. It was puffy, nearly swollen shut.

When they reached the castle wall, Alaric could see only a few of his men still alive. It had been a massacre. Alaric still held his sword, and pushed Dalen forward. "Leave me."

Dalen grabbed Alaric's arm. "No, we cannot lose any more."

Alaric had tears in his eyes. "The shame would kill me and my family."

"There is no shame in betrayal, and revenge can still be ours. We have to hold the city at all costs, but we need you to do it." Dalen put Alaric's arm over his shoulder and helped him along.

Alaric did not argue as he looked back at the bodies of Elnoran soldiers lying dead in the marsh. The flutter of arrow fire and the screams of the wounded and dying filled the air and followed them for a long, long time.

CHAPTER 51

THE PEDESTRIAN DOOR was open at the west gate and they helped the wounded Elnoran soldiers through. The city was filled with people huddled in the streets, armed with anything they could find.

Dalen held Alaric upright as they limped down the market road toward the castle. "There are more men than I expected," Alaric said. "I see at least a dozen with us just now. There might be more."

Alaric closed his eyes, his spirits crushed by the defeat they had just endured. They had the Elgin army routed, and the Dulimore army betrayed them. The only thought in his mind was rallying his men and finding a way to turn the tide once again in their favor.

There were women dressed to nurse the wounded in the courtyard. They had a triage camp there. Alaric felt his heart sink when he noticed young Emery covered in bandages, lying on a cot. So much blood, so many wasted lives, and all because of Dulimore's treachery.

Commander Eric waved to Dalen. "Commander Alaric, we can take you to the manor."

Dalen followed Eric up the stairway to the castle. The manor was in panic as people ran from the rooms to gather anything to help the wounded.

Eric was dressed in full armor and his helm visor was raised, exposing only his face. "They are moving north to the flat. It appears they plan to siege from that direction."

Alaric held his arm tight to his chest, growling through his pain, "How many men?"

Eric went ahead of them and opened the door to Alaric's room. "Three hundred, maybe more. I think it is mostly conscripts, but it is enough with our paltry defenses. The lack of stone has left the north wall soft."

Dalen helped Alaric to lie face-down across the bed. The arrow shafts still protruded from his back like quills. Dalen climbed onto the bed, straddling Alaric, one knee on the mattress, the other against Alaric's back. "This will hurt," he cautioned.

"Do it," Alaric grunted. "It can't hurt more than it already does."

Dalen pulled the two arrows from Alaric's lower back, and then the one from his shoulder. Once the arrow heads were removed, freshets of blood flowed freely from the wounds.

"Gods." Alaric leaned to his side. "I was wrong." He felt lightheaded and sick. Dalen held bandages to his wounds and a nurse came in, slathering ointment everywhere he had been cut. She noticed the wound beneath Dalen's eye and covered it with ointment. "Infection is worse than the fighting. Get this man a room."

Dalen brushed back his hair as they led him out of the room. Several nurses tried to bandage Alaric, but he flailed and kicked, pushing them aside. "Get me a sling for my arm. I want to see the king."

Eric stood in the doorway. "Elias will see you. He is on the battlements."

The women put a wrap over Alaric's shoulder and looped his arm. He stood shakily and leaned against the wall. He steadied himself, nodded, and followed Eric.

Alaric pushed aside offers of assistance, refusing to show pain or weakness. He walked with Eric to the stairwell and up to a door. It opened onto the walls. Elias stood on the northern ramparts with Brian.

Brian wore leather armor and gripped a spear's haft tightly in his hand.

"You make one odd soldier," Alaric observed, and stood at his side.

Brian slowly turned his head to look at him. His eyes were red and swollen, and his face was etched with grief. "They found my daughter's body in the woods. Lord Edwin's as well. There is little left for me. I hope to die here."

Alaric recoiled at the news as if he had been slapped. His eyes filled with tears and he could only watch as Brian wiped at his nose. At last he found his voice and said, "I cannot even fathom the horror of this. We are beaten. What happened?"

Brian cried as he leaned on his spear. "There was a trap for them in Crosshill. It must have been Elgin. That bitch Elena escaped from the dungeon. Gods be damned how."

Alaric closed his teary eyes, damning Elena under his breath. "It will not be long now."

Brian had to turn away. He gazed out over the wall. "What do you mean?"

Alaric opened his eyes and looked out across the field, unable to look at Brian in his grief. "When Lucien comes, all the men you see in the field will be dead."

Brian cried and laughed. "Gods, I hope I live to see it."

King Elias's mail rattled as he walked the battlement. He wore all chain with a tabard over his chest, adorned with six spokes of a wheel. His steel crown rested on his mail coif. "I tell you, I wish I could say I was surprised. Nothing can surprise me anymore. Maybe this is Tryphon's blessing, the suffering before the glory."

Alaric wiped at his eyes. He plugged one nostril and blew a wad of phlegm over the battlement, then the other nostril. "How long 'til Elnora receives word of Edwin's death?"

Elias sighed, looking out over the field below. "Not long. The ships left in the night. I should never have trusted Oswald. He freed Elena and they fled together. What an old fool I have become."

Brian sniffed and composed himself. "Trusting others is never a mistake unless you know they are scoundrels. We had too much faith or hope in him. It turns out he was just a turd all along."

"That explains why they helped them. I can only wonder what Oswald gets out of the deal, or Icel." Alaric continued to stare at the field below. It would be filled with the dead when Lucien returned. He held his wounded arm against his chest and leaned on the crenellations to see clear of the walls. In the field in the far distance, the men from Dulimore were building a siege machine.

Elias extended his arm to indicate the soldiers at work. "A trebuchet," he said. "You can see the timbers there."

Alaric looked where he pointed and there were several large timbers lying near a very long one with a rope-sling on the tip. He knew these patchwork walls could never hold up to an assault from such a weapon. "Lucien better hurry or there won't be anyone left to save."

Elias scratched his head. "I just cannot figure out what is going on, no matter how hard I try."

Alaric stood back, cradling his arm. "What do you mean?"

Elias shrugged and spread his arms out to his sides. "The spies said they had ladders, but where are they?"

CHAPTER 52

J AN PACED THE throne room, stopping momentarily to
think. Then he continued to pace, the sollerets of his armor
ringing on the floor and echoing off the walls.

"Gods, I think I will be sick," Anne yelled out. "Your pacing
is going to wear a hole in the floor!"

Petric, sitting across from Anne, laughed as he peeled an apple.

"Well, my lovely lady, I am facing the loss of everything my
family has ever had. It is a cause for general concern, I think."
Jan raised his chin defiantly.

Haim appeared in the doorway. He cleared his throat. When
Jan looked his way, he said, "My lord, men have been spotted
on the north road."

They all ran to the ramparts of the north wall. Jan looked
out over the fields that bordered the road. "Ladders," Jan said,
and looked to Anne.

She scowled. "Dulimore has betrayed us. Those soldiers are
carrying banners for Prince Oswald. That slimy toad-turd has
joined with Elgin."

Jan smiled crookedly. "Those are not Prince Oswald's. They are King Oswald's. Look again at the banners."

Anne looked again, shaking her head ruefully. "The traitor, at last. I wonder what Elena promised him."

"Her bed, no less."

Anne laughed. "Gods, Jan, you are unbelievable. We are facing down death."

"A hundred or two hundred men against my forty. I like my chances." Jan grunted and waved to his men standing on the ramparts. They hurrahed, and he stood proudly. "I say to any man who kills more attackers than me, he shall receive a cask of wine and a girl in the bathhouse."

The men all cheered and laughed.

Jan leaned close to Anne and whispered, "You can leave anytime. There is a boat still in port. I would prefer not to worry about you getting killed on my account."

Anne's face became red. "I am not sure I want to hear sec-ondhand stories of this battle. I expect a lot of embellishment from a scoundrel like you."

"Certainly not. We are all gentlemen with the ladies here, but a cruel butcher we shall be with the enemy," Jan said, his voice growing louder with each word. His men cheered.

Petric smiled and embraced Jan. "It shall be a glorious day."

Jan signaled and his men on the walls let fly the few arrows they had left. He laughed, watching the men of Elgin and Dulimore run as the arrows rained down on them. He smiled and mused aloud, "Well, two ladders will be quite slow going. I just hope the gate holds." He looked toward the gate, where every wagon and barrel in the entire castle had been stacked against it.

The Dulimore and Elgin forces looked to be heavy in number, but their clothing was mostly leather armor and spears. There were around two hundred, and most of them stood close to the walls while wave after wave of arrows rained down on them. The enemy struggled to raise the ladders as they avoided the arrows.

"Gentlemen and Lady," Jan said, donning his helm on and lowering his visor; "I believe the pampered life we have led may, in fact, finally have a bill come due. Let us say we pay that bill in blood."

There was a hurrah as Petric raised his axe high. "I have lived in luxury since you brought me here, Jan. Today I shall kill ten men to repay you, and ten more to prove twice my worth."

Jan grabbed his shoulder. "I will kill ten as well, and I believe every man here can kill at least ten, if not more. I hope you animals are not too greedy and leave some of the butchering for the rest of us."

Haim and two soldiers brought barrels of linens up to the walls. The end of the ladder reached the top of the battlements. Men collected below to start the climb. Jan leaned over and watched the soldiers getting closer to the top of the wall. "I believe I'd like a little music," Jan said calmly. "Haim, I think it is time the enemy serenade me with their screams."

Haim grabbed the linen rags filled with warm pork fat. They ignited them with a torch and tossed them on the men below.

The burning rag landed on the face of a man halfway up the ladder. His head was almost instantly shrouded in flames. He screamed, grabbed at the rag and lost his grip. He fell, taking the man behind him down with him. The fall was high enough that they broke several bones when they hit the ground, but not high enough to kill them. They writhed below in agony as two more flaming linens were thrown down, burning more of the soldiers.

The second ladder came to the wall and Jan dragged a large hook with a chain down away from the stone battlement. He gestured for his men to spread apart as nearly twenty attackers scaled the ladder.

Jan swung the chain in an arc over his head, then threw it. The hook caught the side of the ladder and knocked a man off. He screamed all the way to the ground and then was silent. Jan's men grabbed the length of chain and pulled. There was a mighty cracking sound as the ladder broke in half. Dulimore soldiers fell screaming down to the rocky ravine, but the falling ladder pulled the hook chain with it.

The enemy soldiers had made it to the top of the other ladder and began to jump to the ramparts. Spears impaled them as they fought a pitched battle.

Jan swung wildly, hacking the arms and legs of the soldiers that dropped down in front of him. The battlement swelled with enemy soldiers as they quickly piled over, making it impossible to swing a blade.

Jan held his shield up and screamed, "Push, lads! We got our first catch of the day!" The men pushed, leaning outward. Their numbers worked against the attackers; they could not get a solid foothold and they slipped to the inside wall and fell to the courtyard below. More than twenty men dropped to their deaths, but there were still many more left in the battle.

The soldiers continued to pile over the ladder. Petric smashed their heads open with his axe as he swung straight over the top. He hacked off their arms and crushed their spines, screaming like a raging beast.

Jan stabbed and cut at their legs from below, and the dead began to pile on the walls so much that they fell to the courtyard. Blood splashed Jan's helm as he stabbed and cut the throat of a soldier, and then wrestled with him as he died. He threw the body aside.

Petric's hands and arms were so covered with blood that he worried he might lose his grip on his axe if he were to swing it. He hooked their legs with his axe head and dragged them to the ground where he smashed his spiked shield into their faces. The crunch of enemy skulls shattering pleased him. He took a moment to wipe his bloody hands on a dead man's clothing and tested his grip on his axe. He nodded, satisfied.

Anne stood behind, watching the melee. The Dulimore forces on the ground crowded the ladder to attempt another climb. She could not tell who was winning because so many of the men were coated in blood. Anne lifted one of the spears littering the ground and threw it at the first man on the ladder. He was just stepping over the ramparts when the spear buried itself in his thigh. He slipped and fell back, taking two others with him. She tried to get to another spear and the men on the wall were forced back as the enemy swelled.

Jan could feel the battle turning against them. He killed a man with a stab to the stomach and cut the arm from another as he pushed to the wall. Petric deflected blows with his shield, then smashed his axe into his attacker's face.

Jan shouted to him, "We have to get that ladder down!"

Petric screamed wildly and dropped his shield. He gripped his axe with both hands, swinging again and again, crushing the skulls of soldiers. He killed half a dozen men as he chopped them like firewood. He took a slash to his stomach, and Jan plunged his sword into the eye of the man who struck the blow. The wound did not slow Petric; he continued to butcher men as he fought his way to the ladder. Jan tried to cover him by drawing the attackers to himself. He slashed and stabbed, throwing men from their advance. He took a stab to his leg and a gash on his shoulder. Petric ignored a deep cut to his leg and swung his axe over the wall. His axe struck the top rung of the ladder, splitting it. The ladder tilted and swayed to the right, and Petric swung at the man at the top, severing his foot.

The soldier's scream climbed up through the octaves with crazy ease. He put his bloody stump down but his leg locked in the ladder. He fell backwards, his leg still trapped, and the ladder tilted a little more. The ladder passed its tipping point and went over, throwing men in all directions. Their screams were brief but seemed to hang in the air for a long time.

There were only eight enemy soldiers left on the wall. Petric collapsed with his back to the stone. Jan took up Petric's shield and pushed the enemy back toward the battlement. "Kill them!" Petric cried as the men surged forward. Jan pushed two men over the wall, but the remaining few pushed back. He split the skull of one, from the crown of his head to his jaw, and slashed the leg of another. Jan's spearmen impaled several and tossed them from the wall to the courtyard.

Jan ran the final attacker through his stomach. The man wailed in pain as Jan twisted and jerked the sword free, pulling a length of intestines with it.

The men of Porin were covered in blood. Several sat against the battlements, moaning in pain.

Anne had blood and sweat on her face, but had been far enough from the main battle that she did not look nearly as horrific as the others. Jan knelt by Petric. "Old friend, I'd say we bought some time for ourselves."

Petric's armor was in tatters and shreds and his body was covered with ghastly wounds. His breath came in short pants and gasps. "We won the day, but they will return. I wish to die on the wall. Don't let them lock me away like an invalid." His eyes were wide and bright with panic at the thought of dying in bed.

Jan nodded and placed his hand on Petric's shoulder. "Rest; we all could use it."

Haim pressed his palm to a wound on the side of his face and stood beside Jan. "My lord, the enemy has retreated to the road."

Jan ignored his own pain and looked out over the wall. The Elgin and Dulimore soldiers had retrieved the broken ladder pieces and retreated north.

Anne stood next to him and looked down at the pile of dead attackers. She said, "My men will scout their camp. We may have a day or less until they attack again."

Jan sighed tiredly. "All right, men, let's toss this shit over the wall and get our wounded to the infirmary."

Haim leaned closer to Jan. "My lord, we should strip the bodies and collect weapons. There are men from the fields below that we can conscript if they're properly equipped."

Jan grunted his assent. "Collect their equipment, but we need to assess our numbers before we arm peasantry. Get Petric below and treat him first. We will need him tomorrow."

Petric smiled as the men lifted him, and Jan winked at him. Anne followed Jan down to the infirmary building. There were many men lying in the hallway and along the wall inside.

A man with a long beard and habit applied ointment to wounds, then wrapped them with bandages. A young boy assisted him. Jan stood watching over his shoulder. "Vogel, do you know the extent of the casualties?"

The elderly man looked up to him. "Seven dead, nineteen wounded, not counting yourself, sir."

Jan scratched his chin and looked around the room. "How many of the nineteen can still fight?"

Vogel handed the bandages to his apprentice and stood. "I believe all can fight in a day, possibly. The victory has lifted their spirits. Petric is the worst of them. I suspect he will not be fit to fight for days."

Jan looked sternly at Vogel. "Get them ready to fight, and when the scum return, I will hoist Petric to the wall myself."

Vogel nodded as Jan walked out of the infirmary. Anne followed after. "Do you think you can keep the ladder from the wall again?"

"I don't know." Jan walked to the throne room, removed his bloody gauntlets, and threw them on the table. "I won't leave, if that is what you're thinking."

Anne placed her hand on his arm and stared pointedly at Jan. "They took heavy losses. It would be the height of folly to attack again so soon. It is possible to beat them on the walls."

Jan struggled to remove his cuirass. "I just wonder what the hell is going on in Dawnbridge, and where your cousin is. I had hoped to see his lordship in all his glory when the battle came. Yet, here I stand, wanting."

CHAPTER 53

VIOLA STRUGGLED AS she awakened. Her entire body was wracked with pain and she lightly touched the swollen flesh around her eye. It was morning and the sun was barely on the western horizon.

She sat up in bed and was startled by Prince Henry. He looked horrible and his face was warped with a sadness so deep that it seemed to have been etched there with acid.

Viola could feel in the pit of her stomach that he had terrible news. "What has happened?" Her voice was weak, as if she could barely speak. "How long was I asleep?"

Henry looked away, fighting tears. "Edwin is dead, and so is Kate. My sister will not wake."

It felt like an icy fist was squeezing her heart, and anguish flooded through Viola's body. Tears flowed from her eyes and she lay in bed, overwhelmed by despair.

Henry wiped at his tears and sniffled. He got up and sat near her. "I am so sorry. There is news that Dulimore betrayed us. They have sided with Elgin and beaten the Elnoran army."

Viola did not respond; she could not. There were simply no words. It had all been such an adventure when they first started out, and now Kate and Edwin were gone. She could not believe it, but Kate was so badly wounded when last she saw her that it was impossible to not accept it.

She wiped the tears from her cheeks and put her hand to her mouth. "Where is he? Can I see him?"

Henry stood, holding out his hand. "Yes, the bodies arrived late in the night. They were wrapped and placed in the college tomb. No one will disturb them there."

Viola covered her face with her cloak and followed Henry. The castle was filled with soldiers as they went. The level of security must have been raised by news of the attack at Dawnbridge.

Soldiers stood guard in the courtyard, and the college circle was filled with more of them. Henry held out the key to the tomb as they entered a passageway behind the circle. "I will trust you with the key. Elnora will want Edwin's body, and we will hold Kate's until the siege in Dawnbridge is over."

Viola unlocked the door to the tomb, then held the key tight to her chest. Henry pushed the door open and Viola walked in. There were several candles burning in little alcoves around the walls. Henry took a torch from a wall sconce and followed her.

The bodies lay on top of sarcophagi in the middle of the room. Viola went to Edwin's corpse. It was completely wrapped in linen. She looked to Henry. "It is all right," he said softly; "you can open it." She gently uncovered his head and looked at him. She studied the face that was becoming dearer to her by the moment and kissed his forehead. Tears fell from her eyes onto Edwin's face. She wiped them away.

Viola swaddled his head again and went to Kate. Her face was badly bruised and showed visible wounds on her head. Viola softly traced her fingertips down the wounds and kissed her forehead. Viola sniffed and took a deep breath to try to keep her voice from breaking. She said, "I hope they won't be disturbed. When they are moved, I wish to travel with them. It will be our last journey together. One final adventure, and done."

Henry looked away from her. When Viola stopped she sat on a stool near a small table with a candle. He wanted to comfort her but just stood there uneasily. Viola looked up at him and saw the pain in his face. She realized she was not the only one suffering, but at least she might be able to do something to lessen Henry's grief. "Take me to your sister. She may yet live."

Henry and Viola returned to the castle. Zara's room was high above in the royal quarters. The stairwell wound around and took a long time to climb.

Henry stopped at the doorway; several people were already inside. A man in fine clothing stood over Zara's bed and the queen stood at the foot. She noticed Henry and came to the door. "It is awful," she said, wringing her hands in helpless frustration. "She will not wake up."

Viola looked to the woman. "She will. It will take a day, maybe a week, but she will recover."

The queen looked at her with the same annoyance one saves for a bothersome insect that won't be shooed away. "Who are you?"

"I am Princess Viola. I am surprised you do not recognize me from your husband kidnapping me," she answered sharply, then felt guilty. The woman was clearly in agony, caused by the deaths of Edwin and Kate and her fear of losing Zara.

Queen Priscilla looked chagrined but quickly recovered enough to say, "I am so sorry. I know what Edwin and Kate meant to you."

Viola's face twisted and collapsed into a ruin of sadness. Henry held her to his chest as she wailed with grief. Priscilla backed away into the room. Henry held Viola until she pushed herself away. She looked up at him. "Where is Lucien?"

"He sent Edwin and me to the south gate along the Free Marsh's border. I have no idea where he went from there."

Viola's brow creased with worry. "He will come here when he finds out. You must be wary of how he will react."

Henry shuddered involuntarily. "Do you know what he will do?"

"No, but when he comes, you should let me keep him under control. I can at least try to comfort him. He will be destroyed and I will do whatever it takes to keep him from going mad. It is what Kate would have wanted." Viola held her hands to her chest and leaned into Henry.

CHAPTER 54

DELVIN SAT IMPATIENTLY on the throne as Andres spoke quietly with Josephine. It had been over a day and Lucien had yet to wake. A messenger arrived and Delvin knew the news was dire.

Andres approached to his left, and Josephine stood to the right of him. Delvin shifted on the throne, nodding and scowling at what was obviously bad news. "All right, you two have been whispering in the corner for an hour. How bad is it?"

Andres looked to Josephine. "Lord Edwin is dead. He was killed in a battle at Crosshill, in Westfall. Lady Aela was also killed. I think it is important to tell Lucien as soon as he wakes."

Delvin stood and blew out an irritated breath. He turned to Andres with his fists clenched and his face hectic with red patches. "What, exactly, are you telling me? That Lucien will go mad with rage and tear the continent apart? That it is best to tell him as soon as possible to get it started?"

Andres scowled at Delvin. "He is weakened now. If we tell him, he will not be able to do much damage."

"Enough! Gods be damned, how did this happen?" Delvin punched his palm with his fist and paced under the dome.

Josephine cleared her throat, the sound of someone with bad news to deliver and not wanting to do so. "There is more, sire."

Delvin turned to her, his face still burning red. He nearly had tears in his eyes. "Gods, how could there be more?"

Andres walked down the steps and stood in front of Delvin. "Dulimore has joined with Elgin. They have begun a siege of Dawnbridge. Our army was destroyed. They were betrayed just as they had victory at hand."

Delvin raised his chin. His lips were set in a haughty pout. "You are wrong, those fools deserve Lucien. Let him rest, and when he wakes, he can wipe them from the surface of this world." He started to turn away, then turned back abruptly. "What word is there of Alaric? Does he live? I am not sure I can stand to break the news to his wife and children."

Andres looked down, an unconscious tell that Delvin knew well. His eyes widened. "There is still more?" He laughed as if he had gone mad. "That bitch Elena is more cunning than that weasel-shit father of hers."

"Alaric is alive, but Lady Anne is trapped in Port Porin. They have a siege there. I am not sure if either city even stands as I speak. We are a day behind." Andres looked meekly at Delvin.

Delvin approached the stairs to the throne. He looked up at Josephine. "Where have they taken Edwin and the girl?"

"Charbel; Princess Viola and Princess Zara were taken there. They were both badly wounded. With the frost coming, they will hold the bodies until it is safe to return them."

Delvin tugged his beard and looked to Andres. "Recommendations?"

Andres glanced at Josephine. "What can we do? Do you wish to lift the siege at Port Porin?"

Delvin dropped his gaze to the floor. "I cannot save both. I am less than a quarter the man I used to be. If this is a trick to draw me out, or Lucien, the island will be defenseless."

Josephine stumbled over her words and took a step toward Delvin. "You cannot...will not...leave us defenseless."

Delvin held his hand up to her. "Calm yourself, I have no intention. We must push them back. We cannot let them take everything. Andres, raise my levy and ready the ships."

Delvin stormed out of the throne room. Andres watched him leave and then turned to glare at Josephine.

Delvin went to Lucien's chambers and drew back the curtains.. Sunlight beamed into the room. It was bright and illuminated his face. He stood impatiently, feeling his pulse pounding behind his eyes and in his neck. He grabbed Lucien and shook him. "Wake up, we are running out of time and you lie there sleeping!" Delvin threw him back on the bed, and Lucien's red eyes opened with great effort.

Lucien's insides were raw from all of his recent exertions. Everything inside him felt dug out. Clearing his vision he saw King Delvin standing at his bed, his face angry and touched with more than a hint of madness. "What -- ?" he began.

Delvin grabbed him again, digging his nails into Lucien's flesh. Lucien opened his eyes wide. "They are dead! Edwin and Kate! We have no time left. You have to go to Dawnbridge to save what is left of everything. My dream, our dream, is falling apart."

The raw tearing at his stomach was replaced by an endless cavern of despair, and Lucien could not contain his sadness. Nor did he want to. His eyes prickled with tears, and he reached out his hand for his father. "It can't be true?" he asked weakly; it was almost the voice of a child asking for hope or comfort. He received neither.

Delvin slapped his hand away and stood defiant and proud next to the bed. "It is true. Lady Anne and Alaric may already be dead. Dulimore has betrayed us. They have stolen our dream. You must lift the siege at Dawnbridge, and go to Charbel. Viola lives and she will let you see Kate and Edwin's bodies."

"My dream is dead. I have nothing left to live for." Lucien wailed in agony. He pushed his face into the pillow, trying to keep from dying inside.

Delvin grabbed him and pulled his face close to his. "This is just the beginning. They will always take from you. You have little left to live for, and even that will be gone soon if you do not crawl from that bed. You will rise from that pit of despair and find a reason to go on."

Lucien opened his mouth to speak, but the sadness gripped his chest and there were no words. They were all too small for something this vast. His face twitched as he fought his tears. Delvin released him. Lucien sat on the edge of the bed.

"Here, there is not much time. Lift the siege at Dawnbridge. I will relieve Port Porin. I don't care what you do after that." Delvin tossed Lucien his cloak.

Lucien rocked on the side of the bed. He pushed thoughts of Kate's smile from his mind and replaced it with images of her bloody and broken body. The anger built in him, replacing his despair, filling his emptiness with a burning rage and implacable need for revenge.

With a push of pain, he teleported to Dawnbridge.

CHAPTER 55

T HE WHINE AND crack of timber filled the still
afternoon air. The rope popped as it released, and the
boulder seemed to momentarily float in the air. Then,
gravity took hold and the boulder plummeted to earth. It
smashed into a roof, collapsing two buildings. One may have
been a privy.

A red cape fluttered in the wind. "You missed again. That
is four throws you have missed. I refuse to wait another day for
boulders. You have just twelve left. The wall is nearly collapsed."
Rabin snarled and barked at the men.

The soldiers loaded another boulder onto the rail; the creak
of wood and groan of rope could be heard as the trebuchet
ratcheted back to be reloaded.

The soldier looked up at Commander Rabin. "I am sorry,
lord, but these boulders are not of the same size. It is hard to
measure the distance when the weight keeps changing."

"Try harder," Rabin commanded.

The soldiers pushed the boulder into the sling and then stood
behind. A crack and whirl of the arm as it twisted and tossed

another boulder high into the air. It fell well short of its mark, tumbling and bouncing along the ground before coming to rest against the city wall.

Rabin sneered and shook his head. "You imbeciles."

The trebuchet sat idle as Elias watched from near the high tower on the wall. His vision was not what it once was. Brian stood next to him. He appeared more at ease today. His face was washed and his clothes cleaned.

"I think the lad in the cape is giving the crew a what-for, from the looks of it." Elias squinted, looking out over the field.

Brian suppressed a smile. "Uncouth rabble, my lord."

Elias leaned over the wall and looked at its façade directly beneath them. There were huge pockmarks throughout the patchwork of stone and wood. It was nearly half-collapsed. The city had several fires, and many buildings had fallen in the streets. "What a mess."

Brian turned to assess the city below. "Nothing we cannot repair."

Elias raised an eyebrow and sniffed imperiously. "I do hope that you have not been getting into the wine. I will be hurt if you did and had not shared."

Brian smiled. "No, my lord, I just feel that we are in a good position still. There were over three hundred enemies killed in the battle at the east gate. Alaric has taken command of the remainder of his army and the castle guard is still at full strength. Things are looking up, and I have an unquenchable thirst for revenge."

Elias leaned back as Alaric approached; his arm was still in a sling. "Lords, I have nearly a hundred and fifty fighting men. What is the latest count of our enemy?"

Brian turned, nodding to Alaric. "Around four hundred. They are a patchwork of Dulimore and Elgin forces."

Alaric smiled. "That does not sound too bad. They are having trouble with the wall. We are getting rested while they look like fools." He leaned forward to see the damage to the city. He considered and said, "Still, they are making a hell of a mess."

Alaric grabbed Brian and Elias turned. He pointed to the courtyard. "Lucien."

CHAPTER 56

L UCIEN GRABBED HIS stomach and fell to his knees. He had ported to just in front of the castle. There was dust and smoke in the air around him. He covered his mouth with his sleeve as he coughed. His sleeve came away with blood.

The port took so much from him that he could barely stand. His knees threatened to buckle as he climbed the steps to the castle. The gate was open and there were people huddled inside. The entire room was filled with refugees and items that people had saved.

Lucien did not recognize anyone and walked leaning against the wall to keep from falling. He turned only for someone to embrace him. "Gods be praised, you finally showed up. I wasn't sure if we were going to pull through this."

The man released him and Lucien found himself looking into the teary eyes of Alaric. Alaric knew as soon as he looked at his face that Lucien knew. "I am sorry." They embraced as Lucien held tight to him.

Lucien saw Brian approach behind Alaric. His face was stoic.

"I need to lift the siege. I can barely stand. Someone help me to the battlements." Lucien put his arm around Alaric. They walked and Brian grabbed Lucien to help him up the stairwell.

Brian grunted as he carried Lucien. "I think we have a ton of questions, but we can start by telling you how grateful we are to see you."

Alaric managed a smile as they reached the top. They walked out near the tower just in time to see another boulder sail high over the wall.

Alaric ducked as it passed by. "Gods, if those fools had any accuracy we would be in a world of hurt."

Lucien leaned forward, bracing himself against the wall and looked out over the field. There were several rows of soldiers standing by as the crews worked the siege engine.

Alaric leaned next to him. "What do you think?"

Lucien thought for a moment. "I will burn the trebuchet. That should slow them down. I barely have much energy for anything else."

King Elias moved between Brian and Lucien. "If you burn that, we will be safe for days. I doubt they will continue; their morale is low already."

Lucien turned to Alaric. "What do you think of the plan?"

He studied his eyes, trying to find out how he really felt. "What then?"

"I will see Viola in Charbel."

Alaric held Lucien's shoulder. "If you cannot make Charbel, port near the walls. We will get you."

Lucien's eyes filled with tears as he pushed the sadness aside. Time for that later. All the rest of his life, in fact. He blew out a shuddering breath. "I will. We will get our revenge."

"I look forward to it," Brian said, clapping Lucien on the back.

Lucien stood away from them, and ported to the field by the trebuchet. The men did not even notice him. He simply walked the short distance to the siege engine and touched the timbers at the base. They quickly turned to smoldering embers and the siege engine collapsed to its side with a roar like some great beast dying.

The men turned to see Lucien's red eyes glaring at them. They shouted in terror and ran. He casually ignited the rest of the timbers, and flames climbed like burning vines on a trellis. It was a full conflagration in moments.

Astride his horse, Rabin pulled his sword and charged. Lucien simply vanished.

Blood ran from Lucien's mouth onto the stone street. He lay looking up at the college circle archway. Soldiers gathered around him, stunned by what they just witnessed.

CHAPTER 57

JAN STOOD BEFORE the men in the courtyard. Haim had salvaged what he could from the dead soldiers and disposed of their bodies over the wall. The seven men of Porin who died were buried inside the tomb beneath the small chapel.

Jan surveyed the men. "A wild lot of rabble, if I do say so."

Anne scoffed and folded her arms. They were twenty farmers, but now armed as soldiers. It was a sorry sight; most barely could stand up straight.

"Drill them. It is nearly sundown and we need every eye on the walls to make sure they don't sneak in while we slumber. Two-hour shifts." Jan nodded as he finished instructions to Haim.

"I have an idea." Anne said, following him into the castle.

Jan waved his hand over his shoulder as he made his way to the throne room.

"It might work," Anne wheedled.

Jan stopped and turned to look at her longingly. "Girls, you? You're a true beauty."

Anne looked insulted. "Who told you?" Realization dawned on her face and she pointed to the chambers above. "Ah. Lucien, I am sure."

Jan grinned. "He is a man of true honor. I always fancied you. You were something and I was a cad. There could have been music between us."

Anne rolled her eyes. "I am...you are a scoundrel."

"Devilishly handsome though." Jan gently clasped her hand. He leaned close, whispering, "I could pleasure you...endlessly."

Anne shook her head. What a character Jan was. "You know you're the only man to ever speak to me this way. It must be part of your privilege of being archduke. How, I wonder, did you turn out to be such a rogue while your father was a perfect gentleman?"

"Switched at birth with the maid's son, I'm afraid. My father was a bit stuffy, and I am sure Celia is a chip off that weathered block. I like to keep it lively." He saw she was not going to rise to the bait this time. "All right, fine, give me this plan of yours." Jan crossed his arms, giving her a heavy dose of skepticism.

Anne laughed deviously. "I want to send my spies to the enemy camp in the dead of night. They will put a digestive relief potion in their water and soup cauldron. By morning they will be in a right state."

Jan sighed and shook his head vigorously. "I am glad you care for the enemy's colon so much, but how exactly does that help us?"

Anne looked puzzled. "Did I say digestive relief? I meant digestive release. They will be at the privy for hours."

Jan laughed and clapped, but then grew serious. "Do it, and double the dose for Petric's sake." He continued with a silly grin.

Anne shook her head as she left the room. Jan sat with his back to the table, watching her backside sway as she left.

"A travesty."

CHAPTER 58

E LIAS AND BRIAN both laughed as the trebuchet burned before them. They could not help but lift their arms and holler as the men ran from the sight of Lucien.

Brian screamed to them, "That is just the beginning, you worthless scum, a foretaste of the hell you will spend eternity in! You will all burn soon!"

They could see Rabin wave his men from the field and it appeared they were withdrawing. Hurrahs and cheers rang around the walls of the castle and men hugged each other. King Elias held Brian by the shoulder. "I fear they will be back soon enough, but we can rest for a day or two."

Brian patted him on the chest as they both moved to the southern portion of the wall. Brian looked down. "I will get the carpenters to work."

Elias held his hand to Brian's chest. "Send men to Dulimore, and why not take some stone? I think it will be our reparations."

Brian grinned broadly. "As you wish, my lord. The masons will be pleased to have the work."

Alaric stood silently as he watched the Elgin men break camp. He did not celebrate. Elias walked to stand beside him. They looked out over the field together. Elias put his hand on Alaric's shoulder. "We won, but we paid a heavy price."

Alaric put his hand on Elias's shoulder without looking. "In a day or two, Lucien will return. They will wish they never lived. I am not sure he will leave any alive."

"What comes will come. Lucien has a great power and like his father before him, he will learn how it is never enough." Elias stepped away from Alaric's touch, leaving him alone on the wall.

CHAPTER 59

THE GUARDS SCREAMED and ran through the streets. Lucien's body was taken to the castle as men yelled to summon the prince.

Henry ran through the hallways and pushed open Viola's door. Smoke billowed from the doorway and filled the room. "Gods," he said, coughing; "what has happened?"

Viola tried to fan the smoke away. She yelled from the corner, "I forgot to open the flue. I have the windows open."

Henry rubbed his stinging eyes, trying to look around the room. There were flasks and vials lying everywhere. Both of the fireplaces were roaring as pots and cauldrons lay around their base, and the bubble of boiling liquid filled the air "What the hell are you doing? It is like a witch's laboratory."

Viola yelled at him angrily, "There have been no witches for five hundred years. Stop with that nonsense. I practice science, plain and simple."

Henry covered his eyes, trying to move toward her voice in the smoke. "Fine, fine, but what the hell are you making?"

Viola saw him approach through eddies of smoke and pushed flasks around on the table near the fireplace. "I lost the love of my life. I need to keep busy so I have a sense of purpose. I am making some soups and potions. I found so many ingredients around the courtyard and the college that, if I didn't know better, I'd say there used to be an alchemist here."

Henry had homed in on her voice through the smoke and stood close to her. "There have never been any witches here."

The swelling around Viola's blackened eye had receded, allowing her to roll her eyes at him with contempt. "Humph, what do you want? I am very busy, as you can see."

"They found Lucien lying in the street. I wanted to know if you would let him stay in here. You said you wanted to watch after him, in case...well, in case." Henry frowned into the smoke and realized he was talking to the bed post. Viola had walked away.

Henry stumbled over some flasks as he tried to locate her again. "Viola?" He finally made it to the doorway just as she took the stairwell at the end of the hall.

Viola opened the door and saw the guards were carrying Lucien's body inside. "Quickly, take him to my room. It is up the stairwell."

The men struggled on the narrow stairway as Viola followed behind. They reached the top. Henry watched with his hands on his hips when Viola passed. She shrugged with a superior smirk and kept pace with the men. The smoke had spread from the room and now filled the hallway as they approached her chambers. Inside, it had cleared enough that the men could see their way.

Viola pointed to her bed. "Put him there."

The men looked at each other and then at her. "Isn't that your bed?"

Viola tilted her head with annoyance. The men shrugged but laid him on the bed. Viola quickly pulled off his boots and his trousers.

The men watched, dumfounded. She waved them away with a flip of her hand. "Be gone, I am working."

Viola struggled to get his shirt off and finally did. Lucien lay in just his underwear. His face and stomach bore wounds that were not fully healed. She looked him over and selected one of her flasks. She lifted his head and poured just a small amount of the contents into his mouth.

Lucien sputtered and coughed; he could barely open his eyes. "Where am I?" He looked around the room, finally focusing on Viola. "I am so sorry. I should never have left her."

Viola cupped his head and pushed her body close to him. She put her cheek to his. "It will be all right. Just don't leave me too. It is just us now, and everything will work out, I promise."

Lucien moaned, unable to move, and his eyes grew heavier and harder to keep open. "What did you feed me? It tasted terrible."

Viola held up the flask, smelling it, "I am insulted. That was my turtle soup. I only gave you a sip." She drank some from the flask and smiled with enjoyment.

She sat the soup down on the table and brought another potion to Lucien. His eyes widened as she tilted it into his mouth. "What is this?"

Viola smiled deviously. "Something to make sure you don't wake up for a while."

Lucien struggled and tried to stop from drinking, but she held his head firmly and poured until he swallowed it, coughing and choking. His struggles lasted for just a moment, then grew weaker, then stopped altogether. He lay motionless on the bed.

Viola shook her head as she scrubbed at the spot where he spilled some soup on her sheets. "You're just like Edwin," she scolded. "Everywhere you go, you make messes."

CHAPTER 60

THE WIND BLEW hard from the east. Jan's men were covered with blankets as they looked out at the composite forces below. The cold morning air was a welcome relief. It would keep the men from another attempt at the walls.

Jan had observed the enemy digging latrines in the frosty ground for most of the morning. Haim stood beside him as they both turned west to see the sun rising. "Do you think we have another day?"

"At least," Jan answered. He smiled at Haim. "Those men will be filling the latrines most of the day. The weather has given me even more confidence." Jan walked along the wall, surveying the men. He nodded to Haim. "Leave only a quarter of the men on watch, and rotate every two hours. I want them fresh for when they do attack." Haim turned and walked along the battlement, moving men from their positions.

Jan took the stairwell down to the infirmary. He circled the room, inspecting the wounded. It had been a day since the attack and only nine remained in need of treatment. Petric took a horrible beating and was still the worst of them. Jan stood next to him as he slept. His body was covered in a crisscross of bandages. The cloying smell of ointment and salves hovered over Petric's sleeping body like a foul mist.

Vogel approached with a young boy who was in apprenticeship. "Good day, my lord. He is doing well," he said, looking down at Petric. He adjusted a bandage that had come loose, then nodded his satisfaction.

Jan turned, surveying the room. "The others?"

"They should all be on their feet by tomorrow."

Jan once more circled the room to see their wounds. "Be sure to clear the room and prepare for triage. There will be more wounded in the morning."

"We will be ready," Vogel promised solemnly.

Jan entered the hallway, and Anne was there. "Well, it worked. I saw them digging latrines this morning."

Jan laughed, "Don't get carried away. That western wind did just as much to stop their attack. I think we might have another day."

Anne followed Jan to the throne room. She watched as Jan took a roll from a plate. He took half of it into his mouth with a hearty bite. He sat back and hung his leg over the armrest of the throne. "So, darling, what is your plan for today?"

Anne rolled her eyes, looking away. "We wait."

"Wait? That is the best idea you have come to yet," Jan said, spraying the air with speckles of the roll he was chewing.

"Is there word on Dawnbridge?"

Anne took an apple from the table. She sat down, crossing her legs. "Yes, Lucien lifted the siege. A rider took all night to get here."

Jan sat upright in the throne, eyes wide. "That is interesting. Did they say where he went?"

"They did," Anne said, her voice breaking. "Edwin is dead, and so is Lady Kate. He went to Charbel to see their bodies."

Jan sat back in his chair, staring at the other end of the room. He looked disgusted. "I would ask what happened, but with the betrayal and the siege, I can imagine. It seems there is no white knight to save us."

Anne put her apple down and looked at Jan sternly. "We have a strong chance to hold. They have just over two hundred men left. We have nearly fifty men now."

Jan leaned forward, wiping at this chin. "We have thirty-three men, half of whom are wounded. There are twenty peasants dressed like soldiers who will be ground into pig feed if we put them in combat. Those men are farmers, horse breeders, and laborers. They are this city, and I won't piss them into the wind trying to meet the enemy on equal numbers, no matter what Haim thinks. We use them as guards, and if we are losing, they can fight if there is no other option."

"I guess you could tell what I was thinking. I did not think a surprise attack would be on your mind," Anne said with a frown.

"No," Jan said firmly as he stood. "What of Elnora? Would they send us no aid?"

Anne sighed and admitted, "I don't know. The wind to the west would keep the ships from approaching anyway. They would be stuck at sea waiting for better weather, even if they were sending any."

Jan laughed and said, "Well, let us hope the wind of fortune will blow on us, then."

CHAPTER 61

VIOLA CONTINUED TO pace her room, making busywork for herself by moving flasks around. She emptied her satchel on the table and put four flasks inside. Opening the door to the hall, the guards turned to her. She growled at them testily. "I wish to visit Zara. I really wish I did not have to check in everywhere I went. I have nowhere to go other than here and the tomb at the college."

The guard said simply, "Or Lady Zara."

Viola ignored him and walked down the hallway to the stairwell. She had been to the royal quarters only once before. It was a maze of passageways.

The guard outside Zara's room barely looked at her when she reached the top of the spiral stairwell. The door to Zara's room was open and the apothecary was washing his hands in the basin.

Viola stopped at the door to wait for him. He looked up with a smile. "You may enter."

Viola sat down gently next to Zara on the bed and the apothecary stood beside her. He introduced himself: "I am Samuel, or you can call me that. She does not appear to wake. The wound has shown improvement, however."

Viola looked at Zara's leg. There was still a swollen groove, but no signs of infection. The injury had stopped bleeding and appeared to be healing.

Samuel stood over her, watching with keen interest. "What are your thoughts? I am told you have done healing before."

Viola laughed nervously, making a show of moving her flasks around. "No, I just make soup. It helps keep up the spirits so people can heal."

"Soup, right. It is not a crime to be a witch."

"I am not a witch," Viola shouted. She stomped her foot and threw her hands up.

Samuel raised his hands in mock-surrender. "I am sorry, I meant herbalist. It is not uncommon, given the lack of access to resources, for people to dabble in making their own medicine."

Viola looked away, her face still red. "And you, I am sure you only follow rigid medicine."

Samuel chuckled warmly. "I do what is necessary, just as you would. If you can heal her, I would suggest you do so. It would show a lot of goodwill for the family, and I can tell you are uncomfortable here after the...erm, I suppose I should say... kidnapping."

Viola felt a tightness in her chest. She was not in favor here, and they would not let her leave. If Zara did not recover, she would never leave this place unless under guard as a bride to one of the princes.

Viola pulled her hair back into a tail. "If you leave me, I will heal her. She may not wake 'til morning, however."

Samuel nodded. "I will not disturb you." He left, closing the door softly behind him. Viola watched the door, listening intently for any sound from the other side that might indicate she was being spied on, but there was nothing.

Viola leaned her ear close to Zara's nose and listened. She reached in her satchel and took a small wood vial out. She dipped her pinky into the vial, then held it under Zara's nose.

Zara shifted in bed and moaned. Her eyes were yellow and unfocused when she opened them. That was her only reaction.

Viola leaned close and said softly, "Try to stay quiet. I need you to drink some soup."

Zara did not move as Viola raised her head and poured chunky liquid from a flask into her mouth. She was careful to pour just a small amount and wait until she swallowed. Viola repeated this until the flask was empty.

Zara had a pleasant hum to her as she drank the liquid. She closed her eyes. Viola leaned close and, in the same soft voice, said, "I will come back in the morning. Just lie still and be quiet 'til then."

Viola gathered her bag and went to the door. She opened it and stepped into the hall. Samuel stood across from the door and approached her. Viola noticed Henry coming. She whispered to Samuel, "Leave her be 'til morning. I will return."

Henry's brow furrowed as he pushed Samuel away from Viola. "What are you doing here? Your instructions were to stay with Lucien or visit the tomb."

Viola took a step down the hall, trying to slowly move away. "I wished to see her, is all. We became fast friends before."

Henry put his hands on his hips. "Fast friends? You seduced me and escaped with her help. You are both criminals by all accounts. You are not to see her alone."

Viola's heart raced and her face reddened. "Samuel was with me the entire time. He only left for a moment, as I needed to check womanly things with Zara."

Henry's arms dropped and he rubbed the back of his neck. His eyes avoided hers. "Oh, well. I did not know. I wish to speak to you in private. Maybe we can go to your room?"

Viola did not want to speak to him, but what could she say? She turned and he followed her down the stairwell. She had thoughts of putting pace to her steps, getting ahead of him, reaching her room first and slamming the door in his face. He was kind to her, but she knew what his father wanted from overhearing the conversations around the castle. James, his scoundrel brother, needed a wife. With Edwin dead, they wanted to keep her here permanently.

Viola entered her room quickly when they arrived. She hesitated a moment too long, and Henry was in the room and closing the door. He looked down at Lucien, perturbed. "Why is he in your bed?"

Viola fumbled about, trying to solve several problems with one answer. She decided to wing it and said, "Um, I...well, I hate to admit such a thing. We were secret lovers. Now that Kate is gone, we can finally be together. Lucien just turned seventeen, so we will likely marry." Viola fluttered about the room, moving things and putting them back.

"You...and Lucien," Henry said without emotion. He could not help but make the statement sound ridiculous. "Nearly every person who has seen you together swears you despise him."

Viola wandered around the room, looking for something that didn't exist as she thought. "Well, we are very good at hiding our lust for each other. Edwin certainly never knew."

Henry crossed his arms, tilting his head to the side. "It is convenient that you are lovers, seeing as I am in search of a wife, and so is my brother."

Viola let her hair down and tossed it about with a nervous laugh. "I had no idea. Lucien and I are just so randy for each other that I never pay attention to such things."

Henry's eyes narrowed. "I am sure you are." He stood beside the bed, studying Lucien. It was difficult to believe Viola could be in such a relationship, but who could understand the female heart? Henry smiled coyly. "Why not kiss him, then? You have not seen each other in some time," he suggested smarmily. "I would feel more confident in the truth of your statement if you kissed him." He paused for effect, then added: "On the mouth."

Viola nearly gasped, but caught herself at the last moment, making an odd, purring sound instead. She moved on tiptoes to the edge of the bed. She side-eyed Henry the entire time as she slowly lowered her face to Lucien's and pecked him on the lips. A bird catching a worm could not have pecked more quickly.

Henry laughed. "That was a very sweet kiss…if he was your brother. I want you to kiss him for real."

Viola put her hands on her hips. "I am not an exhibitionist." She looked at Lucien and really saw him for the first time. He was cute lying in her sheets, and it had been surprisingly thrilling to strip off his clothes.

Viola leaned down and put her mouth over his without hesitation this time. She moved her lips over his, tasting him. She gently sucked his lower lip, then released it. A little reluctantly, she realized. She looked up, focusing the anger for herself at Henry. "I hope you're satisfied."

Henry gasped as his eyes widened. "I am very satisfied. It was difficult to believe."

Viola laughed obnoxiously. "Thank the gods, because this marriage between us or James, that is just not possible."

"We'll see about that," Henry said with an undercurrent of menace, and opened the door. He spun back to Viola as he closed the door. "Lucien won't sleep forever."

Viola bit her fingers worrying over Lucien. His lips were soft and sensual, and she felt something while kissing him. It was in her heart now that he was always nice to her and fun in a jester sort of way. The idea of someone besides Edwin had never occurred to her.

Viola brushed his hair back, feeling the butterflies flitting about in her stomach, her chest, but then worry quickly killed them. *What will he say when I tell him of my ruse? How will he be without Kate?*

CHAPTER 62

THE SUN WAS in the east as Alaric walked the empty field. His arm was no longer in the sling, and he periodically straightened and flexed it, moving it to regain mobility. His shoulder was painful and stiff, but he could grip a sword and the tightness was beginning to loosen the more he moved it.

The Elnoran bodies from the east gate had all been loaded onto wagons so they could be taken to South Pier. Alaric watched as the wagons made their way along the road far to the south.

He walked along the flat, grassy plain north of Dawnbridge. There were random articles of waste, clothing, and a few weapons. Several soldiers combed the ground with their swords.

He turned northeast; the opening to the castle extended until it came to a swampy marshland on the border with Westfall. The ground was soft and spongy as he reached the Dulimore camp. There were a lot of articles left behind: pots, pans, and other things that the soldiers duly loaded into crates and sacks. A horse wagon already stacked high with goods headed to the city. There would be another load ready by the time the wagon returned.

Alaric walked through the camp, searching the ground and looking into the tents that had been left. A soldier approached carrying a crate. "It is some scrolls from the command tent."

Alaric looked in the crate. There were several scrolls and he took one at random and unrolled it. It was a map of the mountain. He did not recognize anything there. He put it back into the crate and looked at the soldier. "Walk this to the city and to the adviser's house. Do not give them to anyone but Lord Brian O'Neill. You are to stay there until he arrives, and hand them personally to him."

The soldier nodded. "Yes, commander."

Alaric watched the soldier hurry along with the crateful of scrolls. He hoped they contained something useful. He continued searching through the camp until he heard a soldier call to him: "Commander, you better see this."

A soldier waved Alaric over to a tent. Two other soldiers were at the tent flap, and they led him inside. There was a Dulimore soldier lying on a cot. His leg was smashed below the knee.

The man lay panting as he struggled with pain. "Lord, please help me. I will cooperate and tell you anything. I was just a baker when they took me. That sinister machine, it fell when the demon boy burned it. I was too slow to flee, and my lads helped me here. Rabin - I don't know who is worse, him or the demon boy - told them to leave me."

Alaric knelt next to the man. His leg was in bad shape, but Alaric had seen worse. He stood and gestured to the soldiers. "Search for the blacksmith or bloodletter. I want you to get a cart and horse here to take him to the city. See if we can help this man."

Alaric pulled an animal skin from his waist. "It is water. What is your name?"

The man grabbed the skin and drank the water, spilling almost as much as he swallowed. His stomach roiled uneasily. "Cesik," he answered. "You are kind, lord. I will tell you all I can."

Alaric had more questions than he could ask in the tent, and Elias would have his own. He put his hand on the man's chest. "Rest. They will want to know everything."

CHAPTER 63

THE SUN HAD set and darkness fell on Porin. The moons were obscured by overcast sky, and the wind from the east had died down. In the distant north, guards on the ramparts could see torches moving south toward the castle.

The guard nodded to the man at his left. "Fetch his lordship; they are preparing to attack."

"I do not see what you get out of the relationship," Jan's elbows were on the table, his head in his hands. Anne sat next to him at the long table in the throne room.

Anne smiled and leaned in as close as a pickpocket. "Use your imagination," she suggested slyly.

Jan smiled his own sly smile and lifted his eyebrows. "I can imagine a great many things."

A soldier threw the door open. "My lord, there are torches coming toward the castle from the north."

All thoughts of romance and seduction vanished. Jan jumped to his feet and began gathering his armor. Anne helped him. "How many?"

The soldier shook his head and shrugged. "All of them, lord. I swear, it seems like they have doubled in number"

"Gods," Jan said, and pulled the cuirass straps tighter to his neck. "Gather the men, I will get Petric."

Jan ran to the infirmary. It was already alive and bustling as the men had begun preparing. He nodded his approval and went to Petric, who sat on his bunk as men helped pull his armor over his head. "Well, old friend, it looks like we have another battle to fight."

Petric smiled. "Too much easy living has made me soft."

Jan tried a weak smile but couldn't quite manage it. Instead, he gave a nod. "Well, there won't be too much more of that." Jan gave Petric's shoulder a comradely pat. "Get him to the battlements." The men continued to work on Petric and Jan left the room. He climbed the stairs to the walls and looked out over the field. The ladder was nearly to the wall as the men gathered along the battlements.

Jan yelled to his men: "Steady, they will have that damned ladder up again! Gods, you'd think this was a brothel, as determined as they are to get in."

They had been lucky in fending off the ladder from the wall, but the invaders would know their defense tactics now and would be prepared for them. The clunk of the ladder hitting the wall below bought Jan out of his reverie. He ordered his men to raise their spears.

The men gathered around the ladder as several lit torches were thrown over the wall at them. Some men were struck in the face, while others' arms, thrown up in defense, were set on fire. They panicked, screamed, and ran, only making the fire burn brighter.

"Water, get water to the wall!" Jan yelled. He ran to pat out the flames on one man, but more torches flew over the wall and landed in their midst.

They fought with the flames. Jan looked up and saw Dulimore soldiers coming over the wall at him. Jan drew his sword, cutting the man's leg in the same fluid motion. He pushed him off to the courtyard below. Another came and Jan slashed his throat. He made a liquid sound like he was gargling, then collapsed at Jan's feet.

Men one by one climbed to the wall from the ladder. The defenders were pushed steadily back, no matter how many attackers they killed. Petric stood with his axe high, then brought it down to chop the head from a soldier. The Dulimore soldiers pushed several defenders from the wall as they struggled for position, and with every defender they pushed back, the Dulimore numbers swelled.

Petric hacked the arm off of a man and then took another's hand at the wrist with his axe. He had suffered several grievous wounds, but continued to fight, continued to wreak carnage with his great axe.

Jan's men struggled to hold ground as Petric's side of the breach collapsed. Jan could see Petric jump to the stable roof as his men were cut down. The few men left with Jan fought as they paced backwards, ever backwards.

Jan stabbed a man through the neck and slashed at the legs of another. He deflected a blow with his shield, then sliced through the stomach of his attacker. He parried another and disarmed him. Jan kicked the man's knee, breaking it and causing him to fall forward, where Jan impaled him on his sword. He looked into the man's eyes as he died.

Anne stood at Jan's side, cutting and stabbing the invaders, killing nearly as many as Jan. It all turned bad in just a moment. She took a stab to her stomach, and a spear sliced through her side. She stumbled and fell.

Jan helped her up. The enemy had over fifty men on the wall by now and Jan could sense defeat. "Take everyone in the keep and block the doors."

Anne pressed at her wounds, trying to staunch the bleeding as she limped down the stairwell to gather the women and children into the keep.

Jan felt the end growing near as the men to his front fell one by one to the courtyard. He backed up, parrying and thrusting. A blue light on the ocean south of the castle caught his eye. He sliced the throat of a man and looked again. There were three Elnoran ships heading for the coast. "Retreat! Every man to the keep, now! Move," Jan screamed as he turned to run.

CHAPTER 64

"MY KING, THEY appear to nearly be defeated," Andres told Delvin, watching the battle from his place at the bow.

King Delvin stood in brilliant silver armor. Aquamarine stones decorated the plates throughout. Delvin held a staff with a runestone the size of a man's fist that burned with blue fire. The guard approached from behind and placed a crown on his head. The crown was made of gold with aquamarine stones on the tips.

Delvin faced away from Andres. "Use your men to clear the castle. I will deal with the men in the field."

Andres said, "Show them no mercy."

King Delvin's eyes burned a powerful, glowing blue, as blue as the stones in his armor and crown. His teeth crackled with energy. "When have I ever shown mercy?" He raised the staff and a pedestal of water rose from the sea. Delvin stepped from his ship onto the platform of water. It lifted him into the air and carried him to the shore.

He raised his staff and the water spread out, lowering him to the ground. He tilted his staff flat and the water spread to the enemy soldiers. Veins of water crawled across the ground and they formed into snakes as they traveled.

A hundred men or more stood at the base of the ladder attempting to climb, but turned to run when they saw the glowing blue light. They screamed in horror as the snakes of water came writhing toward them.

Delvin leaned his staff to the sky. He tilted his head and the snakes wrapped around the men and swelled into serpents. They twisted and tore the men apart. The popping and crushing of bones could be heard even over their terrible death-screams.

Delvin walked toward the screaming soldiers as others still tried to escape past him. Raising his hand high in the air, a massive snake formed and bit down, cutting a man in half.

The water returned to Delvin and formed under him, lifting him into the air. His staff glowed brightly and shot a blast of energy like sun rays that cut the rest of the fleeing men to pieces.

Andres' men battled with the overmatched soldiers at the castle walls. Delvin panted heavily as his mouth filled with blood. He had to keep spitting it out. He leaned on his staff, fatigued. He watched as Andres routed the enemy; many more fell to their knees in surrender.

King Delvin wiped the blood from his mouth. He used his staff for balance as he approached Andres. He was giving instructions for the prisoners.

"The walls are secure," Delvin said, and released a strained breath.

Andres put his hand on the king's shoulder. "Routed with ease, your majesty. You can take quarters in the castle once we get the gate opened. Jan took the defenders inside as we approached."

Delvin nodded and walked to the gate. There were bodies strewn about the courtyard, and his men tended to the wounded. Petric was conscious as they lay him next to the stables.

Delvin's men pounded on the gate, crying, "Open up, it is Elnora! We have them routed."

The dragging of metal and a thud was heard on the other side, followed by voices. The gate opened. Jan's worn and battered face peered out cautiously. "We have wounded here if you can help. We took a terrible beating."

King Delvin gazed upon Jan. "I believe the enemy has been dealt with."

Jan looked concerned. "I had not expected such a visit, your majesty. We can make quarters for you and Andres here in the manor."

"No need, my men will clear the hill north. We will camp there." Delvin spoke sternly, and his words were curt. His temperament was impatient. "Where is Anne? I wish to speak with her," Delvin said, and scowled.

Anne stepped forward from behind the door. She had two bloody wounds on her side and bruises on her face. "My lord," she said; her voice was worn and frail.

"You will take Celia to Elnora and stand as regent until I have returned. If I return incomplete, you will serve until I am ready to take over," Delvin spoke to Anne, but his eyes were firmly on Jan.

Jan was emotionally destroyed by Delvin taking his sister. The only tangible asset he had for alliance had been swiftly and effortlessly taken from him.

"Yes, my lord." Anne moved to the interior to gather Celia.

Delvin turned to leave and Jan called to him, "I expect her returned, your majesty, when things have returned to normal."

King Delvin looked back over his shoulder at him. "Perhaps, but I expect concessions for our actions here today. I do not step foot on the mainland without exacting a toll." He could see Jan fighting not to show his crushing disappointment and despair.

"Do not worry, Jan, I will trade fair and in kind. You may yet come out of this with gain."

Anne held Celia's hand as they approached Jan. Celia looked unspeakably sad as she hugged him. His face twisted in desperation as he grabbed Anne's arm and pulled her to him. "Marry me, for the sake of my sister?"

Anne laughed. "That...that is all you can say to me?" Her eyes betrayed her feelings much more eloquently than her words could have.

"It is my only hope to see my sister again, and have any ownership of my life," Jan pleaded. "You can frolic with whomever you wish. I will never say a word to you about it. I need it politically."

Anne frowned and held her hand to his face. He was prepared for anything but kindness. "No, you should have faith. Lucien will return, and he would certainly not let anything happen to your sister. I promise you, he will right the wrongs done to you. Besides, I think King Delvin may surprise you."

Jan sighed, watching her take Celia away. Celia looked back one last time as they left the castle bailey, and then they were gone. Jan grimaced as he watched the people around him tend the wounded. In the distance, he could see Petric being wrapped nearly head-to-toe in bandages. "I hate surprises."

CHAPTER 65

ALARIC STOOD WITH his arms folded, watching as Brian unrolled a scroll on the table in the adviser's house. "What is it?"

"A map."

"I can see that much for myself," he said. "But a map of what?"

Brian fumbled with the scroll, rotating it, trying to find a direction. "It is Drommer, I am nearly certain. It is a complete map of the city as it was a year or so ago, judging by these marks. The enemy commander must have had it for plans to siege."

"Rabin," Alaric scoffed. "What about the others?"

Brian took out another scroll and unrolled it across the first. "This looks like a map of the mountain. It appears to be near the mine gallery. It has a good plan for the area north where the tribesmen have their camps."

Brian glanced at Alaric, who seemed uninterested. "There are seven in total. I am not sure how they help, other than they are good evidence of what this Rabin was doing. They are maps of the areas in Crosshill, the mountains, Dawnbridge, Drommer, Porin, and the Temple of Dulimore. The seventh I do not recognize.

It is a temple in the east, judging by the mountains. It could be in the Vale or in Elgin."

Alaric studied the image of an interior map with odd markings. It was meaningless to him. He thumped the table in frustration. "What of the prisoner?"

"He received treatment and should be questioned today. The king will do it in the throne room." Brian looked up from the maps to Alaric. "He doesn't trust information that has been repeated from others. I am sure you can understand."

Alaric stood silently for a moment. "What?"

"You should go," Brian said, and waved his hand; "If you want to hear what is said from the prisoner."

"If you find out what the seventh map is, let me know."

"I will." Brian turned away as Alaric left.

Alaric walked the courtyard to the main castle entrance. His men were stationed in the barracks outside the gate. They appeared in better health over the last day; many were taking shots at the archery targets as he paused to look through the outer gate. He went up the steps to the foyer.

The throne room was up a stairwell at the opposite end of the dining hall. Alaric allowed himself a smile at his fond memories of throwing dice with the guards during the gala there. When he reached the throne room, the prisoner stood in the center. Nearby stood Eric as the king listened. Alaric had not seen Arnold in the castle, nor Martin, for some time. It was curious they were not here.

Sergeant Dalen gave a nod as Alaric approached him. "What did I miss?"

Dalen leaned close in a whisper, "Not much, he just told us what he did in Drommer and how he was conscripted. They did it in the night with bags over their heads, like a kidnapping. A hell of a way to run an army. It is no wonder we whipped them, even outnumbered five-to-one."

Alaric chafed at the thought of the betrayal at the east gate. The battle was all but won and those traitors stabbed them in the back. He wiped his mouth with the back of his hand.

Elias spoke very methodically in his questions: "What happened to King Icel?"

Cesik swayed slightly, his footing uncertain. He leaned on a crutch; his leg below the knee was gone. The bandages were heavily wrapped at the wound. Dark patches of blood stained the wrappings. "I never saw what happened to him. The men said he was dead. I took them at their word." Cesik tried to look surreptitiously around the room at the other nobles and guards.

"Elena, what is her relationship with Oswald? Oswald somehow was able to escape with her in the night. I was a fool to trust him so long, but he was rather cunning for a man who could easily pass for a halfwit." Elias smiled smugly as the gallery laughed at the insult.

Cesik shifted himself. "They are to be married. There was a big celebration planned in the city after our expected victory here. I do not know anything beyond that."

Elias struggled to not smile. "Married," he parroted. "Elena must have lowered her standards considerably." The gallery laughed again, and Elias did smile this time, even as he struggled to look stern. "What of this Rabin? You mentioned he was a demon, nearly."

Cesik nodded; his words came out in a stutter and rush: "A horror, my lord. He beat us, kidnapped people in the night, and drilled us night and day. I have seen him kill men randomly in our camps for no reason. He talked of nothing but revenge."

Elias looked curious. "Revenge against whom?"

Cesik shook his head. "I have no idea. It was revenge, he said, revenge for all that they had done. I know nothing of what he spoke. The man was mad."

Elias stroked his beard with thumb and forefinger. He looked inquisitively to Eric at his side. Alaric and Dalen looked uneasy, as they both knew of Rabin and Richter. They had terrorized the continent in the wars and both hated Elnora for opposing them before Chaplain Hill.

"Where did Rabin take the men when they retreated?" Alaric asked as he approached Cesik from the side.

Cesik turned to him with a warm smile. "Kind sir, thank you for saving me. Rabin took the men to Drommer. He said he would levy more men and return with greater numbers. He seemed to care nothing for the men he left behind, or any of it."

King Elias stood. "You can rest, Cesik. I think we will discuss amongst ourselves."

The guards helped Cesik leave and Alaric and Dalen approached the throne. Elias sat down and clasped his hands together. "That is dour news indeed. Any idea how long it will take for him to collect more men?"

"Men. They are slaves, from the sound of it," Dalen quipped.

Alaric gave it serious thought. "It would take time. I am not concerned. I am sure Lucien will get to him before then. What word is there from Porin?"

"No word, but we expect something in the evening or tomorrow morning. They had a horrible battle a day ago, and were able to win just barely. I am not sure they can hold another attack." Eric shook his head, trying to remain confident.

Alaric held his fist to his mouth. They needed to buy time, or hope for them to hold. "Lucien won't be back for days. I suspect he needs a month to get to full strength, and I am not sure if Elnora would send aid. They are at least a day behind the happenings here. I hope they have done something."

"King Delvin would not abandon your majesty, or Port Porin," Dalen spoke, his voice rising.

King Elias looked skeptical, and raised the corner of his mouth.

CHAPTER 66

ZARA GROANED AS she turned in bed. Samuel stood watch with an expression of astonishment. Zara's eyes fluttered open just slightly, looking up at him. "Where is Viola?"

Samuel knelt down close. "She is here, do not strain yourself. You have been unconscious for nearly a week. You have to tell me what Viola gave you."

Zara lifted her hand to rub her eyes, but didn't have the strength. Her hand fell back to the covers. "I have no idea. I want to speak to her."

There was a knock at the door and Samuel opened it. Viola stood there, holding her satchel.

"I have returned, like I told you." Viola glanced back at the guards outside. Samuel gently led her into the room, then checked both ways down the hall before closing the door.

Viola knelt by Zara's bed. She was weak and could barely keep her eyes open.

"I brought soup," Viola said. She held up a flask and sipped from it.

"I hope it isn't a day old," Zara said, smiling weakly.

Viola laughed. "No, fresh this morning. It will help you get your strength back."

Viola lifted Zara's head and let her drink from the flask. Samuel stood to the side of the bed, watching with obvious fascination.

Viola could feel his eyes drilling into her head. "It is just a healing potion, Samuel." She did not look to him, but he edged closer to better observe everything.

"I am grateful, but I also am torn to know how you healed her." Samuel rubbed the side of his nose.

Viola shrugged dismissively. "I made a powerful potion and she drank too much. It put her to sleep for nearly a week. I hope the family won't hold it against me. She did heal well. I would not let her on that leg for a few days, though."

Samuel observed the wound on Zara's leg. It was healed, but the skin over it looked pinkish and still not completely grown. The bone was surely corrected and repaired, but it was best not to test it too soon.

Samuel touched Viola's back with the tips of his fingers. "I will tell the family that she is awake and well. It will be all your credit, though I hope you mention I was a help."

Viola laughed. "Well, I am grateful for your confidence. I will give you equal credit. The family just needs to let me leave with Edwin and Kate when the time comes."

"Agreed, I will tell them not to disturb Zara for a few days, but her mother will want to see her." He nodded and turned quietly to leave.

Zara listened for the door to close behind Samuel. She looked up at Viola. "Kate...is she...?"

Viola seemed to implode at the mention of Kate's name. Her eyes filled with tears and she had to pause a moment before speaking.

Her silence had already answered the unfinished question. "Kate is gone, and Edwin too. I do not want you to worry; it will be all right."

Zara couldn't help but weep for them. She barely knew them, but she could see the pain in Viola's eyes. "I am so sorry. I wish I had left you in that room and her in the dungeon. We were tricked, and I feel like it's my fault."

Viola took Zara's hand and twined their fingers. "It will all be all right. I know we are sad now, but it will turn around. But there are...complications."

Zara's eyes narrowed. "What has happened?"

"I need you to tell Henry and James that Lucien and I are together." Viola's gaze burned into Zara's, trying to indicate just how serious she was.

Zara gently nodded. "I understand. My father is probably still mad with fear of the Valdivians. I am not sure he will let you leave."

Viola brushed Zara's hair back from her face. "Exactly, and I need to try to control Lucien as best I can. I don't want him going insane and committing genocide. Kate would never forgive me for that."

Zara's grip tightened on Viola's hand. "I am so filled with anger, I would almost rather he did."

Viola smiled weakly. Zara could only sigh softly. "Well, I am not certain Lucien can tell enemy from friend when he is mad. He will awake today, and I hope to convince him to not go try to kill Elena or anyone else."

Zara turned her face to the wall. "Would it be so bad if he did?"

Viola stood, putting her flask away. She was not sure arguing would help, because she wanted revenge too. "Just rest, I will come back when I can. Please cover my lies for me as best you can. I keep Lucien in my bed, but there are spies watching."

"I will, and give my condolences to Lucien." Zara made weak fists and rested them on her chest.

Viola stopped at the door and turned back to say, "One more thing: if they find me out, I plan to say you and Lucien are lovers and it was all your idea because you carry his unborn child."

That was enough to cut through Zara's torpor. She gasped and coughed, but Viola had closed the door behind her before Zara could say anything more.

Viola quickly walked the hallways and corridors back to her room. She was certain they were following or watching her wherever she went. In the morning she had gone to the tomb, and several guards had followed, only to turn down blind alleys. That was not a coincidence.

In her room she still had supplies, flasks, and pots lying about; there were also cooking ingredients she was working on. Lucien lay silent on her bed, but he had begun moaning more lately. When she approached to check on him, he stirred and opened his eyes. She looked at the red of his eyes, shaped to focus on her. It was an incredible sight. She looked at him completely differently now, now understanding nearly everything that Kate had said. He was something else entirely different than either of them had ever seen.

The more she looked at his weak, sleepy stare, the more she felt sympathy and affection for him. She crawled next to him in bed, holding him close. She wanted to protect him from the world and its slashing claws and casual betrayals, and from himself. "It will be all right."

Lucien gasped and twitched as he came suddenly awake. It took a moment for his muddled mind to realize it had not been a fever dream, that Kate was actually irretrievably gone from this world and his life. The warmth of Viola lying next to him was difficult to contemplate. His senses were dulled, but he could feel an echo of her fear and sadness.

He grunted in pain as he sat forward in bed, his head resting in his hands. Tears ran down his cheeks as Viola tried to hold him. "I swear, it will be all right. You have to believe me. I don't want you to suffer or make a terrible decision. I need you."

Lucien's body was hollow inside. Kate was his true love, she was everything to him. Regret clouded his thoughts. "I should have taken her while I had the chance."

Viola put her head against his neck. "No, you did everything right. She wanted to be free, and you let her. You are not responsible. She would not want you to seek revenge by killing innocent people for her. You must know she would never forgive you."

Lucien laughed with tears streaming down his face. He was not sure whether to laugh or cry, so he did both. "What does it matter now? Nothing matters in this world. Let it burn. Let it all burn."

Viola cried, holding him. "I need you here. You are all that is left. Do not abandon me in your sorrow. I swear to you, it will be all right if you just hold on."

Lucien pushed her aside and got out of bed. He found his clothes on the table and dressed. Viola circled the bed, grabbing him around the waist. "Don't leave me here alone. I cannot survive. William will not let me ever leave."

Lucien's expression was cold. "Then he will be the first I kill."

Viola put her hands on his chest, trying to push Lucien back. "No, you won't hurt anyone. Kate would not forgive you and neither would I. Please, just calm yourself and rest with me in the bed."

Lucien stood oblivious to her pleading. "Take me to her. I want to see what they have done. How can you know she lies dead and not seek to destroy them?"

Viola could see the despair in his face, and the anguish. "You will not harm anyone. We will walk to the college. I am the only one with a key, and I am responsible. No one has bothered them here."

She backed away from him. He wiped at his face, and felt his sadness being replaced by rage. Hatred coursed through his mind and veins, and he pressed his powers to Viola, to search her feelings. She was mysteriously opaque to him. His power was not even half, and it was badly dulled. He could feel his anger reflect from her and his rage and sorrow were replaced by shame. Lucien tied his blindfold so tightly that it stung on his temples.

Viola knew Lucien could not be turned from seeing Kate, so she slowly walked from the room and he followed. They had assembled quite a collection of guards by the time they reached the tomb. First they were followed by the guards on duty in the hallway outside Viola's room, and they were quickly joined by the stairwell guards, and still more soldiers from the courtyard fell into line behind them. Her chest was tight and her breathing constricted as her worries that Lucien might lose control at any moment increased.

When they reached the tomb she unlocked the door, letting Lucien inside. She followed and quickly closed the door, locking out the guards. She took Lucien's hand and walked him to Edwin's body.

Lucien looked at Edwin's body where it lay atop the sarcophagus. "I want to see his face. I want to see what they did to him."

Viola held her breath as she uncovered his face. Edwin looked so alive. He barely had any wounds on his face, but his skin was pale.

Lucien stared down at Edwin, struggling to speak, "Old friend, what have I done? I failed you as I failed her." He rested his palm against Edwin's cheek. Even then he had trouble believing Edwin was really dead. Lucien wiped the tears from his eyes. "I want to see her face."

Viola covered Edwin's face gently and followed Lucien to the other sarcophagus where Kate lay. She watched Lucien as she slowly unwound the shrouding covering Kate's head. Kate's face slowly appeared; Lucien's face was unreadable.

She stepped back and slipped her dagger into her right hand, ready to strike.

He leaned his head to rest on her cheek and felt his body empty. His heart was as cold as a river stone, pumping freezing water through his veins. Everything inside him felt broken and crushed beyond repair. Seeing her lying dead robbed him of his strength and he slumped to the floor next to the sarcophagus. "I will kill them all. This world does not deserve to exist."

Viola knelt beside him. He sat on the floor with his back to the stone plinth. She watched his face fill with anguish as the reality of Kate's death finally set in. "I am here. It will be all right, we will survive, and you will find a reason to live."

Lucien was lost in rage and despair. "I have to get to them. Elena, she must die. I will make sure everything she has ever known is destroyed, and I will make her watch as I tear her world apart. Only when she begs for death will her suffering truly begin."

Viola took off her cloak; she wrapped her dagger in it and tossed it to the side. She sat on Lucien's lap, pressing into him as she kissed him deeply on the mouth. His eyes were wide with surprise and confusion, but a moment later, he responded and took her in his arms.

A part of him wanted to push her away, but the weight and warmth of her on his lap and her lips on his overrode that impulse. Kate's smell and warmth was gone. If he could be with her again, it would all go away, all the pain, all the anguish.

Viola released him and gasped for breath. He dug deep into her for emotion. She had nothing, complete emptiness.

It was as if she was invisible at that moment. His senses were weak and dull, but he felt as if it was all taken. Lucien cradled his head. The ache of emptiness and the dulling of his senses flooded him.

"I can love you and take care of you. You must listen to me. If you slaughter countless thousands to kill a single woman, no one would ever want to be around you again. They would hunt you and it is not what she wants and you know that." Viola held his head in her hands.

Lucien could feel the sadness and pain inside him, but the silence had cleared his mind briefly. He was so drained of emotion that he could easily get lost in Viola's eyes. Her scent of sage and fire smoke intoxicated him. The erotic warmth of her body pressed to his lap made him want to throw everything away to be with her. It wasn't real. She wasn't Kate, just a poor facsimile.

"I could lose myself in you," Lucien whispered, surprised to hear himself say those words.

Viola felt her heart pounding faster. She did not know what to say. If she could only get him to stay with her until he was calm. She put her palms against his chest and looked into his eyes. "Stay here with me. We can wait until things calm down and go south together. The countryside is amazing. We could take our time and explore it."

Lucien put his hand to her cheek. "I must find Elena. Drommer betrayed us, and Oswald must be found as well. They were in this together."

Lucien lifted her off of him and stood. She was much shorter than Kate and her chin rested on his chest when she looked up at him. "Don't murder people trying to get to them. You need to think of the innocents."

Lucien had stopped crying and wiped at his nose and eyes. "I won't randomly kill them, but I will be methodical and merciless."

Viola did not know what to say or do to make him stop. She reached for her cloak and held her dagger, still hidden in its folds. If she stabbed him, she was not sure what would happen if she failed. He might kill her right there. She wrapped her arms around him, her head against his chest. "Please, don't go."

Lucien took her in his arms, resting his cheek against the top of her head. "Come with me."

Viola pushed back from him roughly, struggling until he released her. She backed quickly away from him and said in a panicked voice, "No, I can't leave this place. You have to stay with me here."

Lucien sighed, "I can't. I must go. You will tell them I went south to face Elena. I will return when I have finished." He paused, turning away from her, and quickly covered Kate's face. He could not stand to see her face again. "I promise I won't leave you here alone."

Viola clutched her dagger as she watched him. She had no idea if she had done enough, but she had done all she could, and he had made up his mind. "I will be in my room. If something happens to you, I will be trapped here forever." Viola tried to swallow, but her throat was as dry as a dirt road. "They will make me a whore if you don't return."

Lucien stepped to her and she instinctively took a step back. "I will return and I would never harm you. Maybe I can know you better."

Viola's face burned with embarrassment. "Make sure you don't kill everyone. I don't want to be afraid when I am around you."

Lucien could not believe he could smile, but he did. "I won't."

Viola watched him disappear, surprised and relieved she had survived. She dropped the dagger and wrapped her cloak around herself, shivering from more than the cold of the tomb. "Gods, he is dangerous."

CHAPTER 67

LUCIEN ARRIVED AT the Dawnbridge castle manor. His room appeared undisturbed. It was hard to imagine Kate had been there with him once, in his bed. He closed his eyes tight, wondering why he didn't do more.

The windows were uncovered and the sun had climbed high overhead, casting sunshine in the room. He could feel again as he stood there. The city was anxious at the thought of the oncoming attack, and Elias's guards worried about a return to fighting.

Lucien opened the door and stepped into the hallway. He sensed Alaric nearby. He descended the stairwell into the corridor leading to the throne room. There were no guards in the halls as he walked. He opened the door to the throne room, and Elias was there with Brian, Alaric, and Dalen. They all were at the table at the far wall.

Elias saw Lucien and smiled broadly. "Well, speak of the devil."

Dalen and Alaric turned as Brian raised his head to see him. Alaric smiled as Lucien approached. "I hope you have a plan?" Alaric took a shuddering breath. "We are desperate for some good ideas."

Lucien was dour as he stared at the four of them. "I have no plan. I want to go to Drommer and tear the place apart until I find Elena."

The men looked to each other and Brian stepped forward. "Do you need a second? I am happy to join, and I need this."

Lucien struggled to meet Brian's eyes. "I would rather go alone. It might not be pleasant seeing what I plan to do."

Brian gritted his teeth in anger. "I need to see what you will do. I need it more than anything in this world."

Lucien shook his head, trying to manage his pain. "I know you want to, but destroying a city is not something you will enjoy when your rage passes."

Brian buried his face in his hands. Elias stood from the table. "You plan to face Elena in Drommer, but I would imagine she is waiting for you there. It could be a trap."

Lucien nodded. "I expect that she will have something planned. I will soften the city first before attacking."

Alaric put his arm around Lucien. "I have twenty or so men; let us come with you. We can go east and make camp in the swamp west of the city. In the morning, we can give you cover."

Brian quickly looked up, his eyes widening. Dalen was smiling. Elias scratched at his beard contemplatively.

Lucien was not strong enough and still needed to rest. The plan was sound. If anything, it would be good to have Alaric there to pick him up after he collapsed from exhaustion. "I agree. You can bring the Elnoran soldiers."

Brian's face twisted. "Wait a damn minute. I have to come with you."

Alaric put his hand to Brian's chest. "You are no soldier. Your daughter will be avenged, but your mind is better here where you can help rebuild Dawnbridge. If this goes in our favor, you might even have to rebuild Drommer once we are done."

Brian grumbled but sat back down at the table. Elias put his hand on his shoulder to comfort him.

Lucien turned to Alaric and Dalen and announced, "I want to leave immediately."

CHAPTER 68

"WE CAN MAKE camp here," Alaric decided, pointing to a flat, dry area ahead.

He dismounted with Lucien at his side. The two gathered items from the horses to make camp. The men began to raise tents in a circle. Lucien helped Alaric with the command tent.

The wagons, covered with mud, struggled to navigate the narrow paths through the swampy woods. Some got stuck and had to be emptied, lifted free, and loaded once more.

Lucien finished with the tent just as the men finished building a large campfire nearby. He waved his hand, igniting it. The men laughed and cheered him. It was the one time he could feel appreciation from the men; it was more common to feel their fear while he was around.

Alaric stood beside him at the fire. "Do you feel anything from Drommer?"

Lucien stared through the woods. Far in the distance, the city walls of Drommer could be seen and, soaring above them, the towers of the castle. Drommer stood high on a plateau in the Dulimore wastes. It was visible even from the borders of the Vale and Westfall.

Lucien could feel the dread hanging over the city like an oppressive summer heat. The people lived in terror. His heart ached at the thought of destroying the city to get to Elena, but he wanted to punish her and Oswald for what they had done. "The people in the city are afraid. They know what is coming."

Alaric grunted, his gaze fixed on Drommer. He had just twenty-nine men. It was a fraction of the men needed to take the city. If the battle became too much, they would have to withdraw.

Alaric turned to Lucien but he had vanished. He looked around to see where he had gone, but there was no sight of him in the camp. He looked in the command tent, and as he stepped out, Lucien walked out of the tent behind him, wiping the blood from his nose.

Alaric turned to him with a look of surprise. "Where did you go? You are supposed to be resting."

Lucien stopped and gave him a weak wave. "I went to get my armor. I will need it tomorrow, and better to use up energy now and replenish overnight. Charbel has a strange energy about it," he added. "I didn't feel comfortable there."

Alaric did not want Lucien falling to pieces. He needed to keep his mind off of Kate. "I know what you mean." Alaric walked past him, into the command tent, and Lucien followed.

The tent had four cots set up on each side, and a table with four chairs in the center. Alaric took a scroll from a crate and unrolled it on the table. "This is a siege map of Drommer we found. It might help you clear the city without killing everyone. This here –" he said, tapping a site on the map with his fingertip, "– is the city's stone and foundry works. In the morning, it is empty. I suggest you target your attack there. If you can scare enough people, they may flee before it gets out of hand."

Lucien liked the idea. If people fled, there would be fewer casualties than if they resisted. "Do you know the number of soldiers that Elena has with her?"

Alaric sighed heavily. "So far, no one has seen Elena. A prisoner told us she is to marry Oswald; at this point, she could already be married to him. It could be Oswald behind all this, or...Rabin."

"Rabin?" Lucien looked confused. "He must be sixty by now."

Alaric shook his head. "He was just a young man when he fought with your father at Richter's side. He may be my age, or younger."

Lucien listened to what Alaric wasn't saying. He could sense there was more to the story and asked, "You suspect him?"

"I do," Alaric admitted. "I have no idea how, but he might have imprisoned Richter and taken Elgin all for himself. Elena may be along just to see if she can get some piece of power. Maybe she will reign in Dulimore and him in Elgin."

"She will be dead soon enough," Lucien said, raising his fist. "I will make sure she dies this time."

Alaric crossed his arms. "Rest, make sure you don't fail from a wild killing stroke. I will have to get to you if that happens. She has planned her vengeance and will be ready."

"So am I," Lucien said, and his eyes glowed redder than all the fires of hell.

CHAPTER 69

LUCIEN STOOD AT the tree line watching as dawn approached. He could see the glow of first light on the treetops in the west. The Elnoran soldiers stood at the tree line with shields and full armor. The black of Lucien's armor stood out among them. He placed the demon helm upon his head.

The men could only look in discomfort at what a frightening sight he became. Alaric, standing beside him, lowered his own visor. "You will make trouble in the east side of the city. I suspect the people will flee south, toward Porin. Jan was able to turn the tide there. I didn't want to tell you, but King Delvin lifted the siege personally."

Lucien's laugh echoed in the helm. "I suspect he has already fled to safety at King's Port."

Alaric spoke sternly to Lucien: "They didn't say, just that the siege was lifted and he made quite a display."

Lucien was focused and ignored any concerns of fleeing survivors. "They will run, or they will die."

Lucien held a black obsidian axe with menacing serrations on the haft. He walked out of the woods and felt his rage rise with every step. His eyes burned red from behind the demon helm and the armor creaked as heat radiated in the air around him. He raised his arms aloft and floated high into the air. He lifted himself to the wall and the men saw him instantly, a black shadow backlit by the rising sun.

They screamed in horror, dropping their weapons as they ran. Lucien closed his claw gauntlets into a fist and burned with fiery energy. At the tree line, he ripped six thirty- and forty-foot tall trees up by their roots.

Alaric and his men stumbled as the violent upheaval of the trees around them being torn from the ground shook the earth. The trees rose high into the air. As the trees crested the wall, they burst into flame with a crackling explosion.

Alaric's stare hardened as he watched the burning trees rain down on Drommer. In a soft whisper he implored, "Matresnott, you wicked witch, give us strength for our revenge."

Lucien thought of Kate's cold, lifeless face, and his rage rose higher. He tossed the giant burning trees like torches into the city's stone and foundry works. They crashed and exploded, throwing burning embers, spreading flaming destruction like ripples in a pond.

Lucien shot huge burning arcs from the walls, igniting rooftops. The people inside screamed in horror and ran for their lives. Hundreds streamed from the south gate of the city.

Even from their place in the woods, Alaric and his men could see Lucien's red, glowing eyes. They stood at attention as Alaric waved his sword, signaling it was working. Their revenge was coming to fruition.

Lucien followed along the wall and the soldiers made no attempt to fight him. They dropped their weapons and ran as fast as they could. Some leapt to the roofs below, falling through the thatching.

Lucien reached the door to the north tower. It was locked tight but he burned through it. He entered the tower and followed the stairwell to a hallway. The guards on duty saw him and ran. The heat from his armor ignited carpets along the floors and tapestries adorning the walls as he stalked through.

The fire spread wherever he walked, and Lucien could feel the energy from the heat enhancing his drive, pushing his rage, feeding his power. But fatigue also haunted him as his power drained through the enhancing effects. Blood poured from his mouth as he turned doors to cinders on his relentless march to the throne room.

Lucien finally blasted the last door and found himself standing opposite Oswald. He sat upon a throne raised two steps above him. He wore heavy armor and the golden crown. "I have been expecting you. The Demon Lord, at last," he said with a smile that was arrogant and twisted.

The tables and chairs burst into flames as Lucien approached. He stopped as Elena stepped out of the shadows. She held a rust-colored diamond-shaped shield adorned with a northern dragon. She wore full-body sinter red armor. Lucien held his axe at his side. "The whore, at last. You had to have known I would come after you murdered Kate."

Oswald laughed. "Perhaps I knew all along you would come. I have a present for you." He reached into a box on a small table next to the throne and rolled a human head down the steps and across the floor to Lucien. "It is a gift," Oswald laughed again. "It's all right, no need to be embarrassed if you didn't bring me anything."

Lucien reached down and picked up the severed head by its hair and turned its face to his. It was King Icel. Lucien wanted to feel sadness, but he could only laugh as the head burned. "One less I have to kill," he said, and flung the head aside.

Oswald stood and drew his sword. "I have been waiting for this." He stepped down from the throne to stand facing Lucien, and in a single stroke of a blade Oswald's neck was slashed open. Blood sprayed in wild spurts with every beat of his heart. He dropped his sword and reached for his neck. His eyes were wide with shock and disbelief. He tried to say something but choked on his own blood. He fell forward and was still.

Lucien could not believe what he had seen. Elena tossed the bloody dagger onto Oswald's corpse. Her eyes peered at him from the red helm. "It is just one more of your victims. I have waited for this moment since the gala. You humiliated and scarred me. You left me for dead and at the mercy of my father and this monster. I will scar you in life and death. These bodies are all your doing. They will sing of the horrible, sinister demon that you are, and all those you murdered here today."

Lucien stepped forward, blasting her with molten flames that picked her up and threw her backward into the throne, knocking it to the ground. Elena struck the wall but immediately got to her feet. She stood with her shield and armor glowing red.

She said defiantly, "The people of this world have fought your kind before, and you are a relic of a failed era of history."

Lucien could hardly believe that she could survive such a blast, let alone stand. She held her sword high and approached, swinging to strike. Lucien stepped to the side and slapped her attack away with his axe. She spun and stabbed at him and Lucien swung high over the top, bringing his axe down through the burning table.

The flaming embers exploded, blinding him long enough for Elena to stab his side just above the waist. It was a painful blow that cut deep. He swung blindly, missing her and leaving himself open. She struck his arm; his hand went numb and he dropped the axe.

She struck Lucien in the head and shoulder but inflicted no damage. Lucien could imagine Kate and how she suffered, how Elena conspired to kill her. The rage was the extra push he needed. "You took everything from me!" Flames engulfed Lucien's body as he grabbed her, pinning her arms to her sides. He burst through the throne room wall to the battlements just beyond.

Lucien struck the outer wall. The crenellations were the only thing that kept him from going over the side. Elena had fallen near him. Their armor was badly broken and hanging in shreds and tatters from their impact with the wall. Elena's sword was lying on the walkway between them. They both scrambled for it, but she reached it first, whisking it away just as his fingers touched it. She drove it deep into his stomach; the tip burst through his back. Elena released the handle as Lucien hunched over and fell to his side.

Searing pain exploded through Lucien's body and then, impossibly, kept climbing up and up. His body was locked, doubled over where the sword was lodged. Blood drained from his wounds and from his mouth. His breathing was labored. His vision doubled, then trebled.

Elena pulled a long curved dagger from her belt and stalked toward him. She tore his helm off and tossed it over the wall. Her eyes filled with tears and her voice shook with emotion: "I did not plan to kill that girl. You would never understand. Your father took everything from me. He killed my brothers and drove my father mad. He tormented me after their deaths. His obsession with revenge drove him insane. The people were starving when Rabin finally imprisoned him. Oswald was the only person to offer me anything, and it was to be his whore. I would have rotted in that Dawnbridge prison, humiliated, and abused."

Lucien could barely keep his eyes open. The pain was just a distant echo now and a coldness crept through his body. His legs were numb and he could not stand. He could feel his life slipping away from him. He gasped for a breath that would not come as she stood over him. "It should have been different." She held the dagger tightly in her hand, leaning down and pressing its blade to his throat. "You could have been different."

The ground rumbled and, a moment later, there was a loud rush of water. Elena looked over her shoulder and saw King Delvin riding a wave of water to the top of the wall. His staff glowed with a bright blue flame. The water washed along the top of the ramparts and he stood before her.

Elena turned to run, but Delvin fired a blast of illuminated blue water from his staff that struck her and pushed her to the wall. She grasped at the edge as the water pummeled her, driving her slowly, inexorably back. Her hands could not hold, and she washed over the side. She fell with a scream to the rock face below.

Delvin's eyes burned bright blue as he approached his son and knelt beside him. "You should have waited for your power to return. You squander it when you should be thinking, not fighting." Lucien's expression was one of resignation. He did not move – he could not – but just blinked as his father pulled the blade from his stomach.

Lucien's pride was destroyed to be saved by his father, the ultimate failure. He had failed Edwin and Kate and now had failed to even avenge them.

Delvin bent to help Lucien up and froze, his face a mix of surprise and pain. He reached slowly to his chest where the tip of a crossbow bolt stuck from his punctured breast plate. He could hear the click and wind of the crossbow being armed. He turned to see a man in heavy sinter red armor with a hooked bassinet. The unmistakable red cape fluttered in the air.

"It has been over twenty years, Delvin, but I have dreamed of this day, every day!" Rabin yelled to him. He held the crossbow loop with his foot as he cranked to reload.

Blood streamed from Delvin's nose and mouth as he forced himself to his feet. He held his staff to the air as water circled and swirled, forming a sphere, trapping Rabin inside. The sphere held him suspended above the ground. Rabin still stared through the water prison at Delvin even as he continued to load the crossbow.

Delvin strained and screamed, holding Rabin in the air for a minute or more before he collapsed to the ground. Rabin fell as the sphere dissipated and he lay on the stone battlement. Delvin looked on in astonishment as Rabin climbed to his feet. Water slowly trickled from the bevor of his helm.

Rabin laughed, "Your kind has been fought before, and this time we were ready. The age of the elementals is long past. It is the dawn of a new era." He fired the crossbow. It sank deep into Delvin's stomach above the belt line. The head of the bolt burrowed through his back, spraying the backs of his legs with a splash of blood.

Delvin dropped his staff and fell to his knees. "My kind shall live on this world long after evil such as yours is dead."

Rabin put his foot into the crossbow loop and cranked it again to load. He laughed as it whined. "You do not have what it takes to rule this land or any others. Richter was right about you: you lack the instinct to rule."

Delvin clamped his hands over his wounds, but he knew his time was soon at an end. "Richter has no idea what I am capable of. I have killed more men than you will ever know."

Delvin dug deep into himself and found the strength to stand. He pulled his silver blade with the edge of razor obsidian. He swung, leaving a deep gash in the front of Rabin's armor.

Rabin dropped the crossbow and pulled his sword. He chopped down, striking Delvin's shoulder and used his elbow to knock the crown from his head. Delvin stumbled and swiped right, gashing Rabin's armor pauldrons.

The two stepped back to find their footing. Delvin's breathing was little more than a wheeze and a gasp. Blood dripped from his wounds and soaked the walk beneath him.

Lucien's vision had gone nearly white. He could only see a small faded window before him. The rest was all haze. He gasped as he pulled himself into a sitting position with his back against the wall. He could hear the sparks of armor and the whoosh of blades being swung as his father dueled Rabin. With the last of his fading strength, Lucien shifted himself along the wall to get closer to them.

Rabin struck clean again on Delvin's armor, shooting sparks off to the left. Delvin stabbed hard at Rabin, cutting through his chest plate and ripping a gash in his side. It was the first blood he had drawn from Rabin and Delvin savored it. While Rabin was still off balance, Delvin struck with a chopping stroke that snapped Rabin's wrist down. His hand dangled from a thread of flesh at the wrist. Gouts of blood sprayed both men.

Rabin gasped in pain and switched his sword to his other hand. He parried Delvin's next blow – they were growing progressively weaker – and struck in quick succession. Delvin was exhausted, barely able to withstand the barrage. He dropped to a knee and Rabin struck him with the flat of his blade across the face, knocking him to the ground. Delvin dropped his sword and Rabin kicked it out of his reach. He was defenseless.

The tip of Rabin's sword dimpled the flesh on Delvin's throat. "Emilia was your fault. She died because you couldn't let go."

Delvin rolled to his side, leaning on the battlement wall. "She was everything, and you were nothing."

Rabin gritted his teeth. "She was mine until you came along and poisoned her mind. Her talk of peace and Franz, that fool, listened. You couldn't let it go, and I made an example of her. She had to die to punish you. If not for those religious fools, Richter would rule this continent."

Rabin once again held his sword to Delvin's throat, studying his eyes for fear but not finding it. So focused was he on Delvin that he didn't notice that Lucien had closed the distance between them. "You stopped the war, but could never make it right. We had a plan and a dream. You had nothing."

Delvin's eyes returned to their brilliant blue as he looked ruefully at Rabin. "You are a pitiable damned fool, and so is Richter. Did you really think those priests could poison that many men without someone finding out and noticing? I can turn water to wine, and can turn blood to poison. It took from me more than I had ever given, but I ended it because I knew you and Richter were monsters."

Rabin's eyes grew wide and he trembled with rage. "You lie!"

Delvin smiled and said patiently, "No, the war is like all things; its time comes to an end. I think yours has finally come."

Lucien reached with his power and lifted Rabin, flinging him from the walls like a piece of trash. They could hear his screams as he fell. Lucien watched his father, shaking his head. "You should have told me."

Delvin grunted, holding his wounds. "Would it have mattered?"

"Yes," Lucien spat, his face twisted in rage. He growled in pain and vanished.

CHAPTER 70

D
ELVIN SAT WITH his back to the castle walls, his face a study in failure. He had failed to kill Elena and Rabin, even though they could likely be dead.

Andres approached him and knelt to address his wounds. "Can you stand?"

Delvin grimaced and put his arm over Andres's shoulder. "With help. I suppose your men haven't found their bodies?" Leaning on Andres, Delvin was able to lever himself into a standing position.

Andres sighed, said, "We did not have men on this side. We were fighting in the city south. It has been secured. We have what is left of the council, and the fires are under control. Alaric and his men are searching north."

Delvin sighed and shook his head dejectedly. "What about Oswald?"

"Dead. We found his body. I don't think Lucien killed him. His throat was cut, and the burned mess of what could be King Icel. Well, his head, at least." Andres helped Delvin through the hole in the wall of the throne room. They stood together,

344

surveying the damage. The room was torn apart and half-burned. Black smoke hung in the air like gathering storm clouds. The walls were dark with soot, and the once-colorful tapestries were little more than charred tatters.

A soldier put Delvin's crown back on his head and he acknowledged him with a nod. Delvin limped with Andres as they went to the outer windows that opened toward the city. "What a mess. The council will organize a cleanup effort."

"Already happening," Andres said, and gestured to Dalen, who approached them.

He bowed slightly, stiffly. "Your majesty, may I be of service?"

Delvin shifted his weight and looked to Andres with a smile. "Head south to Porin, and fetch Lord Jan. I think he will be needed here."

Andres scowled. "Gods, has it come to this?"

Delvin laughed. "King Jan has a nice ring to it, don't you think?"

Andres pursed his lips, releasing a sour breath. "No."

CHAPTER 71

ALARIC STOOD LOOKING up at the wall. The battlements had a sharp rock face beneath them that a person could slide from, but there were enough jagged edges that no man would want to try. He walked along the edge, searching for signs of life.

In the pond farther down, his men were up to their knees and waving their swords about in the water, looking for anything.

Alaric scratched his beard, bewildered at how she survived. It was not just her. Rabin had yet to be found. The men farther east were combing the ground. It was an even more treacherous fall from that face. It was straight down to the rocks from there.

A soldier approached. "Commander, we have yet to find any sign of them."

Alaric turned to the east and the men there appeared to have nothing as well. "Take ten men and head east until it is dark. Look as best you can, but be careful. They are far more dangerous than you think."

The soldier waved to gather men as they moved east. Alaric walked along the west side of the pond. The ground was soft there. He looked for footprints or blood spatter as he went from the south around to the north side. There were specks of blood about, but nothing sufficient enough to count as a trail.

"Did you find anything?" Alaric yelled to the men in the water.

They looked from one to the other, their blank expressions saying it all. "Nothing, commander."

"Get the hell out of there. They have vanished, by all accounts," Alaric growled.

He took the rest of his men back to the city. He could not understand how they escaped or where their bodies may have gone.

When they reached the gates Alaric looked south in time to see Dalen riding away in the distance.

Alaric walked the streets. The city was a mess of ash and rubble. As they got closer to the castle, Alaric and his men could hear people in the courtyard weeping over their lost homes and businesses. Alaric could only think Dawnbridge did not look much better.

The halls of the castle were scorched with burns, and the throne room was filled with charred tables and chairs. Andres already had men removing the burned items.

Alaric stood looking around the room. "The king, can we speak with him?"

"This way," Andres said, and led them to the adjacent hallway. It was in better shape, but smoke still hung in the air. They walked down and then up a flight of stairs to the manor. There were several rooms on each side, and guards stood outside a room at the end.

Andres entered. Delvin was sitting on the edge of his bed, grunting as salve and bandages were applied to his wounds. Vesper stood directing the nurses on how he wanted it. The king drank from a ceramic jug, appearing to be in discomfort.

"My lord." Andres stood in the doorway with Alaric.

"Yes, yes, I am sure it is bad news," Delvin grumbled, glancing up. He shifted as the nurses wrapped bandages tightly under his arms.

Alaric cautiously approached the bed and looked down when he said, "We did not find either of them. I sent the men east. The ground was soft to the west and there were no footprints."

"Damn," Delvin yelled, "That woman is going to sit on the throne of Elgin with Rabin at her side. She nearly got everything she wanted, and gods only know where Lucien went. He could very well be dead."

Andres inserted himself between them, trying to calm King Delvin. "She will be nothing but a petty queen, ruling just as her father did."

Delvin still was furious. "A petty queen ruling a people who may find her better than her father. He was a tyrant, by all accounts. She has the resources and the men to raise an army. We have less than we did before. This is nearly the worst outcome we could have hoped for."

Alaric sighed and continued, "It would take her a year or more, and what could she want from Dulimore now? The city is a mess, and so is Dawnbridge. If anything, she will go north and trouble the Valdivians. I would not be concerned. Besides, the walls of Drommer are untouched. She would need a sizable army to take this place by force."

Delvin slammed his mug down on the bedside table. The nurses tried to treat the wound on his face, but he was too agitated and every time they tried to apply salve, they ended up dabbing it on his nose or ear. He cursed, took the unguent, and smeared it on himself. He sighed as he calmed and said, "Bring more men, and maybe reinforce Port Porin. I will return to Elnora, and Lady Anne will take over there. Jan will have his hands full, but we will strengthen Dulimore to deter any more attempts as best we can."

Alaric and Andres both nodded in agreement.

EPILOGUE

ELENA COULD NOT hold her grip on the wall. She felt her fingers slipping, one after the other, and she fell. She flailed frantically, causing herself to pitch toward the right. Her leg struck first, breaking her ankle. She barely had time to register the pain because a moment later, her arm snapped at the elbow.

She tumbled down the rock face and rolled to a stop near the pond below. There was a long slash down her temple that just missed taking an eye. She tried to raise her arm, only to see her forearm was dangling by the skin at her elbow.

The pain was unbearable and purple spots splashed behind her eyes as her vision clouded. In a haze of consciousness, she looked up at the wall just in time to see Rabin thrown over the side.

He screamed and kicked, trying to brace himself for the impact. He landed wrong, his left leg out too far, and it snapped at the knee. His momentum pitched him forward and he tumbled out of control. He came to a stop. Somewhere along the way, his face had suffered a deep gash.

He trembled with pain and shock. He knew he had to attend to his leg immediately. Rabin wedged the heel of his broken leg between two rocks jutting up through the ground and dragged himself back using his elbows. He bellowed and writhed in pain as he forced his broken bone back into place. He was covered in a cold sweat and his hands were shaking, but he took the bindings from his armor and used them to brace his leg straight enough that he could stand.

Hobbled and in pain, he dragged his damaged leg behind him as he made his way to the drainage pond to look for Elena. He found her lying in a mud pit. He grabbed her arm only to see it was barely attached. He picked up her body to shake her. "Wake up if you want to live," he said. His voice was weak from pain but still filled with menace.

Elena heard his voice through her haze. She tried to focus but couldn't. "Rabin? Gods, I can't believe you survived."

"Hatred," he said. "Hatred will help me survive anything they can throw at me. You will have to swim with me. I still need you alive, and they will be looking for us shortly." Rabin grabbed her by the hair and dragged her to the center of the pond. The water was nearly up to his chin. He reached down, feeling. "It is here. I will drag you with me, but you need to stop struggling or I will leave you in the sewers for the rats."

Elena understood but could not speak. She was going into shock. He tied her around his back, and he placed his helm over her head. "It is designed to create a pocket of air when submerged in water. If you breathe calm and steady, you won't run out."

Elena nodded, once. Rabin dived into the pond face first, and swam down into a large stone opening. It led into a tunnel that he followed until there was an air pocket above. He broke the surface and pulled Elena up with him. He gasped, filling his lungs with the stale air.

He took another breath and swam on, letting the gentle flow of the water carry him when his arms grew weak. As soon as he felt his strength sufficiently returned, he stroked his way through the water again. The whole thing took several hours, but it felt like days. His entire body was burning and aching and his battle wounds still leaked, leaving an unwinding ribbon of blood behind him in the water.

At last he lifted his head and saw light in the distance. He swam with his head above the water until he reached the outflow. In the distance he could hear the crash of waves.

Elena trembled in the cold water. "Where are you taking me?"

Rabin laughed, and the tunnel walls echoed his laughter. "I have only just begun," he said.

IF YOU ENJOYED THE PETTY QUEEN LOOK FOR
THE NEXT INSTALLMENT COMING SOON!

WHAT DOES THE FUTURE HOLD BETWEEN
LUCIEN AND VIOLA? WHO IS THE NEW
PETTY KING?

CPSIA information can be obtained
at www.ICGtesting.com
Printed in the USA
LVHW090708100822
725536LV00016B/214/J